Praise for *Road Ou*
by Alison S

"A closely observed, evocative portrayal of place in a time of extreme duress. A warning about who we become and who we want to be in an uncertain future. Beautifully written and essential."
　　—Jeff VanderMeer, *New York Times* bestselling author of *Annihilation*

"Stark, dark and strangely urgent, this is a book that grabs you on the first page and doesn't let go. Alison Stine is a master at the craft. She takes us on a wild ride inside a future that feels all too real, with characters we care about, and a story that we start wishing will never end."
　　—Rene Denfeld, bestselling author of *The Butterfly Girl*

"Like *The Road* infused with feminist grit, Alison Stine's *Road Out of Winter* focuses on the true seeds of hope during a climate apocalypse: the things that nurture both our bodies and our souls. A startling and intimate look at what happens when our planet turns against us."
　　—Mike Chen, author of *A Beginning at the End*

ROAD OUT OF WINTER

ALISON STINE

mira

mira™

Recycling programs
for this product may
not exist in your area.

ISBN-13: 978-0-7783-0992-5

Road Out of Winter

This edition published by arrangement with Harlequin Books S.A.

For questions and comments about the quality of this book, please contact us at
CustomerService@Harlequin.com.

Mira
22 Adelaide St. West, 40th Floor
Toronto, Ontario M5H 4E3, Canada
BookClubbish.com

Printed in U.S.A.

For Henry

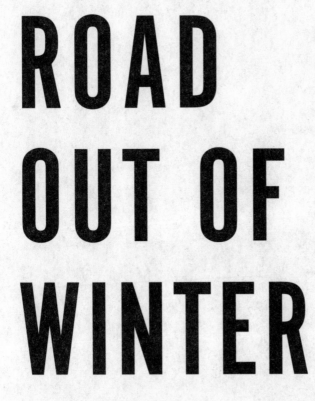

ROAD
OUT OF
WINTER

1

I used to have dreams that Lobo would be arrested. The sheriff and his deputies would roll up the drive, bouncing on the gravel, but coming fast, too fast to be stopped, too fast for Lobo to get away through the fields. Or maybe Lobo would be asleep, and they would surprise him, his eyes red, slit like taillights. My mama and I would weep with joy as they led him off. The deputies would wrap us in blankets, swept in their blue lights. We were innocent, weren't we? Just at the wrong place at the wrong time, all the time, involved with the wrong man—and we didn't know, my mama didn't know, the extent.

But that wasn't true, not even close.

I sold the weed at a gas station called Crossroads to a boy who delivered meals for shut-ins. Brown paper bags filled the back of his station wagon, the tops rolled over like his mama made him lunch. I supposed he could keep the bags straight. That was the arrangement Lobo had made years ago, that was the arrangement I kept. I left things uncomplicated. I didn't know where the weed went after the boy with the station wagon, where the boy sold it or for how much. I took the money he gave me and buried most of it in the yard.

After his station wagon bumped back onto the rural route, I went inside the store. There was a counter in the back, a row of cracked plastic tables and chairs that smelled like ketchup: a full menu, breakfast through dinner. They sold a lot of egg sandwiches at Crossroads to frackers, men on their way out to work sites. It was a good place to meet; Lisbeth would come this far. I ordered three cheeseburgers, fries, and coffee, and sat down.

She was on time. She wore gray sweatpants under her long denim skirt, and not just because of the cold. "You reek, Wil," she said, sliding onto the chair across from me.

"Lobo says that's the smell of money," I said.

"My mama says money smells like dirty hands."

The food arrived, delivered by a waitress I didn't know. Crinkling red-and-white paper in baskets. I slid two of the burgers over to Lisbeth. The Church forbade pants on women, and short hair, and alcohol. But meat was okay. Lisbeth hunched over a burger, eating with both hands, her braid slipping over her shoulder.

"Heard from them at all?" she asked.

"Not lately."

"You think he would let her write you? Call?"

"She doesn't have her own phone," I said.

Lisbeth licked ketchup off her thumb. The fries were already getting cold. How About Somethin' Homemade? read the chalkboard below the menu. I watched the waitress write the dinner specials in handwriting small and careful as my mama's.

"Hot chocolate?" I read to Lisbeth. "It's June."

"It's freezing," she said.

And it was, still. Steam webbed the windows. There was no sign of spring in the lung-colored fields, bordered by trees as spindly as a bread line. We were past forsythia time, past when the squirrels should have been rooting around in the trees for sap.

"What time is it now?" Lisbeth asked.

I showed her my phone, and she swallowed the last of her burger.

"I've got to go."

"Already?"

"Choir rehearsal." She took a gulp of coffee. Caffeine was frowned upon by The Church, though not, I thought, exclusively forbidden. "I gave all the seniors' solos, and they're terrified. They need help. Don't forget. Noon tomorrow."

The Church was strange—strange enough to whisper about. But The Church had a great choir; she had learned so much. They had helped her get her job at the high school, directing the chorus, not easy for a woman without a degree. Also, her folks loved The Church. She couldn't leave, she said.

"What's at noon?" I asked.

She paused long enough to tilt her head at me. "Wylo-dine, really? Graduation. Remember? The kids are singing?"

"I don't want to go back there."

"You promised. Take a shower if you been working so my folks don't lose their minds."

"If they haven't figured it out by now, they're never going to know," I said, but Lisbeth was already shrugging on her coat. Then she was gone, through the jangling door, long braid and layers flapping. In the parking lot, a truck refused to start, balking in the cold.

I ordered hot chocolate. I was careful to take small bills from my wallet when I went back up to the counter. Most of the roll of cash from the paper bag boy was stuffed in a Pepsi can back on the floor of the truck. Lobo, who owned the truck, had never been neat, and drink cans, leaves, and empty Copenhagen tins littered the cab. Though the mud on the floor mats had hardened and caked like makeup, though Lobo and Mama had been gone a year now, I hadn't bothered cleaning out the truck. Not yet.

The top of the Pepsi can was ripped partially off, and it was dry inside: plenty of room for a wad of cash. I had pushed down the top to hide the money, avoiding the razor-sharp edge. Lobo had taught me well.

I took the hot chocolate to go.

In the morning, I rose early and alone, got the stove going, pulled on my boots to hike up the hill to the big house. I swept the basement room. I checked the supplies. I checked the cistern for clogs. The creek rode up the sides of the driveway. Ice floated in the water, brown as tea.

No green leaves had appeared on the trees. No buds. My breath hung in the air, a web I walked through. My boots didn't sink in the mud back to my own house in the lower field; my footprints were still frozen from a year ago. Last year's walking had made ridges as stiff as craters on the moon. At the door to my tiny house, I knocked the frost from my boots, and yanked them off, but kept my warm coveralls on. I lit the small stove, listening to the whoosh of the flame. The water for coffee ticked in the pot.

I checked the time on the clock above the sink, a freebie from Radiator Palace.

"Fuck," I said aloud to no one.

Before the cold came, my mama and I used to fake-lock the driveway gate, looping the chain but not fastening the padlock, so it only looked locked to outsiders, in case Lobo was late and had forgotten his keys again. If he could just push on it to get it open, instead of kicking it in, or throwing his whole body against it, or yelling so loud we would hear from the farmhouse, that would help, some nights. He might not be as angry when he made it up the drive, frustrated at the world, looking to blame someone. But Lobo was gone. Those nights were over. I locked the gate for real, and headed down the roads into town.

High school graduation was a big deal, to have made it that far in this small town—little more than a holler, really, a dip between foothills—where no one would check up on you, no one would notice if you made it to class or not. And where there was always the pull of other work, work that would pay you, that seemed to matter more.

Lisbeth had given all the graduating seniors solos. I wished she had given herself one. How long since I had heard her sing?

The high school looked the same. It had only been four years since I had walked the halls myself, head down, not wanting anyone to stop and ask me for anything. People still asked, of course. Could I get them something, did I have anything, would I bring it to this party? In four years, people might have gone to college, gone away. But that was what people in other places did, not here.

Appalachian Ohio, the heart of nothing at all.

It was illegal, so Mama shielded me. But she loved Lobo, or thought she did, so we'd moved out onto the property to be with him. We had our own place, a tiny shack in a field away from the main house where all the plants were: a safeguard in case the sheriff came. The sheriff never came. A small, narrow house, built on a trailer, it had a skinny kitchen with a gas-powered fridge and a propane stove, a woodstove for heat, a ladder that led to a loft. By the time I was fifteen, the shack was my place, and I slept alone there every night; Mama had moved into the farmhouse. She said it was because the tiny house was cramped for two people—but I knew the real reason: she had chosen him over me.

By the time I was eighteen, I was working alongside Mama and Lobo. They didn't pay me, and I had small, fast hands.

When they left a year ago to make a go of it in California, the farm in Ohio became mine, mine alone—at least, mine alone to manage. I had talked about classes at community college, but who had the money, who had the time, there were chores. What would I do with a degree, except farm? There was a harvest to get in, there was trimming and weighing. There was work in the way of any plans. Money to be made.

At the high school, I parked in the senior lot out of habit. The football field looked dead, brown and tufted. The air cut my lungs, cold but with an undercurrent of wood smoke, as I joined the trudging crowd.

They were holding this thing outside.

Nobody had dressed up—only warmly. My Carhartts wouldn't have looked out of place, though I had changed into clean jeans before leaving the farm, washed my hair under the faucet, scrubbing at the plant scent, heady and woodsy, that clung to my skin. The smell wouldn't come off. I kept a vial of lavender oil on the windowsill to douse myself for days like this. I had dragged a comb through my hair, teeth snagging on stems, put on sneakers in place of my mud-gummed boots. Lisbeth didn't like it if I looked too country; her folks didn't like it.

But we all were country, even those of us living in duplexes and houses, like Lisbeth's, with garages and green lawns. Black rat snakes still found the cracks in cinderblock foundations and slithered into kitchens, box elder bugs still hatched in the sills. In spring, even driveways in town could lose their ends in the rising, brown waters of floods. At least in the springs we used to have.

I felt lighter, less encumbered, without the heavy coveralls, but the chill found its way into my joints. My wet hair crackled around my ears. In the field beyond the high school, the graduates shivered in their thin robes.

Generation to generation, nothing really changed. I knew these kids. They fetched water from springs, were familiar with stalling the electric company. But how many of them had grown up with a handgun duct-taped beneath the dining room table and canisters of money buried in the yard? How many of them slept in the woods some nights? It was safer than being too near the farmhouse with the raving men: customers, friends of Lobo's, who had brought pills or mushrooms; safer than my house with its thin, bum door. How many of these kids ate deer meat for months straight because that was how the hunters bartered for their weed?

I saw Lisbeth's folks. "You couldn't find a dress?" Lisbeth's mama said. Her lips pressed together until they disappeared.

Her parents looked like two pillars in church clothes, clean and pale. They thought my mama was a drunk. I had heard them whispering about it, years ago. And that Lobo was a saint for taking us in. It was safer to let them think that than to know the truth: we were all growers.

My jeans were clean. I swept a hand around my hair and felt no leaves. I sat down next to Lisbeth's folks. We faced the stage, a platform shrouded in mist.

"They always have this outside," Lisbeth's daddy was saying. "They did last year, even though..."

He didn't finish. It had no name.

Last year had been a late spring, the slightest thaw, and the coldest summer. It had snowed in September. And kept on snowing. This year, more For Sale signs had appeared in the windows of shops in town. More of the windows of houses were dark or broken: dingy, one- or two-roomed shacks. Plastic sheeting ballooned out of doorways, porches sagged into rot. Every house still occupied had a fire going, smoke chugging from the chimney. There were no children playing in the yards. On my drive to the high school, I had passed another gas station that had wrapped its pumps in tarps, yet another farm with chains across its driveway and a house that looked cold and empty, a greenhouse with windows smashed. Farms were taking the cold the hardest.

Ushers from the student council had wiped the folding chairs with towels, so the seats weren't damp, but a chill began to seep into my shoes from the ground. I wished I had worn my boots.

"Here, honey." Lisbeth's mama pulled two flat, foil-wrapped packages from her purse.

I slipped the hand warmers into my coat pockets, and my fingers closed around them, cracking them.

The choir had prepared for cold. They wore scarves and hats. Some of the girls had fur muffs, maybe from rabbits their daddies had shot. When the singers assembled on the front of the stage, they looked like something out of Charles Dickens, a band of winter ragamuffins. I was almost surprised when they didn't sing a Christmas carol.

Lisbeth had a great voice: high and true. When Lisbeth sang, people would sit up. People would pay attention. Being part of The Church meant she had to wear shirts that covered her shoulders and arms. It meant that I had never gone over to her house on Saturday night—she had services early the next morning. It meant that we had to meet places in secret like Crossroads.

She never drove out to the farm; she couldn't be caught around that stuff; she shouldn't be caught around me.

They prayed before meals at households in The Church. What Lisbeth believed herself didn't seem to matter. Singing was the reason she stayed, she said. They taught her other things she couldn't seem to unlearn: marriage was coming. Jesus was coming in a fireball that would divide the Earth into the good and the lost. She would have to decide. She would have to be ready to go with Him. She wore sensible shoes, kept her hair long. She was always waiting for men.

I didn't know the song they performed at what would be the last graduation ceremony, the final graduating class; the last time the platform groaned under the risers; the last time the wind tried but could not unsettle the principal's hair, buzzed short on his flat head. The school building behind us was already freezing, empty as a factory. I only listened to Lisbeth's voice, clear and strong alongside the choir, guiding them, blending, but sometimes rising above them.

By the time the principal's send-off to the class rolled around, a few families had left, back to their trucks. The speeches had been interminable in the cold. The sky looked gunmetal gray, a color that seemed familiar but also wrong. The wrong time of year for it.

The principal said, "Go forth. Go forth and don't just plant seeds of change. Let yourself take root."

What was he saying, who was he talking about or to? Go where? Do what? There were more eighteen-year-old local girls in jail than there were in town. I knew if I lingered at the reception in the gym, which I wasn't planning to—red punch that stained, dead boys staring out at me from photographs in the trophy case—some of the new graduates would ask me for work. Or weed.

The principal had a white jutted jaw, a way of droning on. And in the middle of his speech, it began to snow.

The crowd murmured. The principal broke off mid-word. Whatever he had to say, he would never finish it. Some of the seniors stuck out their tongues or turned up their palms to catch the snow, like children.

Snow in June. It was thrilling for a second, before we thought about it. From her seat onstage with the choir, Lisbeth and I exchanged a glance. No spring again. No spring this year.

June passed. The gray sky deepened. Every morning I woke in my tiny house, telling myself I would not have to light a fire, not this morning, not this late, not in summer. But then I felt the ache from shivering all night. I felt the air, crisp as bones. I swung the quilt around my shoulders and crept down the ladder. In the dark I fed wood into the stove.

Through the narrow window, I could see the big farmhouse on the hill, sharper than ever since the trees had no leaves. I could almost imagine a vein of blue smoke above the roof. But no smoke would come from the farmhouse chimney now unless I lit it.

It was quiet on the farm, always, but I began to notice it more. The house and purple finches, nuthatches, cardinals, the birds that would come to the sill for breakfast crumbs—my mama knew all their names—where were they? Morning after morning I stood at the window and realized other things were gone. No woodpeckers thrummed in the trees or thudded their beaks against the house. No owls whooped like boys in the night. I still heard the coyotes, high and cold, that sweet-howl call and response that made my heart freeze, tight in my chest, both beautiful and terrifying at the same time.

But I heard no peepers. Where were the frogs? The two ponds on the property looked low and stagnant. No ducks skimmed the water's surface. Nothing came from the sky except cold rain. Then snow.

My livelihood, my very life, depended on summer, on warmth and sun. Lobo had left me in charge of the farm knowing I could handle it. I could water and rotate, I could keep the plants alive. I could keep my mouth shut and stick to the deal with the boy.

But in July, it didn't get colder, it just kept on not getting warmer, not getting better.

It was strange to celebrate the Fourth without cookouts, Popsicles, and tank tops. I made vegetable soup to bring to Lisbeth's house, and when the sky, which was perpetually dull and heavy like a fistful of dirty wool, darkened, her neighbors set off fireworks. Roman candles, bought across the border in West Virginia.

Then it snowed again.

I didn't want to believe they could happen at the same time, fireworks and snow. The Roman candles dissipated, their sparks extinguished in the cold, wet air. Snow gathered, lacy as ash but mounting on sheds, on the roof of my truck parked in the alley between the houses and an old bar. A man poked his head out of the bar, looked at the sky, then stumbled back into the dark and pounding bass, throwing his drunken arms out for balance like an ice skater. Lisbeth's neighbors were grilling. I heard sizzling as flakes struck the coals. This snow was going to stick.

Lisbeth was quiet. How much longer could we do this, anyway, sit around in lawn chairs in her folks' backyard? People our age were signing leases. If I didn't have the farm to manage, the crop to sell, maybe she and I could do that, get an apartment together in a city, Chillicothe or Marietta. We could take sandwiches to the river where the barges battened kayaks, and fishing lines, threaded with lead weights, hung from the trees, dangling in the water like a girl's long hair.

Instead, here we were, watching the neighbors' thermal underwear stiffen on a clothesline. More than ever, I felt trapped. By my family, by the plants, by Ohio.

"Should'a brought that in," Lisbeth's daddy said about the laundry, taking a pull on a cold lemonade.

In August, people in town, when I shopped for groceries and fertilizer and diatomaceous earth, had finally stopped saying, *What a ridiculous year. What an unusual year. This is one for the record books.* By August, it wasn't funny anymore. The buds never unfolded. The flowers never came.

A letter came to everyone in the county. I opened it at the mailbox and trudged up the quarter-mile driveway back to the lower field. By the time I reached my tiny house, I had read the letter a few times.

In response to the unprecedented cold weather our
nation is experiencing, and under the advisement of
a committee of parents, educators, and administra-
tors, the school board has voted to suspend school
until October 1, at which time this situation may be
reassessed. We will contact you with further updates.

The letter wasn't a huge surprise. I remembered the high
school didn't turn on the heat until the end of October, and I doubted they could afford two extra months of
heating, especially not knowing how cold it would get.
The part of the letter that concerned me was the last line.

We encourage you to spend this time with your
families.

My pocket shook. Lisbeth was calling.

I didn't have reception in the driveway—most of the
farm didn't—but my tiny house sat on its own hill, which
caught some weak signals from the tower in town. She
didn't bother with *hello*. "Did you get the letter?" she asked.

I set the rest of the mail on the shelf inside the door.
"Yes."

"Thoughts?"

I paused. "I don't think you have to worry about those
altos this year."

Lisbeth fell silent.

"Come on," I said. "It'll be like a long vacation for you.
We can hang out together so you won't get bored. Why
don't you come over right now?"

"You know I can't do that. I can't come out there."

"Come to Crossroads at least. Get your grease fix."

She didn't answer, and I glanced out the window by the woodstove. The metal roof of the farmhouse looked silver in a new freckling of snow. In its basement, I knew, the lights glowed warm and white, and the air smelled like a mossy jungle, heavy and spicy and wet. Now, the basement was the only place anything could grow.

I placed my hand above the top of the stove. It was ice-cold. "Lisbeth, I guess I should go. The fire's out. I have to get more wood. In August." I tried to laugh.

Lisbeth didn't laugh back. "Wil, wait." She took a breath, and I knew something big was coming; she inhaled, then spoke in a rush when she delivered bad or hard news. I pictured her holding on to her braid, squeezing it, as she did for reassurance. She didn't even know that she did this. "We're getting out," she said. "The Church is going away and we're going with them. I want you to come with us. My folks want you to. The Church said it was okay."

"Getting out? Where are you going?"

"South. That's all I know."

The news, when I watched it at Lisbeth's house—we didn't have cable or internet on the farm—showed cars waiting to cross into Mexico. The line stretched for miles, longer and longer every cold day, the cars laden with suitcases, gas cans, children's bikes. Whole lives strapped to the roofs. Most of the cars were turned away at the border. Where was Lisbeth going to go?

"What about your job?" I said.

She did laugh then, but it came out barking like a cough. "What job, now?"

What about me? I thought. *Us?* I said, "The entire church is moving together?"

"Yes. The Migration, that's what they're calling it."

"Like birds."

"Wil, you can't tell anyone about this, okay? You can't tell your mama or Lobo, when they call. The invitation is only for you. The Church talked about it, and that was the decision." Silence from me, which Lisbeth felt uncomfortable with and tried to fill. "It's just, we're taking these vans, and there's only so much room, so many seat belts. And there's only so much food."

"You're taking food? What place are you going to that has no food?"

"The Church is prepared. We've been preparing for something for a long time. Not this specifically, but in case something should come, someday, we've been ready. My parents love you," Lisbeth said. "I love you. Come with us. We can protect you."

"Protect me from what? Do you know something? What's causing this?"

Lisbeth paused. "God."

2

The day she left, the vans filled the road, one after the other. It was like the news stories about the Mexican border, except these vans were identical white, their windows tinted. I knew Lisbeth rode in one of them. Even though I didn't want to, even though I hated The Church for taking my closest friend from me, the only one who knew me, the one I loved, I stood out beside the road, in the wild field at the end of our driveway, beside the rural route, and waved at every single one.

Nobody had thought much about The Church until they had moved from the basement of the community center into the abandoned supermarket at the edge of town. Somehow they had enough money to buy the building and fix it up, and somehow they had enough people to fill it every Sunday and Wednesday.

In the holler, we tended to leave things alone as long

as you weren't hurting anybody—and even then, as Lobo liked to joke, there was a sliding scale. Was it your own kin you were hurting? Were they grown up? Had they brought it on themselves, bought the pills, boiled the poppies, kissed your wife or sister?

People were least likely to forgive hurting a dog, Lobo said. That was worse than hurting a woman. If you had land, had bought it or inherited it and held on to it, you could do what you wanted out there, beyond your driveway gate or locked doors. That was your right.

Nobody had thought much about The Church. Except their members kept writing letters to the editor of the newspaper, and they kept having candidates run for school board—and win. They became a part of the town, like a shadow quietly and swiftly spreading over us. Or a disease.

And now they were gone. All gone somewhere. All the white church vans.

The Migration.

I thought I would know which van she was in. I thought she would roll down the window, or I would see her moving behind the dark glass. She would give me a sign—and I would know her. But she didn't. The last van passed me.

The leaves on the trees were supposed to redden and brown, to die and fall. But there were no leaves on the trees. We were supposed to start wearing sweaters as the cold nights stretched on. But we were already wearing sweaters. So we added layers, those of us who could afford more wool and fleece. The charity shop ran out of coats. The Church wasn't there to launch a warm-clothing drive. School wasn't open to feed children hot breakfast and lunch. It was harvest time, supposed to be. The moon looked silver and swollen, and the coyotes howled at night with a sharpness I knew was hunger.

Weed needs a warm, humid climate. Always before, that was what we had in southeastern Ohio; that was our gift. One of the only things that grew well in our old, abused soil, the earth mistreated by years of coal mining and fracking and mountaintop removal, was marijuana. That was what Lobo said.

But the outdoor harvest the year that Lobo and Mama decided to leave had been a bad one. A wet spring, if you could call it *spring* at all. Lobo and Mama had lost their plants that they grew in the wild: in neglected lots, in deep forest, in patches of unused land behind highways, in woody acres belonging to the state or accessible only by canoe.

Some of the plants that Lobo had hiked in on a pack and planted at twilight in the illegal ground had been swept away by rain. Other plants never took. The earth was too wet and chilled. Their roots rotted. Still other plants froze: their leaves folding, blackening, then falling off. Or they were eaten young by desperate animals or the always-desperate insects. Every time Lobo went out in a canoe to check on the wild plants, he returned with his head a little lower, his back more dejected, his jaw tight. I knew he would chew his food silently and angrily, lash out at Mama, kick something down the stairs. I didn't go up to the farmhouse for dinner on those nights. I didn't want to be the thing he kicked.

Outdoor crops were half our income. But after the first cold year, after the loss of everything wild, we didn't even try to plant outside. All we had left was the grow room in the basement of the big house.

As a teenager, I had avoided going in there. It hurt my eyes. I felt it would stick on me, like the scent of weed, be obvious. I thought—like sex—once I had been down in the grow room, people would know. And they *did* know, but for other reasons: it was a small town. There were rumors that were true; people bought from Lobo and knew his girlfriend had a daughter. Our weed was good. People came across state lines to buy it. And they talked about it, about us.

Lisbeth and I became fast friends because I was an outcast and she was a Church weirdo. She had a list of forbidden things, and she obeyed it, at first. She would talk to me without asking, like other kids did, *Do you have any on you? Is it true, what they say, that yours is as sweet as strawberry?*

What I felt, going in the grow room, was *trouble trouble trouble* beaming at me from the walls. Bright lights were suspended from the ceiling. The light bounced off the walls, which were covered in silver insulation, nail-gunned into place, on every side of the room, even the ceiling, to keep in the heat and light. The fans ran daily, ventilating the space. The air was fecund, a lushness you could feel. Someone had to move the plants, heavy in their plastic pots of earth, every day, switching out the plants under the lamps, and the ones closest to the fans, rotating so that every leaf got the same amount of light and warmth, every plant had a chance.

Someone—usually me—had to do the other work of keeping the farm running while the basement hummed on. The daily maintenance, the chores and the crises: always keeping the wild back, keeping the farm from teetering into decay, the weeds pushing at the door of the house like hungry children. I was always beating back nature, bending it into working for me, ripping out the multiflora rose thorns, hacking and burning hemlock, spraying aphids off the pot.

The summer chores were difficult. But winter was dire, made up of essential tasks necessary just to survive. And now winter was everywhere. Winter was always. Winter was the fire, the fire, the fire—keeping the stoves going and the water running, which meant remembering to leave the taps on a trickle at night and sometimes hiking up to the cistern and either chopping at the ice crust on top, or running a hairdryer on the pipes closest to the surface if they froze. Or, if I couldn't unfreeze the pipes and it was biting cold, lugging buckets of fresh water from the cistern back to the house.

But the fire. The fire needed to be fed always, and with Lobo and Mama busy in the grow room—turning the plants, picking bugs off the plants, trimming the leaves from the plants—the fire fell to me.

Soon it all did, all the work. Lobo knew somebody in California. The man had a house and fields, needed a grower. After the first cold year, the year the outdoor harvest died, the first time we skipped spring, Lobo and Mama went on ahead to check it out. They left me alone with the farm.

★ ★ ★

I burned more fuel than I ever had before. Usually we would start in July, chopping wood for the coming winter. It was strange to think about cold when the sun was high and bright, when sweat pasted my hair to the back of my neck, and we drained iced nettle tea in jars. But that was the way of the work: to plan ahead, to be ready. What was coming would eventually come. Chopping a few days a week, a few hours a day, no more, we would have a decent supply of wood by October's first frosts.

But now I couldn't chop fast enough. I was neglecting my chores in the grow room. Meanwhile, the woodpile sank low. Mice scuttled into the house to keep warm. The farm was too much for anyone to manage alone, I thought as I shoved my ax into the truck. I needed more wood again.

I could take Lobo's old truck anywhere, it didn't matter: into the mud, off the road. We would drive it till it died, and leave it where it lay, probably at the bottom of a hill somewhere or in a timothy field, the rusting red hulk of a whale. There was a cutout through the lower field that led into the trees, which the neighbors used for hunting. I drove the truck there to find wood.

The deer were leaving. We had hunted them, we had hunted them a lot. We had finally, when spring didn't come this year, panicked, and went after them with a desperation that knew no season.

People had always poached in the woods. But parking the truck and stepping out into the forest, I saw smaller skulls than I had ever seen before. Deer bones jutted out of the leaves. Does, which were good eating.

But maybe some fawns, too.

I didn't wander too far from the truck; I wouldn't be able to carry the wood. In the cold weather, in the bulky coveralls and coat I wore all the time now, hair stuffed up in my hat, not much marked me as female. But not much marked me as adult, either. I was small, a head shorter than Lisbeth and most of the women in the holler. I wasn't as strong as I wanted to be, as Lobo always thought I should be. *Runt*, he called me. The weakling that came with the real woman he wanted. Good for nothing, he would say. He had told me I had to learn to defend myself. Because of the way I looked, because of who I was, men would come after me.

He was right about some things.

I found a decent tree, a dead sugar maple. I would chop it in the woods, heft the pieces into the bed, drive home, and split it. The work would take all morning, maybe all day, and it was harder, more demanding work than sitting at a table and snipping buds off plants. My back would ache in different places tonight.

But the good thing about chopping wood, your mind wasn't bothered by anything. I could forget missing Lisbeth, missing Mama. What they were doing in California, why she hadn't called for months—he hadn't let her—even the missed spring, I put it out of my mind. It was just me and the ax.

It felt good not thinking, listening to the ax's song. I got warm for a moment. But I heard something. I stopped, buried the ax in the log. I heard a voice calling, not birdsong.

Mama.

That was my first thought. A voice, calling in the woods. What else do you call for?

"Hello?" I stepped off the cow path, let my eyes rove the landscape: hills, speckled with dead leaves, a little snow clustered in feathery patches.

Something detached from a log, becoming not a part of the woods, but a hand, raised up as though I had called his name.

A man lay in the leaves, a hatchet beside him. His right foot was turned to the side, and he held it with his other hand. He looked familiar, in the way all men did: bland features, broken capillaries on his cheeks from the cold or bad shaving. Long dark hair stuck to the side of his face.

I approached him slowly. "Are you okay?" I asked.

"I guess not. I guess I twisted my foot."

"What are you doing here?" I didn't look at his foot. I looked at the hatchet beside him. I looked out of the corners of my eyes and couldn't see a truck, a friend of his. But where there was one man, there were certainly others. I saw notch marks in the log felled beside the man. The marks looked fresh, like the nibbling of a small beast. "A white birch?" I couldn't help myself. "That burns way too fast. That's a bad tree to use for firewood. If that's what you were doing."

He just looked at me, then tried and failed to stand. "Can you help me? Drop me off in town? I think my foot's broken or something."

What was the trick, what was the scam? But nothing in the woods seemed out of place. No branches were broken off along the path. I saw no cigarette butts in the snow, heard no rustling. There was no one else around. Cold whistled in the trees like a drunk.

It was just me out here, me and this man. I heard Lobo's voice in my head, telling me not to be stupid, not to be a girl about this. Not to trust anyone.

"Lean on me," I said.

We hobbled together to the truck. I helped him into the front seat and started the engine. I listened to it turn over, thought about what to say that wouldn't give up too much. "My mama always wants me to carry a first-aid kit with me when I'm chopping wood, but I always forget," I said.

"Me, too. Obviously."

I looked over at him. "What's your name?"

"Grayson. You're Wil. Short for Wylodine, I remember."

"You remember?" I studied him as he leaned back in the passenger seat, teeth gritted with pain as I began to drive. The truck bounced over the rutted path. "Did we go to school together?"

"I'm a year younger."

"But you know me."

"The name," he said.

"Right. The name."

"And…" I could tell he was debating whether or not to say it. "Your family."

"Of course. My family."

But some families grew or cooked worse: poppies, meth.

Some traded in pills. Some drove back and forth to Chillicothe with balloons of heroin, bottles of painkillers. A lot of families got caught. Some were in jail, or died, or were killed. Lobo and Mama at least had been careful.

I looked at the man from the woods again. His back rested against the window, though *rested* was the wrong word. He sat rigid—and not just from pain. He was poised to jump if I did something (*what?*), ready to flinch, roll, or run. I wouldn't have been surprised if his hand was on the door handle.

He would be disappointed to find out I had locked it.

My eyes flicked back to the road. I kept my voice cool. "Did you want to buy something? Is that why you were in my woods?"

"Buy something?"

"Weed?"

"No! I don't do that." He paused. "Do you?"

I could feel him looking at me, gray and intense.

"You must not remember me well," I said.

The parking lot at the clinic was full. I dropped Grayson off at the emergency entrance and parked down by the river. When I returned to the clinic, I found Grayson slumped in the very last chair. I crouched down beside him.

He seemed surprised to see me. "You don't have to stay."

"Do you have folks coming?"

He made some kind of sound.

"I'll stay. Nobody's waiting at home for me, either."

The waiting room overflowed. People sat in wheelchairs. A baby cried. Maybe more than one baby. There were several people with ice packs or bandages, several more coughing, but most just looked pale and miserable, red eyes and thin shoulders.

"People don't want to go home," a nurse said, pausing beside us, ice pack in her hand. "They don't have heat there." She bent the ice pack, releasing the chemicals with a crack, and handed it to Grayson. I thought of graduation: Lisbeth's mama and her hand warmers. It seemed like years ago.

Someone moaned in a corner by the gift shop, and the nurse headed off to see to them.

"You want to tell me what you were doing in my woods?" I asked Grayson.

"I didn't know it was your woods."

"I didn't see a car. How did you get all the way out there?"

Grayson folded the ice pack over his foot. He had taken his boot off, and in the harsh, yellow light of the clinic waiting room he looked younger. The beard scruff on his face could have been new. No lines spread around his eyes. "I got a ride from some guys at the restaurant. I ran out of firewood and wanted to go somewhere nobody would notice if I took a little. The guys dropped me off and I hiked into the woods. I thought, if somebody lived in those woods, they wouldn't mind."

"Stores sell firewood, you know."

"They used to." Grayson adjusted his ice pack. "When was the last time you were at Walmart?"

"My idea of hell," I said.

"Well, the space heaters are gone now. They sold out weeks ago. Back-ordered, I guess. There's a run on sleeping bags, blankets. Grow lights."

"Grow lights?"

"Things are getting bad," Grayson said. "You might not know because you're out there on your farm."

It was true. I could go for a week without going into town, maybe longer. I could make the groceries stretch. It was a thirty-minute drive into town in good weather, and I had made the trip less and less since I had been by myself. I wasn't sure what stopped me. Snow or ice. Worrying about the roads. I waited until too late to set out. The sun sank earlier and earlier in the afternoons, and I didn't want to be driving much after dusk, coming back alone to a house both empty and dark.

I think I also didn't go because I didn't want people feeling sorry for me. It was a small town. And small towns talk. Some people knew my family had left. The men at the feed store were already throwing in bags of fertilizer for free, offering to carry stuff out to my car, help me load. They weren't hitting on me. Men who had known me longer than a heartbeat, or who were familiar with Lobo's temper, had stopped trying stuff with me a long time ago. It was pity I saw in their eyes now.

In the waiting room, I looked around at the wheelchairs, the old women in shawls. A child couldn't stop trembling. Being isolated on the farm, I had cut myself off from a lot. My puffy coveralls felt almost too hot in the waiting room. I wore comfortable boots that fit. I was warm and fed. Fine.

Grayson was talking on and on. "Canned goods are going. Nonperishables. Propane."

I pulled out my phone, but didn't dial the number. Lobo's number. My mama didn't have her own phone. Too expensive, he said. If I called, he would answer. He would want to know why I was calling, what had I done wrong. I shoved the phone back in my pocket. "After you're done here?" I said to Grayson. "We're going to Walmart."

Seeing a doctor took all morning. When she finally came into the room where we had been placed—a storage closet, based on the mops and brooms and rolls of brown paper towels crowded in around us—her eyes looked scared. I sat on an upside-down bucket because there was only one chair and I let Grayson have it.

The doctor didn't ask our names. She didn't introduce herself. She didn't even ask how it happened. She had a large brace ready in her hands. She unwrapped it and strapped it around Grayson's foot.

"This is a walking cast," she explained, tightening the straps. "You'll need it."

Grayson looked at me, then back at the doctor. "What does that mean?"

"That means, in an ideal world, you'd rest for a few weeks. You'd stay off your foot as much as possible. You wouldn't walk. I'd give you crutches. You'd give your bone time to heal. But we don't live in an ideal world," she said. "I don't want you to be left behind."

"Left behind?" he echoed.

And that was it. She was leaving. She had spent five

minutes with us, barely. The clinic had not even taken X-rays, not that I thought Grayson could have afforded them. I had been parking when he had filled out his paperwork, but from the sick gray tone his skin was taking on, the way he had kept asking me, *Is it broken? Do you think it's broken?*—like I knew—paying for this visit was going to be a problem.

The doctor moved to the door, then thought of something. She pressed her lips together. She had short, dark hair, tight as if she had curled it, the blood-shadow of lipstick that had faded away. I could tell she didn't have time to tell us whatever it was she was going to say. "Stop by the pharmacy on your way out."

"Why?" I asked. "Does he have a prescription?"

"No. It's going to hurt. But we're all out of prescription pain meds."

"Out? How can you be out?"

"Oh, we were out days ago. Everyone refilled everything they had or could get their hands on. We're waiting on a shipment, but I don't have high hopes. There are shortages everywhere."

"Why should we go to the pharmacy, then?"

The doctor looked at us blankly. As if we should know this already. "Vitamins," she said. "Over the counter pain meds. But especially vitamins. Get as many as you can carry." She opened the broom closet door.

"Wait," Grayson said. "Do we stop by the front desk or—"

The doctor was already in the hall. Now that the door

was open, we could hear crying. An adult this time. "Don't worry about it."

"But I don't have insurance."

"Why bother?"

And she was gone.

What had happened in the slow, predictable days I had spent on the farm, rotating and watering the plants, chopping firewood? How much had gone wrong? How fast?

We pushed through the swinging double doors, Grayson walking with a hitch as he dragged his bad leg. His foot looked heavy in its new brace, like he was towing a log, and his breath sounded jagged. He was trying to get used to the pain. The waiting room had gotten more crowded since we had been in the storage closet, and out the windows, the parking lot looked strange. Too white. It had snowed again.

At the clinic pharmacy, a line of people waited in the prescription drop-off area. But I headed straight for the shelves. I swept bottle after bottle of vitamins into my arms, then I started filling Grayson's arms.

"Hey, those are prenatal vitamins, for pregnant people," he said.

"So?" I thought for a moment, then put the prenatal vitamins, and gummy vitamins for kids, back. I added boxes of cough syrup, bottles of iodine, rolls of tacky bandages, and painkillers.

"I don't have enough money for all this," Grayson whispered.

"I do."

It was a short line to pay; most people were still at the

drop-off desk, clamoring for refills, for something for their pain. The cashier had a look I was starting to think was *the* look, her lids popping open, her pupils the tiniest dark dots. The whites of her eyes looked as shocked as snow. She filled several paper bags with our purchases and shoved them across the counter to us. A man started to bang his cane against the counter to get her attention.

Grayson and I reached the lobby. The nurse who had given him the ice pack stood on a chair and was shouting, "Please remain patient. You will be seen in the order you arrived."

From the crowd, there was a murmur, getting louder. People had spilled into the lobby and through the emergency room doors. People sat on gurneys and newspaper bins. Someone was bleeding, a bright red trail that streaked across the floor. I began to hear distinct voices, popping up above the crowd like Lisbeth's treble when she led the choir. *Not going to stand for this... How much more...*

We went to Walmart.

3

We had to park clear at the end of the lot, by the Chinese restaurant, which was closed. A hand-lettered sign in the window read *No Heat*. We walked quickly. The pavement was frosted over, the reflections of streetlights buzzing in the icy puddles on the ground. Strangers joined us, their shoulders down, a tautness to their jaws like an arrow's string. It made me think of Lobo, Lobo mad. I heard a thudding, which I realized was Grayson's leg in the cast, striking the pavement.

"I should have dropped you off at the door," I said. "I'm sorry."

He would never be able to wear coveralls with that thing. How would he stay warm?

"I have to get used to it. That's what the doctor said."

There was no greeter at the entrance to the store. I

grabbed one of the last remaining carts, whipping it past a woman who cursed at me. I muttered an apology.

"It's only going to get worse," Grayson said.

Inside, our boots squealed on the floor, crossed with slushy tracks. We were only a few steps into the store when I realized I could see my breath.

"They turned the heat off?" I said.

"Probably never turned it on. Big place like this, it must cost a fortune to heat. No wonder the schools closed."

People and carts clogged the aisles. It was more crowded than even the first of the month, when support checks came in, and everyone who could afford to shopped with their tiny bit of money from the state. Mama had taught me not to go to stores then.

Everyone looked gray as overwashed clothes, exhausted and faded, their eyes turning up at the shelves as if they held the answers. This was another reason I didn't like to come to town. There was too much suffering.

There had been suffering here forever, even before the cold came. Long ago, we had been forgotten in the holler, forgotten and left to make it on our own with no jobs, no hope of jobs. Now, cold wrung the worst from us. People snapped at each other, impatient, panicking over milk. All the women looked like my mama: grease-colored hair, faded pretty faces. The bright displays of the store, which had always looked garish, now seemed obscene.

"I don't know what to get," I said.

Grayson took over. "You're pretty set for vitamins now. You probably need warmth and nonperishable food." But in housewares, the shelves had been swept clean of blankets, sheets, even fluffy towels. In the crafts aisle, Grayson shoved bolts of fabric—fleece and hunter's plaid and thick gray wool—into the cart. "You can make blankets if you have to," he said. "You don't even have to sew."

"Good thing, because I don't."

The camping section had been stripped. Hand warmers, lanterns, and portable stoves had disappeared, along with all the heaters, as Grayson had predicted. He put several plastic gas cans into the cart. In the grocery section, I saw a man pulling canned food out of a stranger's cart. He kept taking them until he was caught by the second man's screaming wife or girlfriend. We steered out of that aisle.

The shouting intensified. We curved the cart around a smashed jar of cherries, bright and pink on the floor. It was hard not to feel dizzy, not to think of bad things. Grayson edged between strangers, adding energy bars, jars of peanut butter, tins of meat and fish, powdered milk, and packages of hard candy into my cart, swiftly and confidently reaching his hand between strangers' hands, taking what he thought I'd need.

"You sure you have enough money for all this?" he asked.

"Yeah," I said. "Cash isn't a problem."

Mama and Lobo had left a lot of it buried in the yard.

"You listening to the president's speech tomorrow?" the cashier asked us, scanning our items. We had waited half an hour in line to reach her. "It's something bad, I bet. Chemical weapons or terrorists. You know what I think?"

"What?" Grayson said.

The cashier leaned forward, her name badge clanging against the stand with the card reader. Her name was April. "I think you should all get the hell outta town." She started scanning again, the beeps from the register punching under her words. "I tell you what, I ain't sticking around to give my notice. Not worth it. I'm leaving tomorrow. Mama and me. We're going to Florida."

I tried not to feel anything at the word *Mama*. My own was fine, she was fine. She had gotten out. It was normal for the two of us to go awhile without talking. We hadn't been close like that for a long time.

"Florida's packed," Grayson said. "Besides, even Florida gets snow sometimes."

"That church left. They just picked up and left, you know? All of them, cleared out in the night."

"It wasn't in the night."

"Maybe those wackos were onto something."

"Thanks," I said. I grabbed the receipt, as if we were ever coming back.

Grayson told me he lived in the rolling ridges on the other side of the county. I knew the place. We had lived there ourselves for a few years right before and after my daddy left. The houses were brown and forgettable. A lot of duplexes. Ours had smelled of mildew. On some nights, when the wind blew a certain way, it seemed like the house had a sharpness, a bitterness I could breathe.

Maybe it was my parents' fights. Even after my daddy had gone, anger had a way of hanging around: sulking past the corners, down the drab carpeted hall. Disappointment lingered in the doorways, like smoke or a ghost.

"Do you like living here?" I asked Grayson. I didn't tell him about my old house. I hoped we didn't pass it. I didn't want to see it again.

"It's okay. My allergies are bad around here. The Church was trying to help with that."

"The Church?" I looked over at him.

Grayson pointed. "It's right there."

I pulled into a driveway before a house, indistinguishable from all the other houses. The lawn looked neglected, the grass matted and pale where it showed through snow. When we got out of the truck, I noticed most of the houses had patchy lawns. The cold had killed them, or the homeowners had given up. Newspapers piled on the porch of the neighbor's place. I thought of Lisbeth's house. Had they sold it, rented it? Was their porch filling up with snow?

On the farm, we didn't pretend that we lived anywhere nice. Lobo barely mowed the grass, just a strip by the vegetable patch that he let get thick and high before he wrestled with it, and he only bothered so we could access the tomatoes. Most of the land had grown up into jewelweed, poverty grass, and thorns, gone its own wild way. The farmhouses looked like toys out in the country, dotted on the landscape, tiny pieces on a complex board game. Sometimes I used to comfort myself with the fact that if we let it go, left it all behind, nature would just take it back, bust weeds through the windows, shoot Virginia creeper down the halls. That was back when we had a summer.

We had reached the front door of Grayson's place. I had helped him up the walk. He removed his arm from around

my shoulders and said: "Thanks. This is good. Thanks for
your help."

"Are you sure you want me to go? You should at least
take some of those vitamins with you."

"That's okay. Thanks. I feel like an idiot."

"Well, do you still need wood?" Then I stopped, because Grayson had gotten the door open, and it had opened
wider than he had intended, unveiling a dim and claus-
trophobic living room.

There were pizza boxes on the floor, more gray newspapers and stacks of mail, a smell of sour milk and dust.
Clothes were slung over the back of the couch, the cushions rumpled with sheets. Someone had been sleeping
there, in front of the dark fireplace.

"Is everything okay?" I asked.

Grayson tried to close the door. "Thanks again for your
help. I can take it from here."

"You live alone?"

He didn't look at me. "The Church."

"The Church?"

"My folks couldn't find a renter for the house so…when
they left with The Church, I gave up my place and moved
in here." He sighed, launching into something I could
feel he didn't want to tell me. "The plan was I would stay
here and work until The Church got settled. But business
at the restaurant hasn't been great. My shifts keep getting
cut, and you can't walk anywhere from here. It's not like
there's a bus. The plan was…" He shook his head.

"I'm sorry."

"I guess I'm not doing so great here on my own."

"Why were you chopping wood?"

"The bills were too high. They shut off the gas. I still have the microwave, for cooking."

"But you don't have any heat."

That was the other thing I felt, standing in the doorway of Grayson's house: a cold so sharp it cut me. A chest-hurting cold, cold that made it hard to breathe. That meant the heat hadn't been on for a long time. Cold had crept into the folds of the drapes, into the cracks in the floor. I tried to imagine sleeping in that kind of cold, how it crawled under the skin.

I had been calling Lisbeth since the vans pulled away. Her daddy's cell rang and rang. Her parents wouldn't let her have her own phone—a worldly distraction, they said. Both Lisbeth and my mama, the two most important women in the world to me, were cut off from me. By men. Had Grayson been able to reach his folks?

I looked again at the clothes, the sheets and pillows on the couch beside the black and still fireplace, littered with ash. The sheets were flowered, which somehow made them sadder. The quiet of the house pressed down on me. I thought of my own house, empty, the farm growing quieter and quieter with each cold day. Grayson and I had both lost people.

"Get your stuff," I said to him.

He protested but not for long. He apologized, as if he had done something wrong. Only fallen behind, that was all he had done. An empty milk carton could turn into a trash pile in days, I knew. Rust could take a tool left out overnight. Just for a little while, I told him. Till his foot began to heal. I had the space. And I had heat.

I helped him load up. He didn't want to take much: clothes, books, a backpack with a beat-up laptop. "I should tell you," I said when I saw the laptop. "We don't have internet out at the farm. My mama and her boyfriend—they're old-fashioned. And paranoid. They like the wilderness. Peace and quiet. Being remote. Plus, they didn't want to pay for it."

"Do you have cable?"

"No."

I knew how it sounded. In a town that included The Church, this absence marked my family as the strangest of all. Mostly, even the dirtiest double-wide, the smallest shack, windows streaked with soot from the last cooker blowout, had a flat-screen: giant and blaring. Appalachian halos, Lobo used to call the blue glow that came from all the households watching TV at night. It must have made him feel good—superior—to have resisted this one pull, this single wicked thing.

"It's nice," I said. "You notice things in nature. But we've kind of been sheltered." I thought of one of Lisbeth's old neighbors, near the bar. They had broken windows, no time or money or inclination to fix them, but they also had a hummingbird feeder on a hook, which they always kept full of red sugar. "You get used to it."

"Wait a minute." Grayson hobbled back into the house. Soon he came back, one last box in his arms. Wires poked out.

"What is that?" I asked.

"A ham radio. It was a project for Boy Scouts."

"You were a Boy Scout?"

"Not a very good one."

We drove away from the house. Grayson looked back only once. I felt a strange sort of sadness as he did. It was years ago, when I had lived there, before Lobo, before growing. I had collected cereal box tops for school; watched TV at night with my mama, wrapped in an afghan against her shoulder, listening to the neighbors' fights through the walls. My own folks' fights were over. My folks were over, stale as smoke.

But everyone fought in those hills.

We passed a decommissioned school bus on the side of the road. It had been spray-painted white, almost indistinguishable from the landscape, except for its blinkers flashing red. Someone knelt in the runoff next to the bus and fixed a flat tire. Inside, the bus was packed to the roof with blankets and boxes. They must have been running, fleeing somewhere. An orange cat stared at us out the back window, perched on an upside-down basket.

We had almost reached the farm before I spoke again. "Do you know where they went?" I asked Grayson.

He turned away from the window, looking at me.

"The Church. Your folks. Did they tell you where they were going?"

"No. Somewhere warm. That was all they said, all they were allowed to say, I guess. I wasn't a member, so... They didn't tell me much. But The Church had been planning this, sort of. Planning a move."

"How were they planning it?"

"Well, they were preppers. They were stockpiling things. Guns and stuff. But they weren't prepping for this. They were prepping for, you know—the end of the world. Brimstone. That's a little different, I guess. They weren't prepping for winter. Just a long, shitty winter. Winter forever."

I stared back through the windshield. The road was a monochrome rainbow of white: new snow, gritty packed snow, and a slick salted tongue of ice. It was slow-going. I thought of Lisbeth around a campfire. I thought of her sleeping in her shoes because The Church had taught her that the world might end at any moment, and she needed to be ready to run.

Grayson said The Church had prepared with guns, believing the world would end with fire. When they left for California, Mama and Lobo had taken the one taped under the dining room table.

But there was still a gun buried in the yard.

4

I expected Mama and Lobo to be there, even after a year on my own. Every time I turned off the rural route onto the dirt and gravel driveway—more and more, mostly gravel and ice—my shoulders tightened. I braced for the anger and silence, my mama moving quickly from one drudgery job to the next, her fingers flying. No time for anything, even for me. No time for thinking about what kind of life this was, what we had gotten ourselves mired in. She never stopped, except when she didn't move at all, when she collapsed, chemicals trickling through her blood, eyelids slammed shut like diurnal poppies.

I still thought I'd see Lobo near the house, mute and focused, chopping wood, the ax above his head like a lightning rod. Mama taking laundry from the line strung from the porch to the peach tree, shaking the dried clothes because they had stiffened in the cold. Some part of me was stunned not to hear the ring of the ax.

I pulled up close to the farmhouse. I could see it through Grayson's eyes: gloomy and bare. When things broke, we didn't really fix them. We wedged cardboard where the broken glass had been; we stuffed rags in the drafts from the door.

"Well, this is it," I said.

Grayson didn't say anything. I showed him inside and nodded at the woodstove. "I'll get the fire going. That helps a lot."

I found myself apologizing. Some of the rooms had been shut off this year, to avoid heating them. I told him not to open any closed doors. I told him that included the basement.

His eyes flashed immediately to the door. Small and peaked, under the stairs like a portal, the door to a kingdom.

"Just don't," I said.

He knew what my family did. He didn't need to see it.

I put his stuff in Mama and Lobo's old bedroom, slinging his duffel bag down on the bed, on the quilt they hadn't taken. Get the memories out. Get it over with, I thought. I thought the room might as well be used. I opened up the curtains. A flourish of dust, like a flock of birds taking off. Had it only been a year?

In the yard below the window rusted an old bathtub, once used for watering cows. It was edged in ice. At the bottom of the tub was a puddle of darkness, frozen solid. Once I had seen a fawn bed down beneath the window. I had not wanted to open the curtains the rest of the way, not wanted to startle the deer into running.

It had been a year since I had seen a fawn alive.

Grayson wandered into the room behind me, cast thudding on the wood floors. He was a loud ghost. I left him to look around, and started a fire in the stove like I had promised. I waited until the kindling caught, then fed the first split logs in. When I heard the crackle and felt the warmth, I straightened.

"I've got to go back to my own place," I called to him. "Unload a few things. Phones don't work so great around here. If you need anything before I get back…" I paused.

"I'll come down to your house," Grayson said.

He couldn't, not with that injury, but we left it at that. I drove home, wondering what I had gotten myself into.

I didn't know him; I had just met him; I felt sorry for him. These long days, longer and darker since Lisbeth left—they would only get darker and colder still. Grayson knew what Lobo and my mama did for money, what I did. Everyone knew, really. But knowing and seeing were two different things. I had brought Grayson to the farm, endangering everything.

Now he knew where the farm was. Now he could find it, or lead someone to it, or tell the wrong person about it without even realizing what he had done.

I could hear Lobo's voice saying these things in my head. But what was the danger now? The plants were gone; I had shipped them off. Harvested myself, done the finger-cramping work of trimming alone, though I could have hired waitresses from town—Lobo liked to use girls because our hands were small and quick, and waitresses always need money, he said. I had carefully hung the plants, cut in Y-shapes, onto clotheslines strung around the farmhouse to dry. For days, the house had smelled heady and dewy, like a fairy kingdom. I had weighed and spilled the piles into brown paper grocery bags. The bags felt so light—it was part of the magic feeling; money from nothing—the weed was almost weightless.

But a nothing worth thousands of dollars.

Still, Lobo would have been angry that I had forgotten what our lives were like. What we could and could not do.

I parked the truck in the lower field by my tiny house, and unloaded the groceries and supplies. The house was built on a trailer Lobo had bartered off some guy for clones. He and Mama had liked the thought that the house could be hitched up to a truck and moved. When Mama and I had lived here, he had liked the idea that he could inch us ever closer. When I stayed on in the shack alone, she liked the idea that I could go.

But in all those years, the house on wheels had never moved.

Weeds had grown and died around the hitch, which was rusted. Some of the wheels looked stuck in mud, though I had kept the wheels full of air, at my mama's insistence. Frozen, mud was becoming another substance entirely: solid, unforgiving as stone. You could crack your teeth on it. We used to have mud season in the holler, when the snow thawed and the river and the creeks swelled their banks.

Back then, mud was an annoyance. Mud got everywhere, drying, then crumbling on the truck floorboards, spackling my hair, sucking down my boots. Sometimes, in the kinds of springs we used to have, I felt I could taste mud in my teeth.

But we had never before had such hardness, such cruelty, from mud.

Inside the narrow entrance of my house, I took off my gloves. Not a lot of room left in the nooks and cabinets for the extra supplies. My eyes fell on the pile of mail I had dumped on a shelf and ignored the day that Lisbeth had called, telling me she was leaving. I had ignored a lot since then. Now I sifted through it. Junk, bills—those were still coming; despite the weather, companies still expected to be paid—a catalog, a postcard.

I glanced at the picture, a nothing image, a stock photo of palm trees, flat-fronted buildings, and a green lawn, then I turned it over to see the careful handwriting, printed like a child. Her handwriting. Mama.

She had written. She had found a moment away from him to write.

There was a return address on the postcard. Arcata, California.

I read the postcard. I pocketed it and got back in the truck.

Grayson was staring at the fire. He looked hopeful when I opened the farmhouse door. I thought again: What had I done, what had I done, letting a stranger come here?

I didn't waste time. "There's been a change of plans," I said. "I'm sorry, but you have to go."

He stumbled to get up, his boot clumping on the floor. "What's going on?"

"I have to go somewhere, and you can't stay here alone."

"Well, when are you coming back?"

"It's not like that." I shifted in the doorway, my shadow casting a long finger into the room, a column of darkness falling over him. "I have to be gone for a while. I have to shut up the farm. I'm taking my house."

I had not, until that moment, decided to take the tiny house. But it would save on hotels. It would be safer at night than sleeping in the truck, I realized, and I wouldn't have to worry about squatters while I was gone. My mama and I wouldn't even have to come back to the farm, if we didn't want to, if he wouldn't let us. I had certainly paid for the tiny house in my labor. I could pay for it again, if I had to, in cash, with the money from the last harvest. The harvest I had done myself.

"How's that going to work?" Grayson said.

My hand was starting to feel heavy on the doorknob. "Look, I'm sorry but you have to go back home. Something's come up and I have to leave."

"What's going on?" He wasn't giving up. He had nothing waiting for him. A cold house in an empty neighborhood. A job with no shifts. No car. He couldn't walk very far with that cast. "Where are you going?" Grayson said.

"To go get my mama," I said.

"Can I come?"

Lobo had buried the gun in the yard years ago, when Mama had moved into the farmhouse with him and was worried about me finding it. She and Lobo had had a big fight, screaming that rattled the windows. I hid in the woods. Lobo buried the gun and then forgot, or said he forgot, where it was, so when things were smoothed over again, when he had won that argument, or when he had exhausted and humiliated her from speaking up about it anymore, Lobo got a new gun at the gun show and duct-taped it under the table in the dining room.

This gun would not be so hidden from me, only from intruders, the sheriff. If a business associate got rowdy, it would be within reach. He needed something for protection, he said. All of the dogs had run away.

I knew where the old buried gun was. A handgun.

I had watched him bury it. The fight about it had lasted all day, and Lobo had buried it at twilight, Mama watching from the house, a shadow in the doorway, slender as a bat. He had buried it in the wild, unmowed yard below the house. I hid a few feet away, screened by whip-thin forsythia and joe-pye weed, prickers that sank their teeth into my legs. The coyote chorus was beginning at my back. Later that summer I would find a calf skeleton near that same spot, in a pile by a stump, clean bones folded like clothes.

But I didn't know about bullets, where some might be around the farm. I could buy some, if I needed to—at a gun show, maybe at the flea market. Would I need to?

Grayson followed me out to the yard. The wind wormed its way under my collar. I picked up a shovel from its leaning place by the door, Grayson watching as I pushed my heel on the shovel, slicing into the earth. It was more difficult than I expected, more difficult than it should have been for September. The ground was hard. We could see our breath, and even the clouds of our breath seemed to carry snow.

The buried gun waited beneath a jewelweed bush, the plant dead and pale as a puffball, a tumble of sticks beside a stump, the stump that marked the calf's grave. I remember when I had found those bones, I had thought they were human at first, a child's bones. I had thought Lobo had done something. I would not, though my mama loved him, put it past him, not the slender, knocking bones, laced with moss.

He was capable of violence. I had seen him smash a man's nose, blood spraying across the dining room wall. I had seen him punch and keep on punching, kick and keep on kicking.

I kept the jewelweed in the corner of my eye.

But I dug elsewhere, in a different place—closer by the house, near the pillars for the back porch. I saw the green plastic of the first canister, and let the shovel fall, pulling the canister out with my hands. We always buried the money shallowly.

"What's that?" Grayson said.

I shook off the dirt. "My inheritance."

On the farm, it was easy to forget the world. But the closer we drove into town, the more it came back: how everything had changed. How everything kept changing. A kind of empty feeling had settled over the landscape. Even the foothills of the mountains, crenulations in the distance, seemed hollow, too cold even to hold animals. The playground at the elementary school looked like a cemetery, the seesaws shovels of white. The doors to the building had been chained. The gas station at Crossroads, where I sold weed, had a large, spray-painted sign: NO MORE GAS TODAY.

"How can they be out?" Grayson said.

"Everybody stocking up."

I was taking Grayson home. First I was taking him to run errands: to the bank to get cash, to get propane for the heater I was letting him borrow—to wherever he wanted to go, really. It was the least I could do. Should I have given him money, let him stay on at the farm alone? What were the rules now that the late-summer sun seemingly set at three in the afternoon—the clouds looked so low and thick it might as well have—and we passed more than one house, where family members were roping suitcases to the roof of their cars? I drove by a house whose windows were blank and wooden, boarded up since the last time I had passed.

I thought of something. "It's Friday, right?"

"Yeah," Grayson said. "So?"

The line at the bank was long. The wait for the drive-through snaked into the road, trucks idling, tailpipes gummed with slush. In the lobby we found a similar scene as in the clinic. People filled the room to the corners. The heat was on in the bank, but barely. Some of those waiting were wrapped in blankets. The tellers wore fingerless gloves, skin flashing as they counted out bills.

I told Grayson to get what he needed. I told him I would buy the propane for his heater, then meet back up with him.

It was Friday, and that meant the Filthy Flea: the market in the parking lot of the old roller rink. Usually it stretched clear to the road. I had checked and the tents had been pitched, and I saw a hum of activity near the rink. The market was on. Maybe I could buy ammo for the gun there.

But in the bank lobby, someone was jiggling a shrieking baby. An older woman wept, slumped in a chair, her hand fluttering over her eyes like a handkerchief. I heard one of the employees counseling an elderly couple about their overdrafts.

I changed my mind. "Grayson, get out everything, everything you have," I said. "You should close the account."

He was filling out a slip. "I don't need all that."

"Not now." I tried to keep my voice quiet. "But you might not be able to get it later."

There it was, the way I was raised: distrust running through me dirty and clouded as a creek in the holler. Get paid in cash. Bury the money.

I glanced away from the table with the slips and pens. I felt eyes on me, felt the baby's crying and, even worse, the old woman's crying shake something loose deep inside me. I didn't know if Grayson would listen to me. Maybe the banks were in trouble. Maybe everyone in line wanted to close their accounts. The pharmacy was in trouble. The gas stations had closed.

"I'll go get the propane," I said to Grayson.

But the attendant at the station wouldn't unlock the cage. "Propane is rationed," she said. "Don't you read Facebook? One tank per household every week."

"I guess I'll buy that, then," I said.

"Great. Line starts over there. We start selling at three o'clock." She pointed to the side of the gas station, where I could see it now: another line. Stamping, shivering people in boots and blankets. They glared at me.

I checked my phone. "It's not even two-thirty."

"Some people have been waiting since yesterday. They sleep here, out on the sidewalk."

"Why?"

"When we run out, we run out. That's it until next week." The attendant stared at me. Her hair was crispy, the bags under her eyes sunk so deep they looked like pockets. "Do you want some propane or not?"

"Yes," I said.

"Then you best get in line."

I moved to the back of the line, past the women sitting on the sidewalk, wrapped in sleeping bags, and all the men in hoodies, looking down. A group was playing cards, huddled on lawn chairs. I got into place behind two men watching a video on a phone. The man holding the phone turned to me, tilting the screen, so I could see the video, see the bare limbs. They were watching porn.

I heard grunts on the screen, the slapping of cards from the bullshit players. Someone won and someone else threw their hand down, disgusted.

Grayson came up behind me. Seeing him, the man with the phone turned back around. "What do you need at the flea market?" Grayson said cheerfully. "You should go get it. I'm done at the bank. I did what you suggested. I can wait here now."

"Are you sure? This line is going to take forever," I said. I lowered my voice. "These guys…"

"I can handle it," Grayson said. "It's easier for me to just stand or sit here on the curb, not walk around. And if anybody gives me any trouble." He knocked on his boot. It sounded hollow, like a plastic drum. "This thing's sole is stainless steel."

I left Grayson in line. The card players were passing a thermos around, something steaming that smelled medicinal. Grayson gave me a little wave. It was strange to leave him there, his boot oversized as a cartoon. I thought that was why I felt a little sad, a little lonely, to walk off without him, because I was worried about his foot.

The flea market had changed. For as long as I could remember, there had been stalls selling airbrushed T-shirts, birdhouses, sparkly phone covers. Mama had taken me there to buy my birthday present one year. We had just moved in with Lobo. I remember her telling me to pick out whatever I wanted, anything, even a rabbit fur coat—we could afford it now. And I hadn't. I hadn't wanted anything, not from his money. Not as a bribe.

Trucks had hawked elephant ears and French fries then. Now, I was surprised to see canned goods were for sale, hard sausages, dried meat. Camping gear. The flea market had become a somber, muted place. Even the tents looked gray. Snow pooled in their sagging tops. And the faces of the people, hard and searching, who walked, hands in pockets—they were gray, too.

I passed a stall selling root vegetables. A woman in a matted fur coat, which smelled like it had been in a basement for a decade, picked up a potato from a bin. The potato looked wizened, old and undersized. "How much do you want for this?" she asked.

The owner of the stall hurried to her elbow. "I'll trade you two dozen for that coat," he said.

Before, sellers at the flea market had accepted cash only, cold hard cash, no cards. Checks were unheard of. Even if you knew the person writing the check, even if they lived down the holler from you, you could never really know a person. You could never trust what they might do, what drugs or hunger might lead them to.

But two years running of extreme cold, and bartering had become a system. Along with cash, I saw blankets exchanging hands, food, live chickens squawking in a wire box.

Walking among the tents, with sellers pushing squirrel meat and mess kits and knives, I felt as if I had gone back in time. I walked through a Civil War camp, or one of those pioneer festivals Mama always swore she would take me to but never did. I had gone back, further than my childhood, further than I meant to. I was lost. A cooking smell of onions and garlic drifted from one of the tents. Something sizzled in a huge pan. I bought two bags of roasted chestnuts, thinking I would bring them back to Grayson. I was not even sure what chestnuts tasted like, but at least they warmed my pockets. I hadn't seen any ammo.

I passed a stall selling garlands, festooned with red bows and sleigh bells, and stopped.

"Christmas decorations?"

The woman in charge of the stall said, "Might as well make the best of things. It feels like Christmas, don't it?"

"What happened to Halloween?" I asked.

It was just meant to be conversation, but the woman pointed across the parking lot, to the end of the aisle of tents. "For that, you want the Pumpkin King."

"The what?"

"If you want a pumpkin, you need the Pumpkin King. He's the only one who grew them this year. All mine died." The woman fingered the bows of a garland, her hands going down the row, like a rosary. "Everything I tried died."

"Thanks for the tip."

I walked on, past bows and kayaks, cider and corn. I bought a bag of apples, cringing at the price and at the small size of them: almost as wrinkled as the potatoes, with spots of green and cracked brown skin. A man who sold military surplus items had a stand at the end of the row. My mama had bought me a pocketknife from him that year I had refused to pick out my own present with Lobo's cash.

I knew that a knife was a bad luck gift. It severed the relationship. That was the superstition.

But though the man had backpacks and canteens for sale, though there were duffel bags and utensil sets, I didn't see any boxes of ammo.

The man—I thought I remembered his name was Phil—

nodded at me from a folding chair. "Wylodine," he said. "Good to see you looking well."

"You got any ammo?" I asked.

A slow shake of his head.

I was surprised to feel relief. Maybe I should have it, but I didn't want it. I didn't want to have to figure out what the gun took, how to load it. How to use it.

"Try the Walmart," Phil said.

"I don't want to go back there. What about MREs?"

"Sold out of those weeks ago. Your best bets are canned goods and dried food at this point. Do you have vitamin C?"

I thought back to the clinic pharmacy. "Why?"

"To prevent rickets, child. Scurvy, if we don't have any oranges this year. Don't you read the internet?"

"We don't have internet at the farm."

"Oh." Phil was sucking on a toothpick. "How's your mama?"

My hand stopped on a canteen. The leather casing felt like a living hide under my fingers, bunched with wrinkles, dry rivers of skin. I thought of the calf skeleton again. "Great," I said. "She and Lobo are doing real good."

I drifted away past Phil's stand, and though he may have called something to my back, I ignored it. We were fine; I was fine. I was certainly not out there alone on the farm. I was certainly not thinking of leaving it all behind, leaving the farm unprotected, driving away and locking the gate forever.

I was sure Phil was one of Lobo's customers, or had been. Maybe one of the men who came up to the farmhouse to visit with him and Mama after I was shut up in my place for the night. Was Phil one of the men who had angered him somehow, asked for too much, paid too little, tried to touch something that wasn't his?

Lobo called these customers *problems.* He solved problems with his fists. Sometimes that's the way you've got to do it, he said. People need a lesson they can see on their skin.

The smoke on those evenings was so thick it drifted down like mountain fog to my door. I swore I could taste it in my sleep. I was surprised the drug dogs didn't come after us those nights, alerted to the scent as they stuck their heads out of windows, riding in the staties' cars down the road.

Frost whitened the pavement. I glanced behind me and could see, at the other end of the parking lot, the overhang of the gas station. The line for propane slunk around the wall. I checked my phone. Grayson would still be waiting.

The roller rink was ancient. A friend of Lisbeth's and mine had had a birthday party there when we were in junior high. I couldn't remember the girl's name. Kids would smoke in the bathrooms of the rink, and we came back stinking. After that, her folks forbid Lisbeth from skating again. Or maybe The Church had banned it—along with YouTube, women and girls driving, shorts. Later on there was a fire, but the rink had reopened quickly afterward, tinged with an ashy smell that we found exciting, like riding in fast cars, sticking five sticks of gum in our mouths at once, the choking game. The fire-ghost scent hung around the rink, skulking like a boy. It never went away. I wondered if the weather had finally closed the rink.

Then I found the Pumpkin King.

It was the orange that drew me in. Amid the gray of the tents and snow, in the drab of everyone's coats and the ashen casts of their faces, the pumpkins, small and stunted as they were, glowed like beacons. Orange in the dark.

The pumpkins were stacked in piles in the woods at the edge of the market. I felt myself pulled to the glow.

I ducked into the woods, stepping around blown bits of trash, newspapers, and fast food bags. I wasn't sure why the Pumpkin King, if that was what he was called, had chosen to sell his fruits here in the trees, except he didn't have very many, and like all the other fruits and vegetables for sale at the market today, they looked paltry. He had scattered the piles around to make them seem more impressive.

Coming upon the first stack of pumpkins felt like discovering a prize. I thought of chicken of the woods, the bright orange mushrooms that grew wild in the forest around the farm. Mama and I would hunt for them in the fall, fry them up with butter. They were easy to spot because they were so bright, as orange as Halloween, almost pulsing with fluorescence. But they hadn't come up this season; there hadn't been a season.

I picked up the top pumpkin off a little stack. Tiny as my palm, and spotted with dark, raised warts.

"Those ain't for eating," a voice said.

I hadn't noticed the man. From deeper in the trees, he stood up and came toward me, tall and lanky, moving as stiffly as a marionette. He wore a wide straw hat, better suited for summer.

"Decorative only," the man said. "They ain't even pumpkins. Those are gourds."

"I know. Why are you selling them?"

He grinned, strangely white. Maybe false teeth. There was a funny clicking from his head. "Idiots will buy anything. Especially now. Now's the time to unload all your shit." He tilted his head, studying me in the shadows. "I know you. I know your folks."

"Lobo's not my daddy."

"I know."

Grayson had probably bought propane by now, and was waiting for me. All I had to show for the flea market was a bag of old apples and chestnuts. I shouldn't have gone into the woods. "I should go," I said.

"Wait a minute. I have something better than food."

He would show me a knife, a gun. Something worse.

But the Pumpkin King didn't move a step. He stretched out his arm. When his fist was below my face, he opened it, and I saw, in the cracks of his palm: seeds.

"Pumpkin seeds," he said.

There were six of them, like large pale tears. He saw that I saw them, then he closed up his fist and shoved his hand in his pocket. "Those ain't just any seeds. Those are from a monster, the biggest specimen I got last year. Connecticut Field. Introduced 1800. People bake 'em in pies, but they can get huge." He patted his pocket with his other hand. "This one sure did. Pretty good eating. And they're keepers. You don't have to grow 'em right away. That'll be important now."

I must have looked at him strangely.

"Girl," the Pumpkin King said. "Ain't your mama and stepdaddy telling you anything? Ain't you preparing?"

"For what?"

"These are the only seeds at the market today. The ones folks planted last year died. Froze in the ground. Never sprouted." The Pumpkin King shook his head. "These are from the year before, when we had a season."

"They're old, then."

"You should know better than that. Shit, seeds can keep for years, if they're dry. These seeds are good," he insisted. "They'll grow in the right conditions, grow a monster, feed a family, I guarantee it."

"I don't have a family," I said.

The flea market soldiered on at my back, just a few feet behind me, in the parking lot. Tents flapped. The breeze carried the smell of sausages and oil. People called out the prices of things, and yes, the prices were a tank of propane or diesel or deer meat or a sweater—but I could almost pretend the world was the same, at the edge of the market. In the trees with the Pumpkin King, though, we lived in another time, a changed time, one with gourds for sale, priced like jewels; seeds hawked like magic beans.

"Girl," the Pumpkin King said. If he knew my name, he didn't use it. "If anyone could find the right conditions, it would be you. You know how to make things grow under piss-poor conditions, under penalty of law. It's in your blood."

"Lobo's not my real daddy."

"It's in your *blood*," he repeated.

And maybe it felt that much colder in the trees, in the darkness cast by their laced bare branches—I noticed for the first time how the trees felt like a trap, a closing net—

or maybe the temperature really did drop again. Maybe it was constantly dropping. Maybe we were sliding, swiftly, into a total winter, forever winter, the world riding an ice chute straight to a bottomless well. But I could not get out of the woods, away from the Pumpkin King, fast enough. I said the only thing I knew that would shut him up.

"How much?"

"What you have on your farm."

"I don't have it with me," I said.

Maybe he didn't know that the outdoor harvest had failed last year, that I hadn't even attempted one on my own. Maybe he didn't know that I was late with the new crop. It seemed not to matter urgently anymore. A lot seemed not to matter.

"Well, of course," the Pumpkin King said. "Come back here. Get it and come find me tonight. My trailer's just over that'a ridge." He waved vaguely at the woods behind him.

I hadn't known anyone lived in those trees. No trailer was in sight. He wrote something on a torn piece of brown paper, folded it, and passed it to me.

I shoved it in my pocket without reading it.

"That's the IOU," he said.

"And the seeds?"

He removed from underneath his coat a small leather bag on a string. He opened the leather pouch, and put the seeds from his pocket inside. One, two, three, four. He pulled the cords of the bag shut.

"There were six seeds," I said.

"I gotta keep something for myself." The Pumpkin King

handed me the pouch. The leather was soft. "Put it on. For safety, under your clothes."

I must not have moved swiftly enough because he took the pouch out of my hand. Then, before I could yank away, he touched my collarbone, pulling at the collar of my coat and flannel shirt, and dropped the leather bag over my neck. The pouch disappeared down my shirt. The leather felt cold and greasy, dirty as hands.

The Pumpkin King zipped my coat up tight. "There," he said. He patted my chest, the space of bone where my heart was beating desperately. "Can't see a thing. Keep it that'a way."

The leather smelled like the animal it had been. I couldn't forget it was there, even if nobody could see it. His fingers had been cold. "My friend is waiting for me," I said.

"One last bit of advice, little girl."

I looked back at him. His eyes had an emptiness, dull as dirty silver. And he had wildness about him that I knew well. Meth, maybe. Or opioids. He moved as if he was jerking his limbs awake, dragging his body through a haze thicker than blood, forcing himself to move. I figured he had been napping when I showed up in the trees. He might fall asleep the moment I left, maybe in the middle of talking to me.

Or maybe he was in pain. Maybe he walked haltingly because his joints hurt him; his bones stiff, or injured years ago. Maybe he was only hurting, with his rolling eyes, heavy limbs. His finger, knobby as a wand, was meant to point at me—*little girl*—but really, it was trembling at the trees.

"Don't plant all the seeds now," the Pumpkin King said. "Plant a couple. They'll take. Plant two seeds, maybe. Save the others as currency."

"Currency?" I pulled the pouch tight, till the cord cut into my skin.

"Trust me. Seeds will be more valuable than gold, and the one who can grow them? She'll be a queen."

5

Grayson had managed to get one of the last tanks of propane. But the sky was darkening by the time we loaded it into the truck. Sunset was coming: a cold surprise. Dusk fell earlier and earlier, unnatural and white. Snow was in the future like a distant, glowing city.

One more night, I promised Grayson. He could sleep on the couch in my shack. I would spend the night packing up, leave first thing in the morning, drop him home on the way.

We went back to the farm. I tried to tell him about the Pumpkin King, but the words stuck in my throat. The man had scared me, and I was ashamed to be scared. I was not sure I could name or explain what had happened.

Cleaning up after our meal of wizened apples, eggs, and fried potatoes—Grayson had cooked, better him than me—I washed the plates and set them in the rack. I scraped the burned bits of potatoes into a bowl, wondering how to best to describe what I had seen at the market: the knives and chickens for sale, the woman in the stinking fur coat, the man with a pouch of seeds.

Every evening, I would dump the bowl of kitchen scraps and eggshells into a bucket beside the back door. When the bucket was full, I would pitch the contents onto the compost heap near the farmhouse. It had always been this way.

But, thinking about the market, my hand froze on the spoon. Why was I wasting my time doing this? Collecting food waste, keeping it in a pile, carefully turning it, and monitoring the temperature—that was what my mama and Lobo had done. That was what they had taught me to do. We had used the compost for growing vegetables. But nothing was growing in this ground. Nothing would sink its roots into this rich soil.

"We should just pitch this shit in the woods," I said. "Give some animal a chance at a few more days."

Grayson was fiddling with his ham radio, trying to tune in the president's speech, and didn't answer me. I hoped he never got that thing working. I didn't want to hear her say she didn't know. I didn't want to hear her apologize again.

I was still wearing the Pumpkin King's pouch. I set the spoon down, reached for the string around my neck, and removed the pouch from beneath my shirt. Inside the leather bag, the seeds looked as if they were cupped by weathered skin, a farmer's palm.

"What is that?" Grayson asked.

"Pumpkin seeds." I looked down at them. I could add

apple seeds to them, from our dinner. "They're for plant-
ing, not eating. And there's only four."

"Where did you get them?"

"At the flea market."

"Were they expensive? As much as the apples? Wil?"

I didn't even know. I dug in my pocket for Pumpkin
King's note. He had written his IOU on a torn bit of gro-
cery bag. I unfolded it to see there was a phone number.
And one word.

It was not what I expected.

It was not weed. It was worse.

Grayson looked over my shoulder. He read it. *"Lights?"*

I crumpled the IOU.

My flashlight swung wildly in my hand, casting trees
and bush and bits of the old barbed wire fence that lined
parts of the driveway into sudden, stuttering light. The
driveway was pitted and uphill. In mud season, when the
creek had flooded, parts of the driveway would be washed
away unless we dug out drainage ditches.

When I saw the slope of the farmhouse roof appear on
the hill above me, I felt dread, more than the usual anxi-
ety I had about the house. I could sense the darkness of the
basement room. The logs from my last wood-chopping afternoon were scattered around the yard like bones. Grayson stopped behind me, his hands on his sides, trying not
to pant.

"I forgot about your foot," I said. I had dragged us up
here without even thinking about him. "Are you all right?"

He looked at the boot, shifting his leg in the darkness. He didn't answer me about it. "Are you going to tell me what that IOU meant? What does *lights* mean? What lights?"

I opened the farmhouse door. The house smelled dusty, stale, with an undercurrent of ash. It was also cold. I shuffled past the dark, extinguished stove, not looking closely at anything—not the empty coat tree, not the mirror on the wall, which showed my face.

I had grown to love this house, in a way. I had wanted to be here, with my mama. I had grown to love the remoteness and wildness of the farm. I was forbidden to bring friends to this house, not to the big house, and never around harvest. This would have been a busier time of year—fall—a dangerous time, in a world where spring had come, in a world where there had been enough light and heat to make a harvest.

I walked straight to the wall under the stairs. I opened the small basement door. "Come on," I told Grayson. "Downstairs." We ducked our heads, and he followed me. I heard the dull clunk of his cast striking the wall. "Be careful."

I switched on my flashlight again, illuminating the narrow steps. The ceiling felt very close. The light shone straight down to the bottom: a concrete floor and another closed door. Usually—almost always—this door pulsed with light. Bright white leaked around its seams, a glowing rectangle, like some kind of clean room. I would push open the door into heat, the thrum of the fan, the thick and heady plants, the room teeming with life. And my mama.

It was a magic world behind the basement door. To

come into this world in the dead of winter, to find her, surrounded by life and light—and danger—cast a spell.

We would grow fifty plants, sixty, sometimes as many as eighty, shoulder to shoulder, brushing my waist, turning greedily toward the lights on the ceiling. I thought of their leaves, sharp and pointed as daggers. As a child, I both loved and hated coming here. Each time I felt a rush of danger and love, overwhelmed by heat and the smell of the plants: the spicy, dark musk of them. Each time I thought I would faint from it.

My mama was just as involved as Lobo, more so because it turned out she was even better than him with the plants. She had a knack for it. It was in my blood, as the Pumpkin King had said. She sang to them, that was my mama's secret.

As an adult, it was hard to forget that feeling, to overcome it every time I opened the door. To stop expecting my mama to be behind it. I didn't sing to the plants as they grew. I had nothing to say to them. *Thank you for giving us money for food. Thank you for taking my mama from me. Thank you for ruining my life.*

The door at the bottom of the stairs was dark now. No light leaked around its edges. I shoved my shoulder against the wood to free the tight door from its frame. I switched off the flashlight, and fumbled on the wall for the switch.

"Brace yourself," I said.

"For what?" Grayson asked.

Then light pulsed through the room, blinking back to life from the hanging fluorescents strung low, at my chest, a height that would be just hovering over the plants when they were grown. Light also came from the bulb on the ceiling. And light came back from the very walls. Reflective silver panels shot the light across the walls and floor, back onto the plants, which devoured it.

There were no plants now. Only a few scattered buckets, some dirt on the floor I had neglected to sweep. A handful of dead yellow leaves. And the lights were diminished. Grayson shielded his eyes from the glare, but it was only half-strength, I knew. Five fluorescent lights hung on the ceiling, strung from a complicated nest of extension cords and wires—not the usual ten. Lobo and Mama had taken half when they left for California.

"These are the lights," I said, tugging on the one nearest me so it bobbed up and down on its wire like a mobile. "This is what the Pumpkin King wants."

"The Pumpkin King? Jesus. Is that really his name?"

I bent to the light, working to unfasten it.

"Wait a minute," Grayson said. "You aren't actually going to give them to him, are you?"

"It's a trade. People do that now."

"But lights for seeds? That doesn't seem like a good trade."

"Help me for a second." I had Grayson hold a light while I unhooked it. We lowered it to the floor, and I wrapped the cord around it. "These grow things even in dark, closed spaces with no sunlight. Even in basements." I looked at the light on the concrete floor. "Especially in basements."

"Can we get more?"

You could buy them in town at the hardware store,

but you had to be careful; you couldn't buy too many at once. You had to talk loudly about tomatoes—that was what Lobo did. You could buy them on the internet, but you should probably buy orchids at the same time. "I don't know if you can buy them now," I said. "But I should pack them up, get them ready, anyway. I should take them with me."

Grayson looked at me over the light. He wanted to know. He had been dying to ask. He had been patient, but I felt the questions coming; I knew they would come. "Did you do a lot? Did your folks make you?"

"They didn't make me," I said.

"What did you do? Make deliveries?"

"It's not like that. It's just farming." That was how I felt about it.

That was how they had explained it to me.

In fifth grade, the drug dogs came. The confident deputies, with their bellies and their holsters, had talked to us about bad men, and things that looked like candy. We had had the bad-men talk before. The Earth was full of bad men. They walked amid the holler, as populous as apple trees, studded with acne and cursing without control. Bad teeth tumbled in their mouths. In their clothes lived the devil. But this talk was different. It concerned what we might smell or see at home, and if we saw the plants—brittle, innocent—or the pipes, smoky blue glass, we should tell someone. Tell *them*.

I told Mama. She told Lobo. They set me down and explained the sheriff would take me away if he knew about the plants in the basement. He would want them for himself. He would take the money, kill the last farm dog who hadn't yet run.

There was nobody to come for me. We hadn't heard much from my real daddy since he left. The phone calls had petered out, like water in the old house when we hadn't paid the bill. The plants were a secret, but not a bad secret, Lobo and my mama explained. It was a treasure we couldn't give away. It would deliver us, deliver me. There were promises—horses and bicycles—that never materialized. If only I would keep the secret.

I came to see the plants as the only magic, an end in themselves. They grew so quickly, they were sprinkled with golden dust, they made the ones who were supposed to take care of me transform back into children: selfish, stunned, and mewing for more. This was the marvel in itself, this plant grown from clones or seed. That we could do that: give something life.

How could I explain that to Grayson? Dirt settled in the cracks of my hand like it belonged there. I mounded seeds into the ground, patting them with a promise: I'd come back. They could depend on me, though I had no one to teach me how to love or be loved. The tender way seedlings sprouted, thin as hair. I ended each day coated in a sheen of grit. I had strange tan lines. I went to bed each night exhausted, achy, then got up early and did it all again. Alone with the earth. It had a kind of song. There was no way to explain it.

"I can make things grow," I said. "Even in a basement. But for that we would need lights."

"We'd need power, too," Grayson said.

"We have power. So far."

"I thought the world would just get warmer."

"Well, we were wrong. It got worse."

Grayson looked at the lights. "We can't give these away. Not even for seeds."

"We traded. I promised him."

"You didn't know what you were promising. Did you?"

"No." I had thought the Pumpkin King had wanted something else. Just weed. What everyone wanted from me. To have a good time. To forget. To feel good. "But you don't understand," I said. "It's different out here in the country. Things have a way they're done in the holler. You keep your word. You take your payback, when it's needed."

Maybe what everyone wanted was changing. Not just to survive, but to live.

"We'll bring one light," I said. "And see if we can barter."

If the flea market was filthy during the day, at night—closed up and empty—it was menacing. Sleet started on our drive into town, and ice patched the lot by the time we arrived. The pink glow of parking lights were spaced far apart, gaps of black pavement and blacker night between. Anything could be in those gaps. Anyone.

The roller rink looked dark and hulking, its neon sign, missing most of the letters, as dim as a jumble of scaffolding. When was the last time that sign was lit? There was no one around. I parked the truck. In the distance, we could see the lights of the gas station: a glow above the trees, hazy yellow like an egg.

"There's a giveaway," Grayson explained. "Tonight at the gas station. They're passing out bottled water."

"Why?"

"People's pipes have frozen. Someone told me about it when we waited for propane."

"Why are they doing it so late?"

"That's when the water truck comes."

"Let's hurry," I said.

I had stashed the grow light in a duffel bag and we each hefted one of the handles. Lugging the light between us helped warm us up. It felt like we were moving music equipment, setting up for some band. Or maybe moving a body, cut up into bones. As soon as I had this thought I couldn't stop thinking about it.

I slowed down for Grayson. He shuffled to keep up, his boot scrapping the asphalt. I felt better once we had stepped into the trees, into cover—that *was* in my blood, the impulse to hide, to sneak. If you keep secrets for a living, you start keeping them all the time. You keep secrets for practice, for no reason at all.

We went a little deeper into the woods, to the base of the rise where the Pumpkin King had placed his wares. Their orange glow would have lit up the darkness at least a little, but I didn't see anything, not a single pumpkin. He had taken his stuff home, or sold it. We rested the duffel bag on the ground. Grayson bent to adjust his boot.

"How's your foot?" I said.

"It's fine."

It was *fine* every time I asked.

"Where is he?" Grayson said.

I looked around. Shadows fell into a ditch, rocky with ice and an old tire. I checked my phone. There was no reception, of course. "I'm going to look at the top of that hill," I said. "He told me to find his trailer around there. You stay here with the light."

"You sure about this?"

"I'm just going to that ridge. You shouldn't walk more than you have to. If anyone comes..." I thought of the gun back home in the ground.

"I'll be fine," Grayson said. "Stainless-steel boot, re-member?"

I glanced around the bottom of the rise one more time, then climbed to the ridge.

The instinct for trouble: I searched for a broken branch that meant a man had run through this way, the trampled snow of footprints, a bit of fabric snagged on a twig.

I saw something large and bright on the next hill across the valley. A pumpkin.

But it wasn't on the ground; it was too high.

The pumpkin sat crookedly on a neck.

It was the head of a scarecrow. Plaid shirt stuffed with something, boots and jeans. Why would someone make a scarecrow in the middle of the woods and leave it on a hill? Go to all that trouble—and waste what looked to be warm clothes?

I climbed up the rise to where the scarecrow had been planted. Behind it, I saw the Pumpkin King's trailer. This scarecrow wasn't guarding any crops. Nothing had been planted in a while. The fields on the hilltop looked empty and black, furrows filled with snow. The trailer seemed abandoned, the siding ripped and shot with mold. The wheels weren't just parked like my own trailer. These tires were flat—rotted.

But I knew he lived there.

I saw green ferns inside the trailer windows. The bird-feeder in the plane tree was full. I approached the cinder-block step and knocked quickly at the door. The birdfeeder, cut from an empty milk jug, wagged in the wind, heavy with seeds. I glanced over the seed that had spilled: red millet.

I picked up a handful from the snow. It might sprout someday, if it hadn't been baked. A wind chime clattered: something else hanging in the tree, made from spoons.

I didn't want to leave Grayson alone for too long. What if the Pumpkin King came back to that spot and I wasn't there? I couldn't remember exactly what he had said, where to meet. He wouldn't know Grayson, wouldn't trust him. I put the millet seed in my pocket—I would ask the Pumpkin King if the millet might grow; surely he wouldn't be-grudge me some birdseed, especially if I was giving him a grow light—then knocked again.

Through the door, its window curtained with a dish rag, I could see a slice of room. The Pumpkin King was messy. Dirty dishes in the sink, the stack teetering higher than the faucet. The curtains on the other side of the room had been torn down.

It was too messy.

There were broken dishes on the floor. Plants had been

overturned, dirt speckled with fertilizer, mixing with the plate shards. Something was wrong.

I should text the Pumpkin King. I should have done that first.

I would have to find a spot with some reception. I turned from the door and left the trailer. Still no bars in the upper corner of my phone. I passed the scarecrow on the hill, hurrying now. What were the scarecrow's hands made from? Not gloves. They were tan and red, blotchy. Like skin.

That was no scarecrow.

It was a man, a dead man, with a pumpkin's head.

"Grayson!" I screamed.

The pumpkin had been carved into a jack-o'-lantern: triangle nose, grin, two holes for eyes. And in the eye-holes, someone had pushed into the body below—they must have screwed them into the flesh to get them to stay—two seeds.

The Pumpkin King's last two seeds, the ones he was saving for himself.

He was in there, what was left of him. I knew his face was ruined, whatever remained of it. I knew there was a bullet in his head or chest, or a knife in his belly. He was strung on a pole, his sagging body forced upright.

Grayson came stumbling over the hill. He had left the light. He had run, dragging his hurt foot. "Is he—?"

"He's dead."

"How do you know?"

The body was too still. It emitted stillness. It pulsed with it, like a light.

"What happened? What do we do?" Grayson said.

I stepped closer to the body.

"Wil! Don't touch it. Goddamn it."

Someone had taken the trouble to find the seeds, some-one who knew—who must have known—what they might be worth, if spring never came back. But they had used the seeds, anyway, wasted them. To make a point? To punish him? What else had the Pumpkin King sold—the thing that made his limbs whittle away to nothing, that made his movements jerky, the thing that eased his pain? What had they taken from the trailer—or had tossed the trailer for and not been able to find?

"Wil, we gotta get out of here."

I bent to the Pumpkin King. In the holes that had been cut in the jack-o'-lantern, I could see his body: his human body. It had never been so human. His skin shone silver and green. I saw streaks of black. He wouldn't want me to waste anything, not when there was a chance, a chance a seed might grow, not this farmer.

"Wil!"

I pulled out the leather pouch from beneath my shirt and opened it. Gently, I picked the seeds from his eyes. We had all the seeds now. I added the red millet from my pocket. I wiped my hands of blood and drew the draw-strings closed.

6

We heard shouting when we reached the parking lot. The duffel bag with the light swung between us, Grayson hurrying and carrying it without complaint. There was no question of calling anyone about the body. Who would we call, what would we say? The sheriff would only make trouble, find an excuse to open my bag, search me, seek out the smell in my truck. It wouldn't help the Pumpkin King, anyway, calling anyone, telling anyone about him. He was gone. He had no people, I bet. The men who had killed him were gone, too, their message lost like pills in the river. The law would never work hard for him. A skinny junkie, they would say, who lived in a trailer: an addict who fed the birds.

At the sound of the shouting, Grayson stopped. The lights over by the gas station looked different. Brighter somehow. We both noticed. "What the hell is happening?" Grayson said.

"Just keep going."

In the time we had been in the woods, sleet had kept falling. A coat of ice lay over the parking lot, clear and rippled with air. I slowed my pace even further so Grayson wouldn't fall. Somehow we made it to the truck. Grayson helped me heft the duffel bag into the bed. We got into the cab and I started the engine.

I thought of the body.

Would fruits burst from his eyes, eventually, if spring ever came back? Or would his body just freeze, wasted, not even a gift to the ground? Was this what they did to growers now—killed us and strung us up like dolls?

I put the truck into gear and drove, almost immediately skidding, sliding over the lot.

Grayson shouted, "Stop!"

I hit the brakes. The truck fishtailed and I steered into the skid. We wobbled to a halt, and a black shape ran past us.

"What was that?" he said.

Another shadow came running.

More and more shadows streamed from around the darkened strip mall. A stampede of them. People were running away from something.

Whatever it was, we needed to run, too.

I put the truck back into gear. We drove until we saw what the light in the distance was.

The gas station was on fire. Smoke poured around the overhang. I heard the crack of glass as the windows of the store shattered. People ran in front of our truck without seeing us, without seeing anything. There were dozens of people. Some were shouting. Some seemed to be bleeding. A fist pounded on the hood of the truck, and Grayson gave a yell.

I saw a person on the ground. He lay half in the parking lot, half on the bank of the bordering woods, on his back. Someone seemed to step on his hand and he didn't even budge. I jolted the truck into Park and unbuckled my seat belt.

"What are you doing?" Grayson said.

"There's somebody on the ground."

"We'll be on the ground if we don't get out of here."

"Take the wheel, Grayson."

"There's a mob!"

"Just do it. Come around and pick me up." Before he could protest again, I had opened the door. Grayson scooted over the seats to the driver's side and grabbed the wheel as I ran to the man on the ground.

He was alive: a young man with wire glasses, broken. I recognized him from the holler, vaguely, but I couldn't place him. Not a customer. Not a man who would spill from a truck in front of the farmhouse, coated in driveway dust, wanting weed. This man was out, blankness coating his face. He looked peaceful, not knowing the chaos around him.

I reached under his arms and hoisted him up. Smoke bleared my eyes. My truck had disappeared into it. Where the hell was Grayson going? The man coughed at being moved. At least he was breathing.

I saw two yellow beams through the smoke. Headlights. Grayson passed us, then backed up and braked. I realized he was driving on his left foot—his cast, his hurt right foot, must have stretched into the passenger side. I dragged the man to the back of the truck and pounded the gate with my fist. The gate stuck. Hitting it was the only way to get it open, and sometimes, even a blow didn't work. The man still didn't wake up. I hit it again, and the gate swung down. I hefted the man's upper body onto the gate.

This was what we did now, I guessed: we found strangers, we saved them. He was heavy, but I was strong. I was grateful for those years lugging bags of fertilizer, rotating heavy plants. I climbed in, then dragged the man the rest of the way.

"Go!" I said to Grayson.

He slammed on the accelerator, and I nearly fell over. I grabbed the man and pulled us closer to the cab. The gate clattered open, bouncing as we drove, but I didn't have the energy left to reach over and yank it shut. I inched backward, dragging the man like a bag of seed. Only when my back touched the cab, the stranger almost in my lap, did I look up at the scene we were fleeing.

We were leaving the roller rink and the parking lot behind, leaving the body in the woods, the gas station in flames. A cloud of greasy-looking smoke grew smaller down the road as we fled. But out of the smoke came people, still running.

I turned to shout through the open window of the cab, "Why are they chasing us?"

Grayson kept his eyes on the road. "I don't know!"

Whatever fight had broken out, whatever had caused

the fire, they couldn't get away fast enough from it. Whatever it was they had seen.

"Water." The man in my lap shuddered and tried to sit up. His eyes opened, small and unfocused.

I tried to place his face, to remember his name. "You passed out, I guess. Don't get up." I supported his head on a tarp I found in a corner of the truck bed.

The man coughed again. "We were waiting for water."

Most men looked the same, most men looked like boys I had gone to high school with, boys who would corner me in the hallway and ask for weed, who would be surprised when I didn't want to go to their parties at the trailers of their deadbeat dads, at the bikers' bar in town which never carded.

This man wasn't one of those boys. I could recognize him now. He was someone who never talked to me, someone who went to school with animal shit on his boots—that kept you away from a social scene. He was from one of the farm communes where kids went to school late, if at all; where they were dragged out early, ostensibly to help with the sheep or the hogs or to follow the walnuts or blueberries, but really, just to keep the kids safe from the Man. The Machine. The ideas that were spread through the public schools.

I remembered he had dropped out forever at sixteen, or whenever we could. I had refused to drop out of school myself, still believing that I was meant for something else, something out of here. Believing that I would have to prepare, to be ready. I remembered when we were just kids, a woman had picked this boy up from school, from the class we were in together. She wore long skirts, wafting a scent that by then I already knew.

"The water truck was late," the man said. He had sun-damaged skin—that aged you fast. His beard reminded me of the scruff on the side of the highway. "People were getting mad. Then the truck just turned around. The driver saw the crowd, how big and wild it was, and he just... backed up and left."

"Nobody got any water?"

"Nobody."

I rummaged around the bed of the truck—Lobo's shit was still everywhere—until I found my stainless-steel water bottle. I unscrewed the top and raised the bottle to his lips. He drank, looking at me over the rim. He still wore his glasses. One lens was cracked; the other, missing.

"I'm Wylodine. Wil. Do you remember me?"

He finished drinking. His hand passing the bottle to me shook a little, but he said, "I do. I'm Dance. My folks were hippies."

"I remember."

"Wil?" Grayson said. "Hey, Wil? Where I am going?"

We drove out of the smoke and into the darkness. The chill closed around us. I felt the wind in every inch of exposed skin: the back of my neck between my hat and collar, the bit of wrist laid bare by my sleeves. I told Grayson where to go. When we arrived at the driveway, he left the truck running and we hopped out to deal with the gate.

I met Grayson in front of the truck, the headlights spotlighting us like burglars. I yanked open the padlock and

Grayson unwrapped the chain. In years before, this part of the driveway would be rutted in mud. I would step out of the truck and straight into a puddle.

But the mud was frozen, hardened lava. Ice made the driveway shine. As we worked, snow began to patter us.

Grayson set the chain down and together we lifted the gate. "Who is that guy?" Grayson whispered. "Do you know him?"

"A hippie. He was in my grade at school. He dropped out."

Grayson glanced back at the truck. "What about the dead guy? Why did someone kill him? For seeds?"

"They left the seeds." We had pushed the gate wide enough that the truck could enter. I let go and wiped my gloves on my coveralls. Frost clung to the fabric, prickly as thistles. Nothing was melting. "Maybe they killed him for money," I said. "Or drugs. I'm pretty sure he was on something. Pain pills, maybe."

"Should we tell somebody?"

I thought of the gas station burning. I thought of the hospital, the nurse standing on a chair to shout at the crowd. I thought of the snow—how it was now, after the freezing rain, the smallest of pinpricks, almost invisible, but insistent: white needles.

The small flakes were a bad sign. They meant colder temperatures. The smaller the flake, the colder the air. I thought of the Pumpkin King, covered in white flowers.

"Who's there to tell?" I said.

I let Grayson stay behind the wheel. He seemed to want be useful. He managed the driveway fine, pulling the truck right up to the farmhouse. Only after he had turned off the engine did I open the duffel bag in the back, did I even remember it. I heard a strange sound when I reached for the bag: a crunching. I tried not to worry, but I knew. I unzipped the bag.

The grow light lay in pieces.

Dance leaned over my shoulder, giving a low whistle at the broken light. He knew what it was. If he was surprised, he wasn't showing it. "Those things are valuable now," he said.

Grayson got out of the truck, readjusting his cast. The engine ticked as it rested. Somewhere in the woods, far off on one of the ridges, a coyote howled.

What I had loved most about the farm—what was my comfort, my solace, my companions this last year alone—had been the stars in the big sky.

I had seen eclipses, a comet, too many shooting stars to count. I went outside whenever I had had a fight with Mama, or Lobo had gotten violent again. Whenever I had grown tired of the lies: the smell on my clothes; having to check my hair for stems; having to keep my coat in a sealed garbage bag outside the front door to try to keep the scent off; the money buried in the yard, everything in cash, always in cash, cash only—and where did it all go? Not to me and Mama. To plants and fertilizer and soil and pest sprays. To guns. To breaking even. To drinks and other drugs. To Lobo. We had money buried in the yard like squirrels, and yet, my coat was safety-pinned together. I had reduced lunch at school until I graduated.

Whenever I felt as if I couldn't breathe, like this secret

life was strangling me, I went outside, even in the dead of winter—or what we called winter then. I went to the back porch Lobo had built out of railroad ties and wood he never treated, wood that was going to rot, and I looked up. I breathed in the sky. I felt my lungs opening in the air. I stared.

So many more stars than I could see in town. They steadied me, even as I saw that they were not steady. If I sat out on the porch long enough, I had learned, I would see a shooting star. It was only a matter of timing, of luck. Stars fell all the time. I don't remember what my wishes were. Just for my life to be different, to be my own.

And now it was.

I saw no stars from the bed of the truck. Only white. White skies coming down. White skies endlessly. The snow clouds blocked everything, all the stars, even the moon's dull beat.

I looked back at the men. They were watching, waiting for me. It was the first time I realized they would do this. They would do this a lot. "We're leaving," I told them. "We're leaving as soon as possible."

"We?" Grayson said. He looked hopeful and worried, his body hunched as he stood by the bed of the truck, favoring his good leg.

I didn't want to drive to California alone. I had been alone for so long.

"Why do you want to go to California with me?" I asked him.

"Wil," he said. "Why *not*?"

Dance looked at Grayson, then at me. "Where are you going?"

"California. Arcata. Wherever that is. My mama is there. I can drop you off at home, or at the hospital, if you think you need to go there and get checked out."

"I don't want to go there. I don't have the cash for a doctor."

"That's really not a problem right now," Grayson said.

Dance pushed up his glasses. The broken lens looked like a kaleidoscope, splintering his face. I remembered he had cried when his mama had pulled him out of our grade school classroom. The fall leaves we had carefully cut out of construction paper and the stained-glass crayons melted between wax sheets were tacked on the bulletin board. And my bean seed in the plastic cup on the windowsill had sprouted, but I don't think other kids' had. Did he remember all that, any of that?

"Can I come with you?" he asked.

Another man. Another mouth. It would mean more work.

It might also mean less hassle. I pictured getting out of the truck with men beside me, their beards and low voices. I pictured walking beside them.

"It seems like this place is dying," Dance said. "People acting like they did at the water giveaway. Rioting. Seems like we should get out now, don't you think? Somewhere warmer, a bigger city, might have more resources, you know?"

I couldn't think. "If you come along, you have to do

your share," I said. "You have to cook, wash dishes, clean up. Do you know how to split wood?"

"Wil," Dance said. "I grew up in the Compounds."

"Okay." Grayson was staring at me, but I had to decide. "You and Grayson go through the farmhouse. Take anything you think we might need. Take Lobo's old clothes if they fit you, I don't care."

"What are you going to do?" Grayson asked.

The shovel lay on the ground by the porch. I picked it up. It would be hard work, now that the earth had frozen. I should have done it months ago, as soon as Mama and Lobo had left.

We piled supplies into the bed of the truck. We packed the remaining grow lights in duffel bags, padding them with pillowcases and towels. We did the hard, complicated work of attaching the trailer of my tiny house to the truck hitch—work I had only helped with once before, back when Lobo was in charge. The air was so warm then I remember we had rolled up our shirtsleeves. I remember blue chicory wagged in the breeze. Now the thought of any flower bursting from the earth, any buried seed rising, any bright color breaking up the brown, white, and gray landscape, seemed extraordinary. The fields were white lakes. Snow gathered in the shrugs of trees.

I was in charge. It was my truck, my home, my idea. If I wasn't so stunned, so exhausted and overwhelmed, if I wasn't cycling through the motions of walking, bending, pulling, wrenching, I would have felt annoyed by all the men's questions.

We worked all night. While they were in the farmhouse, I dug out three more canisters of money. The earth was so frozen it felt as if I was chipping at bone. Once I broke through the crust of cold ground, I had to perch on my knees and use the shovel like a pick ax. I saw the tops of the canisters, then wrenched them out with my hands. Cold radiated through my gloves. I was exhuming a grave, I thought. Snow quickly filled the holes I had made, as if even this small blackness was not allowed to stay in the new white world.

Likely, there were even more canisters—Lobo didn't believe in putting money in banks, and I knew Mama would have left as much as she could for me—but I was worried about time. Would the men who killed the Pumpkin King come at dawn? Would they come tomorrow? Would they come at all?

Other men would.

I needed to get to my mama. Her postcard ran through my mind. I had memorized it, it was so short. So much meaning held in the smallest of words. *It's warm here but hard. He's gotten worse. I wish you had come with us. I love you and I'm sorry.*

Those last two phrases twined together like people said poison ivy and jewelweed did: the toxin and its cure. That was a myth, though. Jewelweed couldn't root in dry places as poison ivy could, not for long. But with my mama, it *was* true. She loved and apologized, loved and apologized: the heart and the hurting. They were linked in her. Lobo had a dual nature, too: helping and hurting. He had wailed on me; he had taught me to survive a fight. To survive him.

I love you and I'm sorry.

Dawn came. The truck was packed and ready. Grayson and Dance stood at the edge of the yard, waiting around, not wanting to bother me or ask what I was doing. I wouldn't have told them, anyway. I had shoved the money canisters I had unearthed into a backpack. Then it was time to go back for the gun.

Midway down the wild backyard, under sedge, dead or dying, I tore through the little patch of jewelweed. The roots crumbled, brittle as wind chimes. Lobo had not replaced the earth well or smoothly when he had buried the gun. It was obvious where it was. He had not cared. He had wanted to be right about the gun, about needing it soon.

I yanked the handle up, knocking off clumps of dirt.

"What is that?" Grayson said.

"Get in the truck," I said. "We're going."

We turned from the lower field as the sky began to lighten. When would the holler realize I was gone? I would have to tell the boy with the station wagon. I would have to make other arrangements, at last. Would squatters overtake the house? Would nature: cold cracking the windows, snow pooling on the floor, rodents curling up in the holes they'd chew in the mattresses? I didn't look back at the big house.

I had said my goodbyes to the farmhouse last night, shut it up, locked what I could. The basement room was dark and would stay dark. There was nothing behind its door now, no mystery. In the field where my house had been parked for years lay a matted shape, the grass pale and dead, dirt showing through, a square cut from snow.

We drove slowly down the driveway. Grayson and Dance were silent, waiting for me to say something, to give them a clue of how to feel. The tiny house, unfamiliar and huge-seeming, swayed on its trailer. I concentrated on driving, turning onto the empty rural route. This time of morning, not even the farmers were out with their wagons. The main road was paved. The driveway was not—and instantly, I felt a weird loss. I missed the bumpy gravel and mud of the driveway to the farm. I parked the truck, got out by myself, and locked the gate behind us for real, for the last time.

The padlock cinched with a crack. It thudded against the chain, snow flaking off the gate.

On one side of town was The Church, where Lisbeth had disappeared every Wednesday night and all day Sundays. But on the other end was the Compounds: the acres beyond the railroad tracks, the marshes and hills that held trailers, patched-together houses. Land was cheap because it was hard to farm, mostly former quarries and crenulated hills. Coal companies had removed the top of the mountains so they were no longer mountains but sharp and fallow ridges, like a furrowed, angry face. Shacks perched on the edges. Abandoned mines meant the earth beneath was hollow, unstable. The creeks ran orange with acid damage.

Nobody wanted the land because nothing could be done with it—nothing grew except mud, went the joke—so you could buy acres and acres for cheap, have your own compound with a farmhouse, a couple of aluminum-sided sheds, a few dead cars for parts. Friends could live out on your land in a trailer, an arrangement of a few weeks that often turned into years.

Dance's family lived in the Compounds. What was left of his folks. His older brother had enlisted a year ago, after the first time we skipped spring, and his daddy, always a drinker, drank more once the weather turned.

People were abandoning farms and houses—even whole subdivisions, like where Grayson had lived—but I was not expecting the Compounds to be deserted. Not those people. They held on to their land. They had provisions, weapons, animals. They had been ready—or said they were ready—for the war and for the other war, for coal leaving, coal coming back, coal going away again. They would be ready for cold, or think they were.

The people of the Compounds would not give up easily. Some of them came out from their houses to stand out on their porches and stare at us as we passed. We must have looked a sight: the truck packed to the gills, everything battened down with tarps and lashed with rope. That was maybe not so unusual: heavily packed trucks and cars disappeared down the road every day these days. But on the hitch of our truck was a house.

That was different.

Some of the people who came out to look at us had guns, shotguns mostly. They came with the guns lowered, but at their sides, holding them as casual and easy as umbrellas.

Ready, I was meant to understand. They were ready.

That was acceptable now, that show. Guns had come out of the lockboxes and closets and cellars of the holler;

they had been brought into the light, dusted off, oiled, and loaded. They had been dug out of the ground. I had seen holsters on the hips of men in line at the bank, at the pharmacy, their fingers drifting to the leather swells like Lisbeth twirling her hair: an absentminded reassurance. I had seen the lumps of guns under coats, unmistakable even under the bulky layers we wore now.

I had a heaviness in my own coat pocket. I still didn't have any ammo, but I had Lobo's old gun. Just in case.

I fingered the leather cord around my neck. The pouch felt like a secret, something to guard. Dance sat in the front seat with me. He nodded at these men with their guns— they were all men. He gave a jerk of his chin, fingers flicked in a gesture that was not fully a wave. The men nodded back. We were acceptable. We were in.

Dance said we were headed to a couple of trailers be-hind a ridge. A van on cinder blocks rusted in the yard, though the dead grass was burr-short around it. Farming equipment, orange and sinewy with cobwebs, sat under a carport, support posts tilting against the hill. We passed a burn pile and a trash pile, both peaked with snow.

"My old man took the truck," Dance explained. "Off on a bender. Weeks ago."

"How did you get to the gas station?" Grayson asked.

"Hitchhiked."

He asked Grayson and me to wait while he went inside his place to get his things. I parked and watched him dis-appear inside the smaller of the two trailers, the one with the wooden step. Snow made the cans and chicken wire of the trash pile look cleaner somehow, newer. It gave it a fresh crown.

Grayson leaned in from the back seat. "How long should we wait?"

"I don't know." I looked closer at the piles of junk.

The burn pile didn't have the usual nest of brush and broken chairs. Instead, there were long, thin strands in the ashes, knotted and coiled. I knew what they were: pipes and wires, pulled from the walls of houses. Dance or his missing daddy had been trying to burn insulated wires, to get at the copper scrap.

Grayson said, "Is this even a good idea?"

I craned back to look at him. "None of this is a good idea."

It was snowing when Dance came back to the truck with a backpack and a sleeping bag. He chucked his stuff in the bed, and got into the front seat with me. He had on a different pair of glasses. The bridge of this pair had been repaired with tape, but the lenses were intact. A gust of wind broke over the ridge, rattling loose a piece of aluminum siding from his trailer.

"How did you and your daddy live out here?" I asked.

"Live?" He laughed a little.

"What did you do for money, I mean?"

"We were ginseng hunters. Root diggers. There was a buyer in town who paid cash. No questions asked. Ginseng, morel, goldenseal, black cohosh."

Seasonal work, then. That explained the copper wire

in the burn pile. They had not been able to find and sell roots for a while.

Snow feathered the windshield. I turned on the wipers, and the flakes drifted away, soft as dogwood blossoms. "So, your work is basically over?" I said.

"Yes. My life is over."

I looked over my shoulder and backed slowly down the ridge. I saw faces pressed to the windows of the houses, ghostly as fish underwater. But no one came out onto their porches again. It was too cold. And they knew where we were going.

Away.

Grayson fell asleep in the back seat, after complaining that his foot hurt. "At least this injury is good for something," he said as he bunched a pillow against the window. "I know when it's going to snow."

"It's always going to snow," Dance said. "That's no gift anymore."

I drove. I had to move carefully. Silently, the roads were filling with white. The tiny house on its trailer slowed us as it swayed behind, creaking like an old ship. Getting out of the holler and onto the Appalachian Highway, long and smooth, would shoot us straight to the bridge to West Virginia. It was not far away, but it would mean hills, hairpin turns, narrow roads. This road, out of the Compounds, was barely paved, gorged with potholes.

Dance told me he had left a note, but he thought his daddy wasn't coming back.

"Why would you think that?" I asked.

"I don't know. Some of his things were gone. It's hard to explain. Just a feeling, I guess."

We passed a trailer with sheets of plastic shrouding the front porch. There was a mattress, partially blackened, in the yard. Maybe they had burned it to try to keep warm.

"I wouldn't come back," he said. "There's nothing here." He tensed his jaw.

Lobo did that, but I tried not to connect the two actions. They were different men: one was old; one was young, almost a stranger. There was safety in Dance being a near-stranger. He could turn out to be anyone. He could be just fine.

"My old man was embarrassed to not be able to support himself," Dance said. "So he started drinking to cover it. Then he drank because he was embarrassed to be drunk. And then he was just drunk. He just became a drunk."

I felt I should tell him: "Our folks both left. Mine and Grayson's. Our people are gone, too."

"But at least your mama wants you to follow her. Right?"

"I should have followed sooner."

"But you're following now."

"I never should have let her go off with him. She doesn't even have her own phone. At least when we were on the farm I could keep an eye on her." I trailed off, checked the side mirror. There was my tiny house, a hulk behind us.

I didn't know why I was talking so much. It was something about the road, the blank road rolling on. It made *me* want to go on. And on. The landscape stretched past us, bland. The trees should have been at their brightest at this time of year, exploding with orange and red. Instead, their bare branches rattled together. I never realized, before last year, how dull winter was. How much the same of everything.

"Is your mama around?" I asked Dance.

"No. We don't talk about her. It just makes my old man sad. Or angry, depending on how drunk he is. She named me, though."

"Do you remember her at all?" I thought of the memory I had of her: a woman taking Dance out of school, trailing the scent of pot.

He wouldn't want to remember that, if he didn't already.

"I remember her hair. She had long hair. And bells. Bracelets and anklets with bells on them. She even had bells on her skirts."

I hadn't remembered that part. But thinking back, I thought I did hear something the day Dance left our class, a jingling I had connected to the smell of weed, so much so that I imagined bells sometimes in the basement room when I worked. But I used to imagine a lot of things to make it better.

"She loved music. That's why she left."

"To be a singer?" I asked.

"To follow a band."

Pink snow light changed the sky. I felt unsteady, driving the house, as if the heavy, extra weight might knock us off the road at any point. The roads weren't really salted. Maybe the holler was saving its chemicals. Or maybe they had run out.

The strips of clear pavement grew thinner, narrowing as slush packed the highway. The ditches, fleecy with drifts, overflowed their banks. I drove over a chunk of snow, which crushed beneath the truck's tires. We passed a dog, maybe a mastiff, ripping a dead deer into shreds.

We were going to take a southern route, which would make the trip longer but hopefully safer, with warmer temperatures, better roads. We were passing through West Virginia first, and avoiding cities if we could. I had been on trips before, but most of the states we were going to go through were new to me, and some part of me still felt excited to see them. I wanted to call my mama to tell her I was coming, but I didn't dare. Lobo would pick up.

I couldn't give advance warning, and I didn't trust myself to speak to him at all. Even if I said nothing about the trip and my plan to take her back with me, he would hear it. He would know.

He could tell when I lied, he said. He could tell when I was planning something. He would always know, he said, when we hid from him, me and my mama.

We did hide, in the woods. She had showed me how, how to make myself small, how not to make a sound. We had tried to leave once. I had begged her to try again. But we had nothing of our own. Where would we go, what would we do? We had no jobs, no skills other than growing and trimming. No references. No credit score. No family waiting.

I had planned the route without really planning it. There was only time for me to plug the address from the postcard into my phone. That had always been enough before. But before the bridge into West Virginia something went wrong. My phone screen flickered and whitened.

The map disappeared.

Dance took my phone and peered at it. Grayson had told me he had run out of data weeks ago, and Dance just had a burner.

"What's going on?" I asked. "It's lost the signal."

"Network overextended? Everybody trying to use their phones at once? The towers could be down." Dance tapped the window, where fog smeared the glass. His finger made an etching sound. "The towers could have frozen. Stop the truck. I'll see if I can get a signal somewhere away from the road."

It was nearly dark. Night fell early and heavy. It made me want to sleep, even though we were hours from stopping. It made me want to curl up somewhere warm and safe. Where would that be? I pulled off to the side, tires crunching in ice, and turned off the engine to save fuel.

"I'll be right back," Dance said. He turned up the collar of his coat, and headed outside, holding the phone high as he hiked up an embankment more snow than grass. The glow of my phone screen lit his face.

I shivered. It already felt cold, like a switch had been flipped. Grayson napped on in the back seat. I was about to get out and search for another blanket, when the dome light flickered on. Dance opened the passenger door but did not get back in. "Wil, you better come here," he said.

"What is it?"

He didn't answer. I glanced back at Grayson, snoring slightly, then opened the door and got out.

I had parked on a stretch of rural highway that didn't have any streetlights, or the lights were few and far between. Maybe everything had frozen and burst. The foot-hills made a jagged rim around the road like broken teeth. Roads had been bulldozed through the hills long ago for the heavy machinery that lumbered back and forth for logging and mining—roads that had no names. I could see zigzags of dirt running through the trees.

"It's here," Dance said.

"Did you get a signal?"

"No."

I stumbled over the ground, catching myself just before I fell. There was something in the snow.

"It's dead," Dance said. "An animal."

He helped me straighten up. The thing that had tripped me had fur, tipped with bronze, but it lay still. The fur didn't ruffle in the wind. It didn't move. It was frozen.

"There's more." He pointed to another form in the snow. "And there's a deer, I think, in the pool."

"What pool?"

He led me a little farther into the darkness. We were far from the cars that were passing on the highway. Too far from the truck, I thought.

I felt the weight of the gun in my pocket. The shadows before me arranged into a rectangle. A black pool. It wasn't frozen all the way. The pool had been halfheartedly covered by a tarp, its corners flapping in the wind. There was a chain-link fence, collapsing on one side around the pool, and a shed, its sides blasted with snow.

The wind shifted, and I smelled something sharp and chemical. Even the cold couldn't mask that, even the clean scent of snow. "This is an injection well, for fracking," I said. "This is supposed to be guarded."

"Well, the guard left."

I saw the deer in the pool then, the shape of the deer, which seemed not to be an animal, not to be anything at all, a torso unbound by time—except that there were antlers, a white rack. They almost looked beautiful, bone painted by snow.

But the body had a stillness I could not unsee. It buzzed with it, bobbing in the pond.

I thought of the Pumpkin King, made a scarecrow in his own dead garden. It was more frantic than the most frantic movement: the stillness of death, a frenzy of no longer caring that legs had broken off like icicles, that nostrils had filled with slime. Death had no shame. The deer carcass floated, antlers pointing at the sky.

"Everything's fucking falling apart," Dance said.

We did not get a signal on my phone. The truck started, and we drove in silence for a while.

If the guard had abandoned his post at the well, what else had been abandoned? Most businesses along the highway looked dark. Cars passed us, as frequently as stars, but the roadside diners and drive-throughs that would normally have traffic had none, just parking lots filling with white. We drove by truck stops and gas stations—had they closed for the night, or for good? Was everyone like us, like The Church and my mama, running?

At the first gas station with its lights on, I stopped. I refueled the truck while Dance ran inside. Prices had skyrocketed. Almost seven dollars a gallon. We had to wait in a line of cars for our turn. I had the canisters of cash, but I wanted to save that, for as long as I could.

I was the only one in my family, among the three of us, to have a bank account and card. Mama's idea, and I was not sure that Lobo knew. I was glad now that she had insisted. I had put a little money in the account every time I met the paper bag boy: a little for the bank, a lot for the ground. My card still worked. I watched the numbers rise.

I had finished refueling and just replaced the pump when the digital pad began to blink, the numbers flashing. I heard a click, and the pad went dark.

The gas station had lost power.

Dance came out of the convenience store with his arms full of maps. Steam had clouded the store windows. Someone had laid flattened cardboard down in front of the door to catch the drips of boots. But nothing was melting, nothing was dripping. I saw a shape move at the window. Someone turned the Open sign over to Closed.

The people in line were getting out of their cars. Those still at the pumps replaced the nozzles or shook them as if that would make the gas come out. People were starting to shout, as if that ever did anything, turning to look at the store.

We left quickly. Grayson woke up, grumpy and rubbing his leg. Dance offered to drive while I slept, so Grayson and I changed places, but I didn't want to sleep. I was too wired, too worried. My tiny house bounced behind the truck. The headlights of the cars passing in the other lane fizzed in the snow. I was not sure I trusted Dance to handle the truck on the icy roads, or Grayson to keep him under control. It would be just like a man to tag along, to tell me how to do things I already knew, like how to drive and navigate, to do them poorly himself.

But I must have slept. The last thing I remembered was Dance asking Grayson if he knew how to read a damn map. Then there was light. It was morning, and I smelled fire.

7

I stumbled out of the back seat. The truck had been parked inexpertly off to the side of the road, in a ditch that might hang us up later. I took a wide step over the ditch. The driver-side door dangled open, and in the grass before me, I saw a dead robin. Its beak was tucked into its body, the size of a shoe, head lolling. Its red breast looked almost obscene. Color in the white snow. I knew if I picked it up, it would feel weightless: the magic of its hollow bones. I walked carefully around it.

Dance and Grayson stood in the road.

As I slept, the highway had turned into a rural route again, narrowing to a single lane. Hills rose on either side. We had stopped before a side road, a turnoff to the right.

But we couldn't go forward: an accident stopped us. Two crashed cars had been abandoned in the middle of the main road. Their smashed noses met on the center line.

The cars had burned. One was still smoking a little—that was what I smelled, the chemical melt of plastic. The cars had no glass in their windows anymore, no bodies that I could see. Whatever mistake or tragedy this had been, it was over.

Someone had spray-painted in red on the burned cars: PREPARE TO PAY. The sentence ran across the two cars, linking them like a banner.

Grayson saw me. "That's not everything, Wil." He pointed to a speed limit sign, near the ditch. More spray paint. A different hand, more careful, had written: Pirates.

"We have to take this right turn," Dance said.

I woke up fast. "We are not going that way."

"The highway is blocked."

"Maybe." The smashed cars looked beat-up, cheap. They would go for nothing at a junkyard. They had crumbled easily, meshing together.

"What does *pirates* mean?" Grayson said.

"Looters down the highway?" Dance said. "Maybe the cars blocking the road were the people who came before us. Who got robbed, and are trying to warn us. Look, we have a lot to lose. I'm fine with taking a side road just to be safe. We have maps now."

I glanced at the side road. It looked rough, disappearing into curves, the road glittering like broken glass through the snow. "Seems pretty icy," I said.

"If it's too bad, we can turn around."

"Maybe we can just push these old cars off the highway," I suggested.

The men looked at me, then at each other. But we tried

it. We positioned ourselves at the back of first one burned car, then we tried the other. We shoved on the count of three. Grayson's boot slipped in the snow. The second bumper fell off under our hands.

But neither of the cars budged enough.

"What about driving through them?" Grayson said.

Now it was my and Dance's turn to exchange a glance. We got back into the truck. I told Dance to drive—he had got us into this parking spot, he could get us out of it. We made it out of the ditch, back onto the rural highway, and inched toward the burned cars.

"We should get a running start," Grayson said from the passenger seat.

"We'll slide on the ice," I said.

Lobo's old truck had been off the roads and into the woods. It had outrun his enemies. It had had a tree fall onto its hood and had crashed into branches, through mud and floods. It had been pulled out of ditches with chains. And now it was going to blast through two crashed cars.

Except it wasn't.

The front of the truck grated against the cars. It sounded like the night I had hit a guardrail when, exhausted, driving Lisbeth home, I had drifted to the side of the dark country road. We heard the sickening crunch of metal on metal.

"Stop!" I said. "These cars aren't moving. If something breaks on the truck, we're in trouble."

"I could fix it," Dance said.

"That seems risky," Grayson said. "I smell something burning."

Dance parked with a huff and pulled out one of the maps.

There were shacks in the distance, up on the hills, black and silent. I could not see the squint of any sunlight off their windows. Maybe their windows had no glass. I saw no smoke from a stove or cook fire. Nobody came by on the road.

"Let's back up and take that turn," I said.

"Off the highway?" Grayson asked. "You're sure?"

"I am worried about the ice on that road," I admitted.

"I've driven down worse, plenty of times," Dance said.

"Ice beats pirates," Grayson said.

We took the right turn.

I let Dance stay at the wheel. I sat up in the seat behind him, leaning forward, looking around. Grayson mumbled something about food or coffee, but I hoped the right turn, our shortcut, would be too quick to even think about stopping. And where would we stop? We were nowhere.

Morning meant nothing. The sun was out: weak and watery. It only made the landscape seem colder somehow, more brittle. It hurt to stare at it. The fields full of poverty grass looked sharp enough to crack. No wind waved them. I hadn't seen any animals.

The road dipped and swerved. Each turn unveiled a secret of the road: ice slicing down the middle like a ribbon of fat. Or a chunk of snow, stained red. Or a child's shoe, lost in a snowdrift. The brakes gritted on the ice and Dance swore.

We passed a stretch of land that had once been orchards. Ice encased the trees, shimmery as jellyfish. Row after row of them, shriveled and glinting. This sun wasn't going to melt anything. There were large wooden crates at the edge of the orchard. They had been split, kicked, or splintered open by hungry people, thieves. There was nothing inside.

Pig houses, sullen as coffins, replaced the orchards. I didn't see any pigs. Maybe it was too cold for them. Then something came into view in the distance. Gray and raised: a road, or runway.

Dance saw it, too. "Is that an airport?"

There were people on it, moving too fast to be walking.

"What the hell?" Grayson said.

The way they glided in and out of view... They were skateboarding.

"A skate park?" Grayson said. "Here?"

"Let's turn around," I said.

"How?"

It was already too late. The road was ending.

Our right turn was a dead end.

There was no way to back up, no space wide enough for the trailer to turn. The road had turned to gravel. The sides of it fell away, crumbling, and the hills rose up, steep and spiky with dead grass. There were structures up on those hills. Houses. The road was ending in somebody's land.

It ran right under a gate, which was thrown open. The right turn wasn't a road at all, I realized.

It was a driveway.

This gate wasn't like the one at the farm, a metal gate Lobo had bought at the tractor store. This one was home-made, welded from pipes and twisted from branches, lashed to a fence of wire. I was certain—if this place had power—electricity coursed through that fence. It ran as far as I could see. I had been seeing it as we drove and not even noticing. On both sides of the road, the fence bisected the landscape into nearly invisible squares, razor-thin and biting.

"Pirates," Grayson said. "They aren't on the highway. They're here. It was a trap."

Two men stood at the gate.

They wore hunting caps, vests, and boots. They carried guns, big and black. Rifles. They held them casually, like daughters; they were used to holding them or didn't care how they did it. The men had seen us. They had been waiting for us. Likely, they had heard us coming a mile away on the road, ice crunching under our tires, the rumble on the snow. One of men held up his gloved hand—*stop*.

"Where are we?" Grayson whispered.

"It's a compound," I said. "Lots of structures, a fence. This is their land."

"What do they want? Why do they have their guns out?"

The man who had made us stop approached the truck.

"Fuck," Dance said, and rolled the window down.

The man wore aviator sunglasses. "Can we help you, gentlemen?" he said. He leaned into the open window and saw me. I swore his eyes widened behind the shades. "Lady."

I looked away, at the fence. There was a dead deer hung on it, twisting in the wind.

Dance said, "We're passing through, on our way to find family. We saw your skaters."

It was the truth—but it felt like a lie. They had made us come down this road. They had given us no choice, with the blockade of cars. They had crashed them on purpose. It was these men who had blocked the highway, I was sure of it. Beyond the gate, I could see the skaters again, gliding in the white sky, jumping and spinning. It looked like freedom.

But it seemed off, everything seemed off. The fence was too long, the gate too elaborate. There were bits of broken bottles and jagged glass stuck at the top of the gate. What could I see past it? A sagging farmhouse. Some kind of concrete band shell near where the skaters were dipping up and disappearing down from view. Who would have built that?

And who would skate now, in winter? In the midst of *this* winter?

The man tilted his head to let me know he was checking out the inside of the truck: our food wrappers, blankets, and maps. I knew he was checking me out. I felt his gaze. I was as padded as a bear. I wore jeans lined with flannel, my coveralls, my coat.

But I wished I had worn two coats, wrapped myself in a garbage bag. I wished I had cut my hair short, wished the guards at the gate were women. Wished the world was women.

The other man had disappeared. Then we heard him shouting from the back of the truck.

"Mick," he said. "They have a house back here!"

Mick, the man in sunglasses, grinned, a mouth of yellow teeth and chewing tobacco. "Cool," he said.

Knocking on the passenger side window.

Grayson exchanged a look with Dance, then rolled it down. The second man was there. He stuck his head in, and talked to Mick across the seats, panting a little with excitement. "It's a baby house," he said. "Looks like it's got a kitchen and everything."

"Interesting," Mick said.

"It's not for sale," Dance said.

"I didn't ask you if it was for sale. But I will ask you, what you have for trade."

"Trade?" Grayson said.

Dance was speaking in a calm, quiet voice. "We just need to turn around. We'll be on our way and won't bother you."

"Turnaround goes through our place."

"Listen, sir." Grayson held up his dead phone and shook it. "Do you know what's going on? The weather? Any news at all? We can't get any service."

"Service? We never had service here. Shit. Maybe it's an uprising." The man looked into the distance. "Maybe it's a Tuesday in West Virginia."

"We'll pass straight on through," Dance said. "We won't even stop."

"You don't have to stop," the man said. "If you drive this way, you pay us."

It was a racket. They had dragged the cars over to block the highway, and were hitting up everyone who took the turn. Like we had, dumbly, ignoring the warning spray-painted on the sign. Misreading it.

I stared at the back of Grayson's head, his neck held stiff

and alert. If we didn't produce an item they wanted, the men would start riffling through our truck. They might find the grow lights, the cash, the gun.

I had stuffed the gun under the driver's seat when it had been my turn behind the wheel, hiding it in a hole in the upholstery. Lobo had cut the hole for just such a purpose, digging out the seat stuffing, gray as entrails, and hollowing a slit for money or drugs or anything my mama or I might need to hide. The men at the gate might wonder why we had such things, why we had made a secret place for them. I looked at the men's guns, their long barrels, magazines as big and black as the wings of a giant bird. They weren't just rifles. They were semis—maybe fully automatic.

I sensed the leather pouch of seeds around my neck, warm and soft against my skin.

Grayson said, "What if we give you—"

But Mick said, "Oh, we don't want any of your things. We have plenty of things. We're stocked. We're good to go. We've been ready for something like this for a long time."

"That's right," the second man said.

"We wanna know," Mick said, "what you can *do*."

"Do?" Grayson's voice cracked.

Mick and the other man turned their heads and stared into the back seat. At me.

Everybody looked at me, Dance and Grayson craning back over their shoulders. Grayson looked panicked. Dance, though, had a different look. Resigned. He tightened his mouth. He turned back around in a flash while Grayson was still staring, horrified, at me.

Then they spoke at the same time, both to the men with guns, though Grayson looked at me when he said it. "I can cook," Grayson said.

"I'm a truck mechanic," Dance said.

"What?" Mick said.

Grayson started to repeat himself, but the man said, "No. Your friend. What he said."

"I'm a truck mechanic."

What an amazing liar, I thought, before I realized he was telling the truth.

"That your job?"

"No," Dance said. "But it was my daddy's job, before he got too drunk to do it. And he taught me everything he knows."

"Works for me," the second man said.

In the back seat I said nothing.

The men pulled back from the windows, and stepped away from the truck. With their guns, they indicated we should drive through the gate.

"Pull up to the main house," Mick said. "You'll know it."

Dance rolled up the windows and gave a friendly, fake wave. Once we had driven a few feet away, and I could see the men in our rearview, standing in the frozen dirt, admiring the back of my house, Grayson said, "What the hell did you just get us into?"

"I got us out of a whole lot of shit," Dance said. "They weren't going to let us leave, not without—" he glanced in the rearview mirror "—something. Something bad."

"Can you even fix trucks? Do you even know what you're doing? Was any of that true?"

"It's all true. My daddy was a mechanic once. I can fix whatever they want."

"Well, they're going to want a lot." Grayson slapped the dashboard. "Why did we come this way?"

Dance looked at me in the mirror. "Wil, are you okay?"

I had felt a jolt go through me when I had seen the men, when they had leaned into the cab and noticed me, the way their voices perked up at the sight of a woman, the way they had paid attention. I had a bullet lodged in my chest, ice in my throat. I felt like I was being strangled. How could I tell Dance that?

"I'm fine," I said.

We traveled up the driveway through the gate. We saw the usual collection of outbuildings, trailers, and sheds, each more collapsing than the next, planted haphazardly on the hills like tumors growing out of the ground. I was used to seeing cars on blocks, buildings left to rot, even old farmhouses with trees sprouting through their roofs. But some of the cars parked here beyond the gate were burned, bombed out, and vandalized like the cars on the highway. Some of them looked as though they hadn't been running for years, snow mixing with rust. This place was a junkyard.

Or a graveyard.

The truck bounced over the ruts of the road, knolls of ice along the driveway's eroding edges. They had not dug ditches here. I looked back at my tiny house, still chained to us. Still intact. The driveway grew more difficult, and the house jostled. I heard the brakes of the truck grind. I straightened around to see where we were going.

Something had been built into the hill ahead of us, the ground hollowed out for what appeared to be a giant, curving swimming pool. But it was drained and empty, the curves swept clean of snow despite the white ruin all around us.

This was where the skaters had slipped off the edge of the world, flying into the sky. The big, band shell–looking thing I had seen from the gate was perched at the top— it was not a band shell at all but a dome, resting above a concrete bowl, deep and wide.

"I think that's a skate park," Dance said.

"It's a theme park in hell," Grayson said.

"If you own land, you can act like a king. You can build what you want." I was glued to the window.

We came over the crest of the hill and saw the main house, as the men at the gate said we would: two stories, shingled with rot-black wood. A farmhouse turned flop-house. A sagging front porch hid any people who might be standing there, watching us from the shadows. The roof, sloppy with snow, threatened to collapse onto their heads. An addition onto the house had never been finished, and tar paper flapped, loose in the wind. The pink insulation made that side of the house look naked. It would never be finished now.

Junk was everywhere, tires and beer cans. Fires burned in the barrels scattered around the hills, and in pitted, ashy craters in the ground.

Trash was being nosed about by dogs, which seemed to

roam freely, thin-ribbed and snappish, the kind of dogs that were kicked by men. I had grown up with men like these, slapping off their hands and walking through their comments like it was nothing, faint music from a radio down the street. Men who would not think twice about staring at a woman. Men who carried guns and laid them out on tables when they came inside a house.

Men were coming out of the farmhouse now to look at us.

Then I saw a woman, standing in the doorway of a shed, blond-haired and small, a red-faced baby on her hip. I couldn't see any emotion on the woman's features, any fear or hope. She was shut down, as blank as the sky, a painting of a woman more than the real thing. Even the baby on her hip was silent.

One man broke away from the group at the farmhouse. He stepped down from the porch, spreading his arms wide. The others moved to let him pass. He had a kind of glow about him. I recognized it. He was in charge.

"Welcome!" the man was saying, loud enough to hear from the truck. He wore a fuzzy hat and a long wool coat. I noticed his gun when he outstretched his arms, causing his coat to flap open. A handgun, holstered at his waist. Other than the coat and hat, he wasn't dressed right. Not for work, not for the weather. He wore a muscle shirt under his coat. And—I couldn't believe what I was seeing—he wore flip-flops. "Come out, come out!" he shouted, gesturing to us like we were children.

Dance put the truck into Park. We all looked at each other.

"If we die here—" Grayson said.

"We're not going to die," Dance said. "Wil—"

"Nobody say anything about the seeds," I said. "Or the grow lights. Or me being a grower. Nothing. You hear me?"

"Okay," Grayson said. "You can trust us."

I looked at him. I looked at Dance. "We're going to get out of this," I said.

I opened the door.

First I noticed the smell, noxious and oily. Burned gasoline in the air. The sour smell of the trash. Fire popped in one of the barrels. I thought I heard a baby crying.

"Heard you got some skills," the man said. "My boys radioed ahead."

"Your phones work?" Dance couldn't keep the hopefulness from his voice.

"Walkie-talkies," the man said. "We're old-school here. Well, welcome, welcome. I'm Jake. And this is my utopia." He indicated the unfinished house, the cars, the sheds.

Someone had pulled a TV out onto the patch of dirt in front of the farmhouse. A tractor tire was positioned before it, like a La-Z-Boy, surrounded by empty cans. An extension cord, patched with tape, snaked back into the house.

"What is this place?" Dance asked.

"Paradise," Jake said. "Skating, shooting, drinking, and babes. What more do you want?"

"How long have you all been out here?"

"Oh, we been here forever. But lately—" he winked "—it's gotten real interesting."

"They said you've got some trucks that need work?"

"Do I!" He gestured around the dirty yard.

"All these vehicles—and you don't have a mechanic?"

"He died," a thin man in a trucker cap said, then spat.

Grayson was silent, shifting on his bad leg. He had his hands deep in his pockets, and his head down, turned away from the men. He was hanging by the back of the truck with me, trying to hide. But there was no hiding.

Jake saw him. "Well, you're no good."

"I can cook," Grayson said.

"Of course you can. Why didn't they just shoot you?"

Grayson flinched, but Jake strode right on past him and came up to me. To his credit, Grayson didn't move. He stayed standing in front of me, trying to block me with his hunched shoulders. But he couldn't, of course. Jake would find a woman, find a weakness, a mile away. He stopped before me. He stared at me strangely.

"And you?" Jake said to me. "You dance?"

"Dance?" I thought of the gun in the truck. I thought of how fast I could run. Jake looked me up and down. His face was so tanned it looked stamped. There was a scar under his eye, a white line I recognized as a knife scar. He wasn't much taller than me, but his chest and arms looked bulky and muscular. His neck was veined. He would be strong.

"How many trucks do I have to fix," Dance said loudly, "to get us back on the road?"

Jake turned away from me. When he broke his gaze, I realized I had been holding my breath. I tried to recall his face: the soft spots, the weak spots, the places I might break with my fist. His eyes were small. His nose had already been broken once or twice. He was missing a couple of teeth.

"Don't know," Jake said. "Depends on how good you fix them."

"Let's get started, then."

"All right. I like a man with initiative. Follow me. You." He pointed at Grayson. "Park your dollhouse behind the main house. Girl … What was your name again, darling?"

"Sarah," I said.

"Sarah." He repeated it, staring at me as if he did not believe me. "Right. Sarah, you go along with Jamey now. You'll probably want some girl talk, after being with men for so long."

The woman with the baby on her hip, the silent blonde, flicked a look at me, then deliberately turned and went back into the shed without saying a word. I got the feeling she didn't want me to follow. Jake started to walk up to the main house, his flip-flops slipping in the snow. All the men with the guns were turning away, going back into the farmhouse. It was too cold to stand out here talking.

Dance opened the truck door. "They're separating us on purpose."

"What do we do?" Grayson said.

"There's a gun in the truck," I whispered. "It's not loaded. In a hole in the cushion of the driver's seat."

"Jesus," Grayson said.

"Let's get a move on!" Jake said.

"I can't take a gun."

"There's a knife in the glove box, then. Stick it in your cast when you move the truck."

"Hello!" Jake called from the porch. Somehow he had already gotten a beer in his hand.

"We can't leave Wil without a weapon," Grayson said.

"Less talking, more working!" Jake said. At a signal from Jake, the man in the trucker hat started toward us, hunting rifle slung in his arms.

"I have a knife on me," Dance said quickly. "Take it, Wil."

"They're looking at us," I said. "I can't take it now."

"Here," Dance said. Before I knew what was happening, he had grabbed me around the waist and pulled me toward him. He kissed me, hard and cold. His beard pricked and I felt his hands at my hip, searching.

But I wore coveralls; there was no waist, no way to pass a weapon to me. Men said those things were like a chastity belt. Finally, he tucked something colder than his fingers into my pocket. A knife.

"Damn, boy," Jake said.

"If you touch me again without asking," I whispered to Dance, "I'll kill you. Even if the world ends."

"Just saying goodbye to my girl," Dance said loudly.

The man with the hunting rifle spat.

8

I had lost my virginity to get it over with. I was eighteen; it felt past time. Avoiding the boys in town and their constant requests for weed meant I had missed out on a lot of what other girls went through: being cornered at parties, being led upstairs, giving in. That was how girls talked about it. *I just got tired. It just seemed easier.*

One of the men who bought from Lobo was younger. He seemed different somehow. I got the impression that he had been dragged along, that the price of the ride he needed from his friends or his daddy was a stopover here at our farm, and a long, long wait while the others smoked.

Or maybe I just wanted him to be different.

I first saw him getting out of a truck. He had been sitting in the back with a horde of men. The others spit, adjusted their jeans when they hopped down from the truck bed, but he didn't. And when he got back into the truck a few hours later, he smiled at me, gave a little wave. I guess that was enough, that was as good as I might find in the holler.

The next time he came over, I watched him from the yard where I was weeding. It was summer then. We did things like that, knelt in the earth and pulled things from it, things that had grown green and warm. Too many things had grown, so many that we could be choosy about what we kept and what we uprooted to toss and rot in a pile; we could be careless. He must have noticed me, too. When the teal truck, dented with dings, rolled to a stop in front of the farmhouse in a show of dust and gravel, he came over to me. The others went inside.

"Too hot to do that in the daytime, huh?" he said, nodding at my pile of weeds.

Twilight gave everything a fluid outline: the weeds; my arms; the man's arms in his T-shirt, lined with hair. It was like we were being rubbed away. He had long, straggly brown hair, home-cut from a pocketknife, and a beard that was red.

"Yeah," I said. "Too hot to do much of anything."

It must have been June. The tomatoes were stalky and fragrant but still green and hard. He unscrewed the lid and took a swig from a plastic bottle of water. Nobody around here drank just water, but that's what it was.

I had a window AC unit at my shack then. Maybe that's what I used to get him there, the lure of the cool chemical air. I couldn't remember. Probably I didn't need to use or say much of anything. It was like the girls always said:

men fell into bed with you. It was harder, much harder, to resist than to give in.

I didn't have to do much of anything. He didn't want me to. He wanted to do things to me. But what was I supposed to do, what were we supposed to talk about while I was just lying there, naked from the waist down, and he was kneeling over me in my loft. *You just get into it*, girls in the holler said. *You just let your body take over.* But mine didn't.

"You're so beautiful," he said.

What did that mean? I felt like he meant that I was skinny. I felt like he meant that I was young, which was nothing to do with me. Just an accident that I was in the middle of.

The AC blasted, and my skin felt pickled. Through the window in the loft I could see the plane trees waving in a new breeze. The sun was drowning behind them, almost down.

I looked up at the ceiling. "Sorry, I think I put Bag Balm on my knees. They were really dry. Sorry if it tastes weird." But he wasn't at my knees.

"Are you kidding me?" His voice had the awe of weed, the hush of amazement at the cosmos, at the sound of my name. He was out of himself, brought down to his knees by my nakedness, and I should have realized some power there, but I didn't. I just wanted it over with.

Soon, it was.

It didn't hurt, like girls said it would, but it also didn't feel like anything. Maybe because he kept falling out. He was nervous. He kept saying that: *I'm so nervous.* And I had to comfort him, telling him it didn't matter, and it didn't, but not for the reasons I pretended.

A few nights later we tried again. It hurt this time. He was ready. This was what the girls spoke of, trading cigarettes in the bathroom of the roller rink we would be banned from. Sharp, rending, tearing pain. Stabs, like fishhooks in my body. I felt like a bedsheet being torn, ripped into sections. There was a burning, and my stomach felt tight.

The pain came from where I imagined my soul might be, if I believed I had a soul: my center, that spot where I felt a heartbeat sometimes. Girls might tattoo a circlet of flowers or stars there, a landing pad for the tongue. The pain felt like I was being pulled to the ceiling—and I decided to stay there.

After that night, Lobo wouldn't sell to the man's daddy or his friends. One of the other men must have said something, or maybe the red-bearded man told them: how I had led him to my loft with the flowered sheets and the pink quilt my mama had made for me, how I had practically begged for it, how I hadn't bled or cried.

Somebody said something. Somebody told. After that night, things changed.

Some of Lobo's customers would stop by the lower field on their trip home and try the door of my shack, to see if maybe I had something to sell or give them, too. After the first surprise visit—a heavy-bellied pothead stumbling into my room, already taking off his belt; he was too stoned and drunk to walk straight, and he went out the door hard when I kicked him, surprise bubbling up like vomit on his face—I learned to lock the door. I would brace whatever I had against it: a bookshelf, cords of wood. I used bags of potting soil as sandbags. I stopped sleeping well.

I didn't see the red-bearded man again, but I didn't expect to. I wouldn't sleep with another man who came to the farm, nobody who knew Lobo, nobody who might get my mama high. There were a couple of men in town: one from the feed store, one at the biker bar the boys from high school were too tired to go to now after their shifts, too worn out from children they didn't know not to have. For those men, I took off my clothes in trucks—those pieces I needed to take off—slipping out of one leg of my jeans but not the other, leaving my shirt on but raised. I could wiggle out of my bra without taking off my top. The windows steamed, and the men cried out, and I felt the same thing, the same two things: pain and nothingness, twined together.

Poison ivy and jewelweed.

Lisbeth and I tried it. It was so confusing. The Church forbid everything before marriage, even kissing, and I was stunted by...stunted by—I didn't know, but I was obviously doing something wrong. I was supposed to feel an explosion of longing. I was supposed to open up and feel warm and emboldened, as bright as a day lily, as free as white trilliums. Wasn't I supposed to want this? To want it more and more? My mama had moved us to the farm for this, uprooted and permanently scarred our lives to twist in Lobo's arms, to cry over the dirty dishes for him, and put up with him: his anger, his moods. She wanted him that badly.

And I could barely get through it without squeezing shut my eyes.

"When I get married, I'm going to need to know how to do this," Lisbeth said. She was very serious. "We need to practice, Wil. I don't want to be bad on my wedding night. I don't want to let my husband down."

I lowered my head. Was I supposed to start? I was looking at the floorboards of her bedroom, the dark spots where water had spilled and been left too long. I was trying not to look at Lisbeth's knees, the bony domes of them beneath her skirt, and the folds of the fabric, where it twisted—and then her lips were on mine.

This was different. They were soft, she was soft. It felt really, really sweet—that was what I thought. Tender, hesitant. Her hands were nowhere near me, not touching me or trying to, not searching for a way in. That was different, too. I didn't have anything to bat or twist away from: my wrist pinned to the truck window, my skin burning with a tension men thought was desire but really was me resisting the impulse to run, to fight. With Lisbeth, I just sat there and felt safe. It was just the flutter of kisses, then—

Lisbeth sat back on her heels and opened her eyes. "I didn't feel anything, did you?"

"No," I lied.

At the compound, one of the cars had a pair of underwear speared on the radio antenna, pink and small. On the ground there was a cooler tipped open on its side. A dog licked blood out of the lid.

"Stay safe," Dance said, then went with the man with the rifle.

The woman and the baby had disappeared inside the shed, and I was supposed to follow her, to walk into who knew what. Jake drank his beer on the porch, watching. Grayson looked at me, then got in the truck and drove it away where they told him to go. I hoped he would be able to grab the knife.

I was left alone in the yard.

For a moment, I thought that this was my chance. The air was still and white—the only sound: two of the dogs, snarling over a bit of food. Jake rocked on a chair against the house, too far to reach me if I bolted.

But how far could I run without a car, without my house and supplies? Where would I go? Where were we, other than West Virginia, in a holler darker than my own?

And I wasn't alone. I felt it on the back of my neck, as cold as the knife Dance had passed me: men watched me. Jake wasn't the only one. From the outbuildings, from the burned-out cars, from the woods, I felt eyes. I could not run.

I went to the shed as if it was my choice. Went willingly. Rosemary grew wild against the side of the shed, only half-dead. Herbs could live through a lot. I crouched down and broke off a sprig, still green at the top. I could feel Jake's presence behind me on the porch. I put the rosemary in my pocket.

The shed might have held wood once, or tools. It had a thin plastic storm door, smeared with grease. I pushed it open without knocking and went in.

A smell. A mattress on the floor. Some laundry, I thought.

There was no heat. Ice crystalized on the window in patterns as pretty as a quilt. The girl with the baby stared at me from the mattress. I was wrong to call her a woman. She was young. Her hair was a lank, yellow smear. Her eyes looked huge and hollow, rimmed by circles of blue pencil.

"You want food?" the girl said blankly.

No hello. No names.

I was hungry—but I didn't want to take food away from her or the child, an egg-haired toddler on the girl's lap, her cheeks fat and pink from health or from cold, I couldn't tell. Her belly protruded from her sweater. Her legs and feet were bare and filthy. She stared at me, silent and sullen as her mother.

They were eating out of a can. The baby reached in her small hand to pull out a fistful of runny, cold beans. She smeared them on her face, a few beans finding her mouth. I had to stop myself from wincing when I saw her hand in the can, inches away from the razor-sharp lid.

"I'm Wil," I said.

The girl didn't answer or introduce herself.

I tried a question. "Where are we exactly? What was this place before?"

"Before it got cold? It was great," the girl said. "We had cable. Parties all the time. Lots of bands came through here." She flipped her hair. Stiff with grime, it barely moved. "Metal mostly. Good bands came to play. We paid them and they could skate, too." The baby whimpered, and she began to bounce the child on her knee without looking at her. "Now nobody comes here. Well—" she looked up at me "—except for travelers."

There was something about her glance that scared me, something that seemed not right, beyond the usual hunger and sadness—something beyond what I could attribute to cold and loneliness and exhaustion. There was a leer in her eyes, a flashing darkness. It looked like excitement.

I tried to redirect her. It worked sometimes with Lobo's customers, to get them focused on something else, something not my waist or small hands.

"This is a skate park?" I said.

"No. Not *just* a skate park." She laughed. "You've really never heard of us?"

"I don't skate."

"You're missing out, then." She shifted the baby. "This is a community. We have parties every week. Well, we did before the money ran out. People come to party but they stay."

"They stay?"

"They used to. I did. As long as you work some, Jake don't care." She shrugged, like she was offering me half her bedroom, a trundle bed, a bunk. It was no skin off her back, what she was offering. "You can stay, too, if you want. There's always work to do."

"I can see that."

I thought about Jake asking me if I could dance. I thought of the scar filleting his face, the black doorways where some of his teeth had been.

"You help him out, Jake'll give you a place to sleep, feed you. Take care of you," the girl said.

I didn't like this recruitment, the girl droning on. Had Jake put her up to this? Was this her job, the work she did? She didn't have much to sell the place with. The shed smelled of sickness. The baby was barefoot. What care was he giving her?

"So this is a commune?" I said.

"I don't know what that word is."

She didn't ask me to explain. She told me her name was Jamey, with a *y*. She told me she had lived at Skate State, as she called the place, for over a year, though she said it was harder to keep track now, since it was cold all the time. She asked me if I had any good celebrity news.

"Celebrity news?" I repeated.

"I know it's dumb, but I really like to hear about their lives, you know? They're so much more exciting than us, and since we got no internet..."

"There's no internet?"

"It went down."

"You mean, your network went down?"

"No," Jamey said. "There's no internet anywhere. Jake drove into town and tried the free wireless at the Wendy's. Nobody's got it. That's what they said on the radio. It's gone."

"The internet can't be gone. Maybe some lines got icy, that's all."

"So you don't got any news?" Jamey asked. "Where did you come from?"

"Ohio."

"It's cold there? Like this?"

"It's cold everywhere," I said.

"No internet." Jamey shook her head, a little smile on her lips that was grim or amused; it was hard to tell. "We're on our own, girl. It finally happened."

If she was talking to herself, or to me, or to the baby, I didn't know. I heard a cry then, a catlike whimper. I thought it was the baby, but Jamey didn't look down at her or comfort her, and the child was staring up at me, silent.

The mound of blankets on the floor began to move. A rail-thin arm emerged. A blanket slipped and I saw a head of matted, black hair, a pinched face, and a woman's eyes: rolling and white. Eyes that were sick. Eyes that were not present, not in this world. I knew eyes like that.

Jamey didn't seem concerned. "We're out, Kaylee."

But the girl on the floor had motivated Jamey. She got off the mattress, balancing the child on her hip—the baby clung to her, submissive as a doll—and set the can of beans to the side. She wiped her free hand on her jeans and shook out some of the blankets, plumped the pillows. It was absurd to see her straightening up the filthy, uninhabitable shed.

The girl on the floor moaned again.

"What's wrong with her?" I asked, though I knew.

Jamey glared at me. "What do you think? Damn it, Kaylee, I have to wash those sheets in the creek."

"You don't have water?"

"I ain't gonna waste water on her."

"Who is she?"

"Before everything went to shit," Jamey said, "she was

a stripper. Jake hired her for a party. He let her stay on if she'd dance in exchange for…" Her voice trailed off. She looked down at the girl.

Half of my life was spent ignoring high people. I had seen people on Molly. They acted happy, unconcerned, sometimes wild. It was scary, watching them be happy, because I knew little else mattered to them in those moments: even a child, even me. Even their own child. People on opioids, maybe like Kaylee, didn't hurt you, they didn't want to. They just fell asleep. Sometimes forever.

"You can't take care of her?" I asked. "Help her?"

Jamey shook out a sheet so hard it snapped. "We don't have internet. We don't have heat. We definitely don't have oxy. Or methadone. Not anymore. Nobody does."

"You have to get out of this place."

Jamey was staring at me, numb as the baby. "Jake ain't never gonna let you leave."

Jamey took the sheets to the river, and handed me the baby to watch. I think she thought I wouldn't run away with her baby in my arms: another mouth to feed, another person to take care of, one who wasn't even mine.

The child went willingly with me—too tired, too cold, or too used to it to complain. For a few minutes, I thought about running, anyway, taking her with us to California and away from this, whatever this was, with the skating and the guns and the men who burned cars.

I wondered what that would be like. Where would we find milk for her, if all the stores had closed? Did she still drink milk? What would my mama say, when we caught up with her? I had a sudden memory of Lisbeth, when we were little, kissing all her dolls.

I had to get out of the shed. Even the cold was better than this stinking shack, stifling and freezing at the same time. I wrapped the baby's legs in an adult-size fleece I found on the floor, which looked mostly clean. Outside, the air, even tinged with gas and the smoke from the barrel fires, felt better in my lungs.

I sat on a log in the woods a little distance from the creek and rocked the silent child. It was strange how quiet and compliant she was, unnatural. She took to me instantly. I wondered what her name was. Through the trees, I could hear water running over rocks. Otherwise, the woods were silent. I listened to the soft smacking sounds the baby made with her mouth. She started to play with a thread on my gloves, picking at it until it ran. She made a red zigzag, like a heartbeat.

Something was off in the woods. Other than the river and the child, I heard nothing. No birds. No scuffling of squirrels or chipmunks. Had the men scared them all away, or shot them? We had packed deer meat, frozen hard and wrapped in white paper, from the hunters who had traded game for weed. But we might run out of that eventually. If we did, I was going to have us hunt squirrels: clean, easy meat, though not a lot of it on each animal. But what if there were no squirrels? There had been no frogs singing at night, no turtles sunning themselves on rocks in the river.

Who knew where the frogs were. The days blurred together—they were barely days. The bare trees, the early sunsets... Jamey was right; it was difficult to keep track of time.

I felt the weight of the baby on my lap, and missed Lisbeth more than ever. We used to pretend, when we were very young, what our lives would be like. It was not a game I was good at. For Lisbeth, it was all husbands and children and singing. For me, it was...maybe go to the community college the next town over? They had a clinical herbalism program. I thought I might like to do something with plants that could save lives, that could heal, not just make someone feel good or get relief for a little while. Maybe I'd own my own farm, somewhere far away.

But now we were away—across the state line at least—and what good had it done me?

The child whimpered, and I hugged her a little tighter. I wondered if she was cold, though the shed wouldn't be much warmer. Where was Jamey?

I heard a twig break, the crunch of leaves that had frosted stiff. I stood with the little girl in my arms, preparing to give her back to her mama. But the figure that emerged from the trees wasn't Jamey. It was Grayson.

"Where have you been?" I said.

"Why do you have a baby?" he asked.

I hitched the girl higher on my hip. "Her teen mom is at the creek, doing laundry."

"Well, that's depressing."

"What's going on? What do they have you doing?"

"Cleaning the kitchen." His face looked flushed. "This place is a giant frat house. I have the privilege of making them dinner tonight."

"Well, you said you could cook."

"I was trying to barter for your life."

The baby made a sound, and Grayson leaned over to brush a tendril of hair out of her mouth. The gesture was so kind it derailed me for a moment. "How did you get away from them?" I asked.

"Went for firewood. The cookstove is almost out."

"You have to make dinner on a cookstove?"

Sometimes, when the power went out because of a storm, we would do that on the farm, simmer deer stew on a cookstove all day. The heat felt like nothing else, radiating from the iron surface, and the height was all wrong, too low for work. Bending over a cookstove for hours, I was so hot and tired I forgot to be hungry.

It seemed the drudgery and the work would never end for us at Skate State.

"Oh, there's barely electricity here," Grayson said. "Generator only."

"Has the grid failed?"

"I think they just didn't pay their electric bill. All the power they have goes to the important stuff. You know, flat-screen TV, gaming, stereo..."

I thought of the shed where Jamey, the woman on the floor called Kaylee, and the little girl slept: unheated, freezing, the blankets mounded on the ground. A structure more suitable for junk, not humans, not fit enough for chickens.

"I can only be gone for a little while, or they'll get suspicious," Grayson said. "The woodpile is supposed to be around here somewhere."

"Over here." I had seen it on the walk from the shed. "What's Dance doing?" I asked as we picked our way through the trees.

Ice and snow cast the leaves in silver. It should have been pretty. But nothing in the foothills of Appalachia was just pretty. The snow couldn't cover all the trash, the bits of paper and plastic bags, the hulks of old farming equipment and junk cars.

"They separated us right away. But from what I saw, they have him working pretty hard. There are dozens of cars and trucks here. And it looks like just about every single one has something wrong with it."

"Why do they have so many?"

"Some people collect china figurines, some people collect broken-down cars? I think they're for parts."

"So, when do we get to leave?"

Grayson tore through a plastic bag that got caught on his cast, ripping it away like a spiderweb. "Nobody's said anything about leaving."

We had reached the woodpile. It wasn't a huge stack of wood, not nearly as much as Lobo and my mama and I would have stockpiled by this time of year, in a regular year, for just the three of us. And who knows how many people needed firewood here, how many people Jake was supposedly keeping warm.

The crudely constructed overhang hadn't sheltered the woodpile very well. It tilted with rot. Snow had drippled through gaps in the shingles. The ends of the logs in the pile looked black, which was not a good sign.

Grayson picked up a log and examined it. "This wood is wet."

"It's never gonna burn," I said.

He threw the log down and picked up another one. "This is all wet."

The baby on my hip began to whimper.

"Hang on," he said. "I saw a tarp around here somewhere. Maybe there's more wood underneath it."

"Tarps aren't any good, either," I said. "They collect moisture."

But we went around the side of the woodpile, anyway, looking. There it was: a flash of blue plastic. But it didn't shelter firewood.

Grayson ripped a corner of it off, revealing a dusty hood. The tarp covered a car. The windshield was pollen-yellow with filth, leaf crumbles collecting in the seams.

I thought I had seen more tarps in the trees. Holding the child tightly, I spun around. I could see them now. They looked so obvious in the woods. How had I ever missed them? Bits of color, mounded with leaves. Snow piled on their peaks. There must have been half a dozen tarps scattered through the woods, like a field of bright mushrooms.

"How many spare parts do they need?" I asked.

Grayson was examining the vehicle under the blue tarp. He wrenched the door open—out spilled a tumble of leaves—and popped the hood.

Jamey would be back from the creek soon, wondering where we were. Grayson would be expected back with the wood.

"Wil," he said. "This car looks new. It should run

fine, except…" His head shot up from beneath the hood. "There's no engine. They took it out."

Grayson shut the hood. He walked a few paces, till he found another car. It didn't take long. They were everywhere, amid the trees and the garbage from the compound—beer cans and plastic bags, the blackened ends of bottle rockets.

He uncovered the car, popped the hood, and leaned over the inside. "This one has lines cut."

"What do you mean?"

"I don't know. Maybe Dance would know? But there are cables, sliced in half. Look." He shook something at me. "This should not be sliced in half. There is no reason they would do that." He met my eyes over the hood.

"Unless they didn't want someone to leave," I said.

He slammed the hood. The sound reverberated in the trees. It was so loud I waited for someone to come. I couldn't hear the sound of the creek anymore. I looked around, the baby on my hip. She stayed quiet, her hand twined in my hair.

Grayson said, "Where are all the people these cars belong to? Where did they go?"

"Starla!" a voice screamed out of the trees, so sharp I almost dropped the child. Her fingers laced around my neck in cold little hooks. "Starla, where are you?"

"Mama," the girl said.

I shifted her in my arms. "We've got to go. Grayson. You've got to get out of here and go back to the kitchen before Jamey sees you."

"What are we going to do?" Grayson said.

"You're gonna do what you're told."

I turned and Jamey stood there, balancing a basket of laundry on her hip. She had a cigarette in her hand. Seeing her, the little girl, Starla, whimpered. Jamey set down the basket and sucked in the cigarette, her eyes closed as if this was her one free moment of peace. Then she opened her eyes and stamped the cigarette against a tree. She held out her arms, and I gave her back the child.

Grayson started to speak.

"I don't care," Jamey said. She smoothed the flyaway hair of the baby and kissed her dirty face. "You're nothing to him. You're nothing to Jake. Her, he can at least use." She lifted her chin at me. "That's all he cares about, how useful you are. So you do as he says. You watch yourself." Starla buried her face in her neck. "And you take your first chance."

Grayson looked at me.

"Our first chance to what?" I said.

"Escape. You might only get one." Jamey nodded at the basket of wet sheets she had deposited at the foot of the tree. "Get the clothes, girl. You," she said to Grayson, "get back to work." She turned her back on us, trusting I would follow, and began to walk with Starla through the trees to the shed. Bouncing the baby, she started to sing.

"What the hell is her story?" Grayson said.

"I have no idea."

"Well, when am I going to see you again? How are we going to do this?"

"I don't know. We'll figure it out."

"Girl!" Jamey called over her shoulder.

"Tonight," I said. "We're leaving tonight. There's no way I'm spending the night here."

We hung up the wet laundry, Jamey and I, on a rope strung between a tree and the roof of the shed. We did the work without speaking, Starla playing at our feet with a handful of clothespins. The laundry was worn, the sheets so thin they were almost translucent. The clothes looked like they had come from a charity box, mismatched and shrunken: glitter-sticky leggings, a sweater with a hole the size of my fist. The clothespins clacked together.

When the last sheet was hung, Jamey said, "This'll probably freeze, anyway."

We could hear gunfire in the far-off woods; the hooting afterward let me know it was target practice. The men were shooting at something and hitting it, or celebrating like they were. I supposed there was nothing else to do. There were worse ways to keep warm.

"Why do you live out here?" I asked Jamey.

I wondered how old she was. I tried to imagine passing her in the hallway of a high school. Tried to picture her slamming her locker, exchanging notes with her friends, laughing.

I couldn't see it.

"I don't have anywhere else to go," she said.

I couldn't see her face without the bags under her eyes, couldn't see her arms without a baby in them. "But your daughter—" I said.

"Nobody else would take us."

"We would take you."

Jamey stared at me. I had spoken without thinking, surprising both of us. And as we stood there, the only sound the clack of the baby hitting clothespins and the distant retorts of the guns, I began to run through in my mind all the reasons that was a really bad idea.

But Jamey said, "No."

No explanation, just *no*.

I felt relief. I didn't want her or Starla tagging along, as much as I felt sorry for them. I couldn't see any way bringing them with me would be helpful for any of us. I didn't push it.

Jamey was looking at me. "What's that thing around your neck?"

I pulled the leather pouch out. "This?"

"What you got in there? Pills?"

"Seeds," I said.

"Like vegetable seeds?"

"Why are you helping us?" I asked. "You don't even know us."

"I'm not helping you."

"You're not turning us in. You told us to escape. Why do you care what happens to us?"

Jamey reached down for the baby. "Nobody helped me."

I didn't see the boys again until dinner, when night came to the compound, creeping through the trees.

The day had passed in drudgery and boredom. Most of the men seemed stupid with sleepiness—or hunger— slowed by the beer they drained, throwing the cans anywhere, into the woods. Numb or buzzed, they napped in the open, with a bravery that astonished me. I had never felt that free. I saw men asleep on the lip of the skate park, in the trees, lying where they fell like the war dead, their heads cushioned by cardboard or T-shirts or nothing at all. Were they too drunk to feel cold?

I saw a naked man in the woods by the shed. He was lying on his back, on a collapsed tent, not five feet from the shed window. I noticed the bottom of his feet first, dirt-blackened as though he had held them to a fire, his skinny pale legs, then his cock, slick and pink. The naked men I had seen had been in the dark, in the neon of bar signs, fumbling at me in the truck. Shadows made their bodies manageable, made us both just a collection of angles. The red-bearded man hadn't understood. "Don't you want to see the person you're making love to?" he had asked, kneeling in my loft, his head only inches from the ceiling. The hair on his chest spread erratically, like a rash.

I thought I should take Starla away from the naked man, but she was occupied, not looking, grinding baked beans into the floor of the shed with her fat, grimy palm. Kaylee moaned in her sleep. Jamey was off somewhere, smoking a second cigarette. She said she didn't like the baby to see her smoke.

I stood watch near the window. I kept my hand in my pocket, on Dance's knife.

Jake picked up Starla after the laundry had been hung. When he came shuffling up to the shed in his flip-flops, I looked to Jamey but she only folded her arms and watched his approach.

I felt sure he was coming for me.

But then Starla raised her hands in expectation. He picked her up like a duffel bag, swinging her over his shoulders, holding on to her with only one hand. Not enough, I thought. Not safe. She was squirming, crawling over his neck, but laughing. It was familiar to her, this game.

I never knew a man to be silly with children; no one was with me. My daddy left when I was too young, and Mama had found Lobo when I was already too old, too suspicious to be loved. Or loving. I had been wary of a stepdaddy, but we both kept our distance from each other. Besides, he wanted Mama, to spend time with her, to work alongside of her, to love her. I was a scrawny tadpole, a beanstalk. Runt. I was the extra that came after.

He had other things to teach me.

"Keep her warm," Jamey called.

"Ain't none of us warm," Jake said, and carried the baby down the hill.

"Where's he taking her?" I asked.

Jamey exhaled, bent, and swooped the clothespins Starla had been playing with into a pile, dumping them into the laundry basket. "Skateboard lessons."

"She can barely walk."

"I know. But that's, like, the age he learned, so." She straightened, rubbed her nose, which had turned pink in the cold. "It's better if kids can hold their own, you know? Especially girls."

We watched them reach the patch in front of the farmhouse, what passed for a yard with the tractor tire and the big TV. Jake produced a small plastic skateboard and balanced the child on it as he stood to the side. Holding her hands, he began to run.

I was afraid of what would happen at night.

Jamey said the night meant dinner, partying, music if there was enough juice in the generator, which there probably wasn't. Maybe Jake or one of the other men would take the mic hooked up to the PA system and freestyle, until they tripped over the extension cord or hit their heads on an amp. That had happened before. There might be dancing, she said.

At least one person would attempt to skate, though the half pipe was furred with ice. There were standing puddles in the bottom of the swimming pool, what she called the bowl, and the cement at the top had started to crack. Jamey said the men might joyride my truck, or light Grayson's hair on fire. Maybe somebody would pass around weed. I didn't let my face move when she said this. I had learned not to react.

Jamey told me not to be alone with anyone.

Jake brought Starla back, riding on his shoulders, and Jamey went off to smoke. Twilight passed as I thought it would. The men began to wake up, the naked man taking his damn time about it. The crackle of fireworks and the *pop-pop-pop* of guns echoed through the trees. I heard the squeal of a belt, as a truck got stuck. I heard wheels spinning out and shouts.

The air smelled of gunpowder and ditch weed. Kaylee woke and spent a long time combing her hair. She had a tattoo on her neck of a palm tree. Jamey came back to the shed and did a surprising thing. She sat on the mattress and unbuttoned her top. Starla crawled across the bed and began to nurse. Jamey had a round, soft stomach; it hung over the lip of her jeans. Her breasts were afterthoughts where Starla opened and closed her fists, her eyes drifting shut. I turned away.

There was a knock at the shed door.

"What the fuck?" Kaylee said. "Who the fuck knocks?"

It was strange to hear her talk, after she had been sick or sleeping all day. Jamey's face gave me nothing, no clue as to what to do. So I opened the door.

Jake stood there.

I went outside and closed the door quickly behind me to shield Jamey, naked from the waist. Out in the cold, Jake coughed into his hands. It was hard to look him in the eye, to be that close to him. Energy poured off Jake, a mania I could feel, like sparks. It was that I had seen when we had first pulled up to the farmhouse.

Jake hopped from foot to foot, his skin red in his flip-flops. His hands were red, too. He had lost his hat, and I saw a bald patch in his hair, a hole in the thatch on the side of his head. Someone had shaved him, or maybe he had been burned. I had seen a scar on Jamey, too.

Jake smelled of beer. His tattoos were everywhere and undistinguishable. They looked like lesions, old and green and formless. "Hey there," he said. "Sarah." The name looked strange on his lips. "Wanted to talk to you."

"What's up?" I said. I tried not to act surprised at my fake name. "When are we getting back on the road?"

"Well, here's the thing, Sarah. Your boys have been

working hard, but you? You haven't done shit for me. And I know that's not who you are. I know you're special. I can tell. I have a sense for talented people. So here's what we're going to do. Sarah. We're going to have dinner, like a family, real nice. And then you're going to work for me. Then we'll see what you can do."

He pointed his finger at me when he spoke. It seemed like any word, any protest, any answer at all, might enflame him. I concentrated on that finger, red and chapped. I imagined it burning, the skin falling off, the bone breaking. I pictured breaking it myself.

I went back in the shed and closed the door. There was no way to lock it. I kept my hand on the flimsy handle and watched Jake's shape in the window. He hesitated, maybe listening, maybe watching for me, too. Then he walked away, crunching through the snowy leaves around the shed. I pictured ice clinging to his bare ankles. I hoped it hurt.

None of the women in the shed had moved. Starla pulled off Jamey's nipple with a pop, and a tear of yellow milk slid down Jamey's stomach. She brushed it away like a bug.

"I have to get out of here before dinner's over," I said.

Jamey started buttoning up her shirt. "They wanted me to siphon the gas from your truck earlier." Her eyes flicked up. "I just pretended."

"Don't you ever want to get high?" Lisbeth asked me.

Behind the Church was a parking lot, an old loading dock with Dumpsters and pallets, and behind that, a hill sloped to a ditch. A field stretched on the other side before the river, brown and unchanging. Later, it would change: white, and white, and white again.

We used to sit on that hill after services. Lisbeth hiked her skirt to her knees. Her leggings beneath were white, the knees already kissed green. Grass was green then.

"No," I said.

"Not even a little? Not even sometimes?"

"It's not really my thing. I've seen a lot. It can make people stupid. It can make them forget and get paranoid. It can do good things. It's medicine—I do believe that, and I believe it should be legal, available. But if you smoke every day, every day multiple times..." Every day since you were ten, as Lobo had.

"Well, I wouldn't do that," Lisbeth said. "You wouldn't do that."

"I don't know what I would do," I said.

Lisbeth believed in God and her parents, and that kissing me didn't count. She also thought she should know, at least a little bit, what she was giving up, what she was sacrificing for the kingdom of forever.

She met me regularly at Crossroads for Coke or coffee. We had gone to the roller rink once after it was outlawed, and one of the girls had passed her a cigarette. She inhaled greedily as if it were food, the red tip lighting up our dim corner like neon. One moment of sin. Then she folded over in a fit of coughing. Everybody laughed. It was fun to see the church girl fall.

There was another night I had gone with her to the biker bar in town. It was karaoke night—eighteen and up, ladies always free—and Lisbeth said she had her eye on the prize, two hundred dollars in cash. I think she just had her eye on the stage, a small raised platform in the back by the bathrooms. The stage lights shone out sickly green from the rims of old coffee cans. The host was an old man who had been to our farm. We nodded at each other, in the way of those who know not to say more. Nobody checked IDs.

Lisbeth liked the attention. That wasn't godly, but I knew that about her. There was no way I was going to remember the songs she picked, not that night. I could barely watch her for watching the men, keeping tabs on them, keeping them away from her. They lined up at the foot of the stage, staring up at her. Their faces blurred, glazed with drinks. There were so many plastic cups. The bass was too loud, the floor sticky. Smoke and weed smoke threaded the air. The lights made Lisbeth's pale dress translucent; I could see the lines of her sensible bra. Sweat stood out on her forehead like pearls. Any one of the men could have reached out, grabbed her ankle. Reached up, felt her breast. By the end of the song, she was flushed and gasping.

One of the men did reach up then, through the applause, and handed her a cup. She grabbed it and drained it before I could push through the crowd to the stage.

"It was sweet," she said. "It was sweet, just Coke."

"It wasn't just Coke."

It was sweet, she kept repeating, when she fell into my arms after her next song, when she tripped trying to get off the stage. Her skirt flipped up and some of the men hooted. She was loose-limbed and friendly, running her hand down the prickled face of a stranger who stooped to help me, gazing at him like he was God.

"Don't touch him, you don't know him," I said.

"Does it make a difference?" she said dreamily.

"I like that girl," the man said.

I kicked open the door to the bar, but the cool night air did nothing. There was a drunk vomiting into the road. I thought of my mama.

I had never told Lisbeth about the night I came home to find her asleep on the kitchen floor. She lay in a heap under the cabinets, like she had crumpled where she stood. Her skin was too white, almost purple. Drool glittered in the corners of her mouth. Her limbs looked odd, uncomfortable.

Lobo came up from the grow room, dirt on his hands.

"What did you give her?" I asked.

"Fuck," he said. "She must have tried it."

"Tried what?"

"Somebody brought something. I told her not to. Told her we were going to sell it."

"Tried *what*?"

He shook his head, couldn't keep the twitching smile from his lips even as she lay there, drooling on herself. "Your mama." He got this look when she drank him under the table; when she danced for him and his friends, bottle in one hand, joint in the other. I had seen her, through the windows, her eyes closed, shaking to music only she heard. Lobo was impressed at her verve. My mama, wound up enough to fly away, a music box dancer. She didn't belong to me, to anyone. She was barely in this world. "She's a wild one."

"Is she okay?" I said.

"She will be." We bent to her, straightening her back, rearranging her arms. Lobo got a pillow from the couch for her head. I wiped the drool from her cheeks with my shirt. Lobo knew what to do. "I won't let her do that again," he said.

I looked up at him. "People don't tend to try some things just once. You taught me that."

"What do you know about it? Runt." But then his face twitched again. He changed. "I won't let her do that anymore. I promise you."

That was the thing about Lobo. He was violent, cruel—and he kept his word. I could count on him like a burn: to wound, to fester, to flare up. Then to smooth over everything, like the hurt had never happened. To be a faint scar forever.

There was no plan, no discussion. Jamey put Starla to sleep, singing a country song I didn't recognize, down on the same bed as Kaylee. The only bed, on the floor.

In a clearing by the farmhouse, meat sizzled on homemade spits: a hot dog skewer and a curtain rod. There was deer meat, and something greasy, maybe groundhog. I wondered if Grayson had prepared it. The men sat around the fire in stained canvas chairs or reclined on the dirt. The naked man had wrapped a sleeping bag around himself and put on shoes. The men were drinking—and it was only the men afforded this luxury. The women—because there *were* women at the campfire, Jamey and a few other girls who looked like Jamey—served, tending to the meat, replacing the men's beers. I wanted to ask Jamey: where had the other women come from, why were they there? The men threw the empties into the woods.

Grayson and Dance sat among the men—but uneasily, on the edge of their circle. They were not drinking, either on purpose or because they had not been offered anything. Grayson had grease on his face; he had been working. He also had a fresh bruise on his forehead, and when he saw me looking at it, he tightened his mouth and shook his head.

Say nothing.

Their hands were not bound, I was relieved to see. Almost nothing would surprise me anymore, not zip ties or chains. Not a blizzard. Not a landslide of dust to sweep all of us, every living thing, away. Grayson fiddled with something. Keys.

I hoped they were the truck keys. He turned them over and over to keep his hands from trembling. Dance just sat there, cross-legged on the ground. He looked stunned and exhausted. What had they made him do?

"Stop staring." Jamey thrust a bowl into my arms.

I looked down at the contents: shriveled brown potatoes. "I'm not staring."

"Yeah, you are. Your boyfriend is fine."

"They're not my boyfriend. Either one of them."

"If Jake thinks you like them, he'll do something about it."

I looked up from the bowl. "What does that mean?"

"He'll send them away. They'll disappear. Or worse."

What was worse than disappearing? I tried not to look at the men after that, but I couldn't help it. Men were everywhere, drinking, lighting bits of trash on fire. One man pulled a woman down onto his lap. She laughed, pushed his hands away, eventually stopped laughing.

Jake sat in the center of the circle, the place of honor, in a faded, old recliner, larger than the other chairs. Stuffing vomited out the sides. He looked like the king of shit. His feet were up in those flip-flops. A ratty fleece blanket, printed with a wolf's face, was thrown over his lap, and he was laughing. He turned his head to me, his eyes pale as a dog's. Was this the moment he saw what I could do? Was this the moment he made me work for him?

"Stop looking," Jamey hissed.

I turned my head down to the potatoes. "What do you want me to do with these?"

"You got a knife?"

Did I want to lose it to her? Did I trust Jamey? "No," I lied.

A burst of laughter, like machine gun fire, from the men. Something one of the women did, or was made to do.

Jamey licked her lips, hesitating, then pulled a pocket-knife from her coat. "This is sharp. Cut out the eyes and cut the taters into chunks, then fry 'em in the deer grease."

"I know how to cook potatoes."

"Then act like it," she snapped.

A couple of the women set their serving platters down and began to dance. It was such a slow, languid motion that I did not understand what was happening at first. One of the women unzipped her coat. It fell in a puddle at her feet. Then, despite the cold, she stripped her off her silver T-shirt. She faced my direction, rocking her hips awkwardly. Her skin was a sky stippled with bruises. There was no music. One of the men began to beat on the underside of a pot with a knife or stick. He couldn't keep time. The women moved like hypnotized snakes, drugs or exhaustion slowing their blood.

"I got something for you," Jake said, scrounging in his pockets.

For a moment, I remembered the Pumpkin King. But it wasn't seeds Jake pulled from his pockets. It was quarters. He flung a handful at the women. Coins dinged off their bodies like hail.

He snapped his fingers for more beer.

I turned away. I found a dirty, cast-iron skillet beneath a tree, and snapped off a stick to scrape it out with. I was crouched on the ground, my back to Jake and the women, scrubbing at the skillet, when I saw movement in the woods.

I stood. Behind me, the campfire cast a red glow on the men clustered around it, giving their ball caps and hoodies horns, giving their faces long bearded shadows, even the men who had no beards. There were work lights, powered by a generator, strung up on some of the outbuildings, but about half of the bulbs had burned out. Or been shot out. A pale lantern lit the dome of the skate park, flickering over its curves like a cave.

But the woods around the compound were black and

unfathomable. The movement I saw looked pale as moonlight. There was no moon tonight.

I took a step closer to the trees. I saw cars and trucks covered by tarps, saw more and more each time I looked. Skate State was more junkyard than skate park. But this thing moved. A slender, light shape. It weaved.

I glanced back at the campfire. Men laughed and drank. The quarters on the ground glinted by the fire. Nobody moved to pick them up, or to cover the women. The meat was cooked, and some of the women sliced it off the spits with Bowie knives.

If only they would take those knives and escape. Jake was drunk, all the men were drunk or getting there. The women could overpower them. They could get away. Starla was sleeping in the shed with Kaylee—that woman would be a burden, to carry or convince, to deal with her sickness as we drove far, far away from here. Were there other children in the compound, hidden in trailers and shacks? Would we have enough cars to carry them?

The shape in the woods made a sound, and I looked for it again, willing my eyes to adjust to the shadows. The figure wobbled, tripped. As it came closer through the trees, it no longer appeared graceful. I heard the snap of branches and leaves. I heard a moan.

The men tore into their meat. The women would eat last, if at all; I knew this without even asking. Dance and Grayson would eat with the women. I looked at their empty hands, their eyes as they watched the other men chew. Most of the women had their eyes cast down, or were making themselves busy picking up the beer bottles and bones, trying to stay on the edge of the circle and avoid attention.

But Jamey looked straight at me across the fire. She said loudly, "Where the hell are those potatoes, girl? The men want potatoes with their meat!" She began to stride across the ground to me, purposefully. She touched my shoulder and turned me away from the fire, away from Jake. She lowered her voice. "What's wrong?"

"There's somebody in the trees," I said. "Are you missing anybody? Did anyone run away?"

"No."

"Look. Just stand here and look. Someone's in the trees."

She stood with me, so quiet I thought she was holding her breath, so close I could almost believe we were friends. Together we saw the pale shape stumble forward, almost colliding with a tree. If not for Jamey beside me, seeing it, too, I would have thought I was seeing a ghost.

Jamey said: "That's not a person."

I looked back at the shape as it sank to its knees.

"It's a damn deer." She sounded disappointed.

But then I knew something. "Jamey, we can't eat the meat. The deer meat. If that's a deer..." It was beating its head against a trunk. Dazed, as if dosed. So thin its rib cage stood out like a prow. "If the deer meat came from the woods around here, we can't eat it. Nobody should eat it."

"Why?"

"I've seen this thing before. At one of our neighbor's."

We'd been driving, on our way back from visiting Mama at one hospital or another. Lobo had kept his promise—but my mama hadn't. A wild thing, she was drawn to other wildness: drinks that burned, pills that stilled. If it had been just the weed…but it wasn't just weed.

I had explained to Lisbeth—I couldn't try anything. I couldn't take the chance that something might take, something might stick to me, like it did to Mama. She couldn't shake it off.

The silence of our drive was broken by Lobo swerving off the side of the road. He stopped the truck and drew my attention to the window, to the deer: thin and pale, stumbling in a stripped cornfield. The deer sank onto its skinny knees and just lay there.

We did not accept meat from that neighbor's woods again.

"It's wasting disease," I said to Jamey. "Like mad cow for deer. Or AIDS."

Jamey took a step back. "Is it catchy?"

"Not from touching. Or breathing. But we shouldn't eat the meat. We might get sick from it."

"The meat," Jamey said.

She turned and ran back to the campfire. She raced into the light and sped around the circle of men, flipping tin plates out of their hands. "You can't eat the meat!" she said. The glow from the fire made her face look wild. "The meat's poison!"

Men stood up, shouting, as their plates tipped over, food spilling into the dirt. The woman without her shirt was deposited onto the ground. Grayson and Dance leaped to their feet. Jamey pulled the plate from Jake's hand and threw it into the fire.

"What the fuck," Jake said. "Jamey, what the fuck did you do?"

Jamey looked up at me. "Now," she said.

"Run!" I said to Grayson and Dance. I turned before I knew if they were following, but they were, crashing behind me. I was headed away from the campfire, but beyond that, I didn't know where to go.

"Where's the truck, where's the truck?" Dance was saying.

"We shouldn't be separated!" Grayson said. "I have the keys!"

But we were already splitting off, Dance straight ahead, Grayson to the right. I panicked and ran on instinct, heading to the first hiding place I could see: a huge garage. There was a slanting tin porch attached to the side, supported by two-by-fours. In the dark, I couldn't tell if the building was half built or half rotted away.

I heard shouting. Grayson and Dance had disappeared. But from down the hill came the calls of men and the wild, spinning beams of flashlights. They were following.

I ran to the garage. I shoved into the building, and into the dark.

9

I locked the door behind me, but it was a cheap lock. All the locks were cheap. The men could break the door down, if they wanted to. They could break the building down.

I flung my arms out, almost knocking over a rickety table. My fingers fumbled over a Coleman lamp. I picked it up, found the switch, and cranked it high. Light flicked into the garage. A girl stared at me from the wall. It was me.

I flinched for a moment, startled by my own appearance in the mirror hanging there. There were leaves in my hair, dirt on my face. I touched my collarbone. The cord was still there, the leather pouch of seeds: pumpkin, apple, millet. I thought of them like a prayer to give me courage. I had a fresh scratch on my throat. There was a pink sticker on the top of the mirror. It said: *Dirty girl.*

I looked around. There were mirrors along the wall of

the garage, bunk beds in the corner, and in the middle, a stage with a silver pole, glinting in the lantern light. Sleeping bags were slumped on the floor of the stage.

I heard a cough from the direction of the bunk beds. I spun around, the lantern swinging.

"Jesus, man, the light." A hand came up from the bottom bunk.

I lowered the lantern and saw, raising herself up from a rumpled bed, another Jamey. She had a rounder face than Jamey, stringier hair.

"Where's the way out of here?" I asked.

The girl pointed: past the stage. There was a doorway curtained by plastic.

"Thanks," I said.

I didn't look at the pole. I didn't think about the stage. I pushed aside the plastic, and then the smell hit me: the salty-slick smell of blood.

The doorway opened up on a slaughterhouse. It was a room for butchering, but dirtier than any deer-processing place I'd seen. My lantern flashed into the corners. I saw a table, flecked with blood. I saw red parts, a barrel, knives, a saw. I smelled blood and meat left to putrefy. Something hung dripping on a hook.

"Shit." I swung the light back through the doorway. The girl on the bunk was sitting up now. She looked sleepy, unconcerned. "Why is all that here?" I asked.

She shrugged. "Meat and meat."

The garage door jumped in its frame. Fists pounded and the knob rattled.

"Bitch, let us in!" the men said from outside.

"Hold your horses, hold your horses," the girl on the bed said loudly. "I'm coming, I'm a'coming." But she didn't move. She lifted her chin at me. "Well, get out."

I ran through the butchering room. I ran past the table, holding my breath. I didn't look at the animal parts. Whatever they were, they were dead now. My boots slid on the slick floor, but I didn't look down or drop the lantern. *Come with me come with me*, I should have said to the girl on the bed.

But I didn't. I just ran.

At the back of the butchering room, there was a row of metal roll-up doors. There was also an ordinary door on the side. It was not locked. I flung the side door open, thinking it would lead outside.

Instead, the door opened onto a small, windowless room. I shielded my eyes. The walls in the room pulsed with silver. Grow lights had been hung from the ceiling, over rows and rows of familiar plants.

Something was wrong. The plants were too pale. They looked stunted, diseased. They drooped in the stale and cold air. Dead yellow leaves papered the floor.

The men were in the building now, behind the plastic curtain. I heard them yelling at the girl. I heard the girl yelling back. Then a slap, and no more yelling.

I ran from the grow room, leaving the dying plants. I saw a butcher knife on a long table beside a deer skull; a tall boy rested in one of the eye sockets. I should have grabbed the knife.

But on the floor was a remote control with green and red buttons. I stamped on the green one. With a jerk, one of the garage doors rattled up. I ran out into darkness, into open, cold air. Little fistfuls of snow pelted me like the quarters Jake had thrown at the girls.

The hill ahead was in total blackness, broken only by the gray crowns of trees. I kept my eyes on them. My lantern light was weak. It lit the square in front of me and no farther. Then the ground changed.

I noticed too late. I tripped over the edge of the empty swimming pool—and then I was down, over the rim and tumbling. I bumped to a stop at the bottom of the skate park, and skittered into a small puddle of ice, which cracked. Cold seeped into my clothes. The lantern had fallen, too; I heard it crashing beside me. Breaking.

I tried to sit up. Already my damp clothes felt heavy, and the side of my hip burned, skinned or bruised badly. High concrete sides sloped up all around me. A light burned into my eyes.

Jake peered down from the rim. He held a flashlight, shining it in my face.

I scrambled across the concrete, trying to make it up the side. But the sides were smooth, made slicker with ice. I moved half an inch, then slid back down again.

The flashlight skipped as Jake ran lightly down the ramp into the bowl, practiced and effortless. He moved like a young boy.

"Not a skater, huh?" he said.

I pressed my back against the wall. "I didn't do anything to the meat."

"I didn't say you did."

"I didn't do anything."

"Not yet," Jake said. He walked across the basin, until he was inches from me. "But everybody's got to be useful here."

If I reached for one of my knives, he would see, he would grab me. If I ran past him, he would drag me down, into the ice. I froze. My heartbeat throbbed in my ears and my chest felt tight. There was no exit.

Jake pitched suddenly to the side. His head swung like someone had punched him, a quick flick, eyes rolling back, then he was down.

Whatever had hit him was so fast and surprising I hadn't even seen it. Only a blur. Then Jake was at the bottom of the basin. He rolled, groaned once, and went still. Blood trickled down his face. A skateboard rolled past before striking the sloped side of the bowl and flipping over, wheels spinning.

I looked up. Above me, Jamey stood on the rim, Starla on her hip. She was glowing, lit by headlights. Her free hand, the one that had thrown the skateboard, clenched into a fist at her side. "Shouldn't ride without a helmet. Jake always was a damn fool."

Dance drove, Grayson rode shotgun, and Jamey and I crowded into the back seat.

Starla curled on Jamey's lap, the girl's yellow head tucked beneath her mother's chin. Instantly, whether from exhaustion or stress, Starla fell asleep, though we tore over the hill at a speed that almost made me sick. I knew, from the way the engine strained and the back fishtailed, the house was behind us, somehow, but I didn't dare to look to see if it was damaged, if it had been ransacked or burned.

Grayson, shouting, tried to navigate: up the hill; around the garage with the girl, the meat, and the grow room. Dance clipped the porch as we passed, and one of the support beams buckled. The whole porch roof slid, like a cake falling off a table. It crashed in the snow and we kept on going.

Out the window, I saw running men and torches of fire, waving flashlights. The men had working batteries, or the foresight to stock up on solar-powered lights. Dogs were barking. Men lunged for our truck, and then when they realized Dance wasn't going to stop, leaped out the way.

"Why aren't they driving after us?" I said.

Dance got a little smile on his face. "Not many of their trucks are running now."

Nobody said anything about Jamey. She had helped me into the truck and climbed on in after me, backpack on her shoulders, Starla clinging to her like the sash on a beauty queen. I saw a pacifier in the mesh side pocket of the backpack. Jamey had packed for herself and Starla. She had been ready for a long time.

But other women had helped me, too.

"What about Kaylee?" I asked. "And the girl in the meat house?"

"The *meat house*?" Grayson said.

"We can't just leave them there."

Dance met my eyes in the mirror. "We can't save everyone."

Jamey didn't say anything, didn't look at me. I think she

thought if she spoke up, we would notice her and what a burden she was; we would make her and the baby get out.

I fell silent. I finally glanced back at my house. It seemed fine, a little dented. A few shingles were missing from the roof, but the windows weren't broken, and I didn't see any other damage.

A few of the men were giving chase on foot down the road behind us. One threw a flashlight. It struck a tree and shattered. I turned back around.

The two spray-painted junk cars that had blocked the rural highway, blocked our passage, and forced us to turn into Skate State in the first place had been towed to the sides of the road. But they were on fire. We drove between them, flaming sphinxes.

"The world's gone crazy," Grayson said.

"No," Jamey said, looking out the window. "It was always this way."

10

We kept going, as quickly as we could. On the narrow, icy road, the tires gritted, desperate for traction. We skidded, swerved around ruts. We were driving too fast. Dance gripped the steering wheel tightly and we held our breath, tensing at every spin, every rasp of the brakes. I kept expecting men to leap out of the trees. I kept looking behind us for headlights.

They came, as I knew they would: yellow eyes, burning through the snow. Coming up fast. The headlights were small. "I think it's bikes," I said.

Jamey didn't look. "Jake has motorbikes. They used to race them."

Dance met my eyes in the mirror. He hadn't known about that, hadn't broken those engines.

"We can't slow down," Grayson said. "If they catch us…"

He didn't finish his sentence, didn't have to. I glanced

over at Jamey, but she had turned to the window, her forehead resting against the glass. She closed her eyes, willing it all away. But it wouldn't go away.

We could hear the motorbikes now, the whine of their engines above the wind. The trees by the sides of the road looked like men. Then the trees gave way to fields, which should have been corn or wheat, but the crops had never grown, had never even been planted. In the darkness, the flat bumpy fields seemed like the surface of the moon—that inhospitable, that rough and alien. Nothing could live here.

Dance cut the wheel hard—and then we were traveling over the fields, jerking through them with a recklessness and speed that made my teeth clatter in my head. Starla woke up and began to cry, her face screwing in a red crease. "Don't like," she wailed. "Don't like."

It was the most I had ever heard her say.

"What are you doing?" Grayson said to Dance.

But Dance kept driving fast, his shoulders hunched. The house banged and fishtailed behind us, weighing us down, rocking the truck.

"We're going to roll!"

A tire sank into a groundhog hole. The truck dipped forward and we all slid, Jamey and Starla pushing up against me. Then Dance steered us out of it. Starla slid up on Jamey's lap and popped her thumb into her mouth, silently weeping. Jamey held her tightly.

"We just have to find another road," Dance said.

But there was no another road. We rocketed over the fields. Plain and jagged and endless. I was afraid to look back, to see if the house was safe, if the motorbikes were there. I couldn't hear their engines anymore. Then Dance slammed to a stop.

The truck was blocked by a line of trees, packed so tightly together I had almost missed them. They looked like extensions of the darkness. Starla wailed. I stared at the trees, exposed by our headlights.

The trees made a wall. They had been forced into a dense line. I saw swatches of knotted fabric, the kind of cheap blue cloth used for cleaning. The trees had been wrapped in the cloth, and lashed together with rope and bungees, the narrow gaps between them stuffed with branches, dead moss, rags. Several stumps, uprooted, had been wedged there, making a barrier like a beaver dam, sealed with mud and hard-packed snow.

Someone had done this, done this purposefully. Someone had seen how closely together the trees grew and had used it to their advantage. People had been here, and made some kind of fence, using junk and bits of the forest. What were they trying to keep out? Or in?

Dance looked over his shoulder, planning to try to back out over the rough fields again, but I stopped him. "Maybe we should hide here," I said.

"Hide?"

"Get on the other side of that tree fence, get behind something."

"Where are we gonna hide the truck? The house?"

"If we cut the lights, maybe they can't see."

Dance turned back around, reaching to switch off the headlights, but then he froze.

"What?" Grayson said.

A person stood in the glare of our brights.

They were dressed all in black, almost blending against the tree fence.

"I don't think they're from Skate State," I said. They looked more careful, their clothes calculated for both warmth and cover of night. Black coat, black boots, black hood, and ski mask.

"We need to get out of here," Grayson said.

"Do you know where we are?" I turned to Jamey.

But she was struggling with a crying, thrashing Starla. "No fucking idea."

It was like watching a tree detach from the woods and begin to walk. They came toward us, the person in the headlights. Then more shadowy figures in black came out from behind the fence. They swarmed the truck.

"What is going on?" Grayson said.

"The whole world has gone to shit because one thing has," Dance said.

I leaned over the front seat, looking closer at the strangers along the tree fence. I had seen something, something about the shapes of the figures or the way they moved. Something was different about them. Then I knew.

They were women.

Bundled against the cold, all in dark clothes, their warm things masked them. But I felt movement gave them away: a fluid bending of their bodies around the tree wall, the dips at their waists. I thought of Lisbeth in her long sleeves and long, heavy skirts, wrapped up but unmistakably *her* beneath the denim and flannel and down. Maybe I wasn't disguising myself in coveralls as well as I thought.

"They're all women," I said.

Dance was out the door, stepping into the headlights.

"Don't!" I said to Dance, but it was too late.

He had left the door hanging open. I could hear the whine of the motorbikes again in the distance. Cold flooded through the cab, and Starla cried harder.

"Are you coming here to join us?" one of the women said, muffled behind her ski mask.

"Who are you?" Dance said.

"Are you being followed?"

"Yes!" Grayson leaned across the seat and shouted through the open door.

The woman looked to him, then back to Dance. "All right. Come in behind the fence. No cars. Park to the left. There's an opening in there. We'll hide your truck. And—" her head turned to the back of the truck and she jolted briefly but otherwise did not give much away "—your *house.*"

Dance got back into the truck and did what the woman asked. There was a break between the trees, barely wide enough to ease the truck through, and we drove in carefully. The forest closed up around us, dark and magic with snow.

Starla quieted, looking around. When the trailer had edged its back wheels into the woods beyond the fence, the woman held up her hands for us to stop.

"Here we go again," Grayson said.

"Look, I don't think this is as dangerous as what we just left," Dance said.

"Why? Because they're girls?" Jamey snapped. "Girls are just as dangerous as men."

I watched the women's sides. I hadn't seen any guns. "I don't think they're armed," I said. "Maybe they can hide us for a while, until Jake gives up."

Grayson helped Jamey with Starla as they got out of the truck, and I stretched my hand into the front seat. "The gun," I said to Dance.

He looked around. No one watched us; they were busy with the baby.

"You said they're not armed."

"The gun," I repeated.

After a moment, he pulled it from the slit in the seat cushion and handed it to me. The gun, flecked with rust from its long sleep in the earth, felt cold. It felt heavy and strange. I shoved it deep in my coat pocket.

Dance was looking at me over the seat. I could read the challenges in his eyes. Could I use it? Had I shot one? Why did I have it? "You better get used to me having it," I said.

But I felt those questions knocking around my own head. I should have practiced with the gun. I should have gotten ammo for it. If I needed to use it someday, would it even work?

We threaded through the forest after the women. Exhaustion hit me as I walked. The simple work of following, of watching where I was going to avoid roots or branches, seemed too much. I felt the bruises from my fall into the skate park, a sharp and tender ache. I couldn't remember the last thing I had eaten, and the last time I had slept was in the truck.

I heard a rustling, and looked behind me. In the clearing where Dance had parked the truck, women were piling pine boughs and brush over the truck, covering up the vehicle and my house. If I turned back in a few more minutes, they would be hidden, safe. The group ahead of me went around a curve, and I followed. When I looked behind me again, the clearing and the women were lost to shadows.

What were these women doing in the woods?

Up in front, Dance walked in step beside the woman in the ski mask. She carried Starla in her arms; Jamey seemed fine with it, maybe grateful for the break. Starla was quiet now, wrapped so securely in blankets I could barely see her face, only a tuft of her hair, like a corn silk.

"Did you come from Skate State?" the woman asked.

"How did you know?" Dance said.

"We have one of their pigs. And some refugees."

"What are you doing out here in the woods? Do you live here?"

"We do now," she said.

The path dipped down and I saw it. Fire, tents, a line of laundry strung between trees. There were bales of hay, a large stack of wood.

"We organized after the first lost spring," the woman said. "Some of us started to move out here then, but our numbers keep growing. More and more people want to do something that matters."

What are you doing? I wanted to say. *What matters?*

The dozen or so tents were clustered around each other, hugged by trees; there were fires in the middle. Nosing the hem of a blanket on the line was a large white pig. At first I thought it was injured, a gash in its side. As we came closer, I saw that the pig had been spray-painted with a red bull's-eye.

"They use them for target practice at Skate State," the woman explained.

"Then dinner," Jamey said.

The woman looked closer at Jamey for a moment, then she addressed all of us. "Let me tell you the rules here. We don't cook meat. We don't use cars. We try to be as respectable and sustainable as possible."

"Who are you?" Grayson asked.

Tent flaps had opened up and a few heads had poked out, a few people curious enough about the voices to wander out in the dark. People in their twenties, in clothes that fit. People who looked like they were in college, looked clean and well-fed, shiny. Their coats weren't duct-taped. Their hair wasn't matted. I didn't see any children.

"I'm Mica," the woman said. "We're occupying this forest."

"Mica?" Dance studied the woman. "I'm Dance. Do you remember me? From the tree-sit at Ladd Ridge? My action name was Dirt Boy."

Grayson looked incredulously at me. *Dirt Boy?*

Then the woman—Mica—handed the baby back to Jamey, and pulled up her ski mask, revealing a face soft with youth, black freckles, and round cheeks. "Dirt Boy." She and Dance hugged. "You look different than I remember. Not as thin."

"Well," Dance said. "When you're not stuck in a tree, you can eat more. What happened to that tree?"

Mica shook her head.

"Sorry to interrupt," I said. "But what is all this?"

The tents looked new, slick in the firelight. None of them had patches. Even the laundry, drying on the line, seemed fresh, unstained sheets that hadn't even faded to gray. I didn't see any bikes or cars, any way of getting out quickly. I didn't see any weapons.

Mica looked at me. She was beautiful in a way of seeming not to care. Her hair had escaped the hood of her sweatshirt, as dark as her clothes and wild with curls and a little braid near her face, sleek as a garter snake. I could tell she did care, though. Her boots were leather with a thick heel, and she had lined her eyes. The makeup, so out of place in the woods, glittered in the firelight.

"We've occupied the forest," she said patiently, as if I was a child, as if I couldn't see and understand everything. "When things started to get bad, we made the decision to set up a camp here so loggers, frackers, and capitalists can't take it. We won't let the trees be sacrificed. We're protectors."

"Right on," Grayson said.

I shot him a look and he shrugged.

"What about firewood?" I asked.

"We only burn dead wood."

"What about your leather shoes?"

"Wil," Dance said. He turned to Mica. "Thank you for trusting us."

"I saw the direction you were coming from. Only one thing's out that way, and it's not good."

In the clearing with the fancy tents, it was easy to forget the compound just down the road. (How far down the road? How far had we gone?) A pig had escaped from there, running through the fields. Could Mica and the others hear the gunfire from Skate State? Were they close enough to see the smoke as the cars burned? Didn't the men want their pig back? It was meat.

Two women from the tents approached our group.

"Jamey?" one of them said. "That you, girl?"

The women didn't seem like they belonged with the camp. They didn't look like the others. They wore baggy, ill-fitting coats—hand-me-downs—and the wrong shoes, not winter boots but sneakers. Their long hair was shiny with grease and tangles. One of the women had a bruise on her face.

But Jamey recognized the women and squealed. It was such a strange sound, coming from Jamey. She sounded like a little kid.

"Skate State refugees," Mica said, nodding at the women.

There was more hugging, Starla passed around. "She got so big," the women said.

"Are you hungry?" Mica asked us. "We have tempeh."

"Great," Grayson said.

★ ★ ★

After we had eaten, Mica found places for us to sleep. I wasn't sure if we should sleep, but my limbs felt so heavy. As soon as a bed was offered, it was all I could think about.

Jamey and Starla stayed with the women they knew from Skate State. The rest of us bunked up together in an extra tent near the back of the camp.

Deep in the woods, the group was erecting structures that seemed like they could be permanent, strange misshapen buildings that, in the darkness, looked more art than shed—straw bale houses, homes made of mud—using whatever materials they could find. Amid the shadows of the trees, I saw wood planks and sheets of corrugated steel that could have been lifted off a construction site or ripped from a warehouse. Nothing seemed habitable yet, not in the wind and snow. Loose bits of steel grated against each other, and the packed mud sides of the houses looked wet.

But it seemed like the group was making plans, making plans for a future I couldn't understand. There were sacks of soil and cement, neat bales of straw stacked against tree trucks.

"I'd rather sleep in my own house. Or my truck. I don't know why we had to leave it parked," I said as I punched the sleeping bag Mica had produced for me. It was musty and olive green, like a relic from a Boy Scout camp.

The extra supplies the camp had rustled up for us weren't as nice or new as the equipment they had brought for themselves. My bedroll was patched, thin, and smelled of a basement. When I had unrolled the sleeping bag, dust flew up in the lantern light.

"Their land, their rules," Dance said.

"It's not their land. They admitted as much. They're trespassing."

"Occupying."

"Okay, Dirt Boy."

Grayson snorted.

"Why didn't you tell us about your past?" I asked.

"What's there to tell?" Dance said.

"An organizer? That might be useful."

But Dance shook his head. His sleeping bag was polyester, printed with a cartoon character. It looked even thinner than mine. "I doubt that," he said. "I didn't organize much. I was involved with a few groups, went to a few protests. Even before the first lost spring, when things were just starting to get bad, I wanted to do something. I wanted to try, you know? So I chained myself to a bulldozer, showed up to some rallies, smashed a bank window. That sort of thing."

"You smashed a bank window?" Grayson said.

"It didn't do much good, did it? I met Mica on a treesit. We were trying to stop a pipeline from going through a forest in Virginia. I guess we lost that one."

Nobody I knew—Lisbeth, Mama, or Lobo—talked about what the cold was, or named it. We were too busy just handling it, surviving day to day. It was like living on the farm. You didn't question why the aphids came, you just dealt with the invasion: sprayed the bitter neem oil with its garlic scent, washing the leaves like you would bathe a child; dusted the plants with diatomaceous earth, the sharp white powder that would nick your fingers and get into your lungs unless you wore a mask. We were all just focused on making money, staying warm, staying alive—not naming things, not blaming yet.

But Dance and Mica had named it: *lost spring.* I wondered what the president had said in her speech. I wondered what they were saying in cities.

"Do you think this is our fault?" I asked.

Dance's breath hung in the tent between us, a thin white bridge. My fingers hurt from the brief, frozen moments I had stripped off my gloves to untie the sleeping bag. I wondered if it was snowing again.

"Isn't everything?" Dance said.

He fell asleep first, or pretended to. I lay in my musty sleeping bag and listened to his breathing, soft but deep. I was on the other end of the tent, nearest the side. Grayson had put his bedroll in the middle, between me and Dance: a kid between his folks. Now he leaned over to me and whispered. "Are you awake, Wil?"

"No."

"Can I ask you a question? Why were you upset about Mica?"

I rolled over and faced him. He had his sleeping bag and whatever moth-holed blankets Mica had unearthed for him pulled up to his chin. I wouldn't have wanted that stuff to touch my face. "I'm not upset," I said.

"Yes, you are."

"She has the keys to my truck." She had asked for them, in case they had needed to move the truck in the night, she said, to deeper cover. I cursed myself for handing them over. For believing her. I was so tired my guard had slipped. I was making mistakes.

"We'll get them back in the morning," Grayson said. "Dance trusts her."

"I just don't know Dance very well, either," I whispered. "I don't know if I trust him."

"Dance? He got us out of Skate State, didn't he?"

"No," I said. "Jamey got us out. He drove us in there. And we don't know Mica and these people here at all."

"I don't know what choice we have other than to trust them, at least for tonight."

I peered around Grayson, but Dance was buried beneath blankets and somebody's old coat, breathing in the darkness in his cartoon bag. "I just want to keep going," I said. "To California. I don't want to get stuck here."

"I promise," Grayson said. "We are not going to get stuck. We're going to keep going. No matter what."

The tent radiated with cold. It was sleeting lightly. Faint trails of moisture beaded the tent, pattering on top. I had to keep myself very still. If I reached out my hand to touch the side of the tent or bumped it by mistake, I would send icy streams cascading into my palm.

"Are you going to be able to sleep?" Grayson asked.

Other than the sleet, the woods were silent. No generators hummed. No animals called out to each other in the night. "Do you think it's safe here?" I asked.

"Is anywhere safe?"

Lobo said if she had to try things with anyone, he was the best person. He would sit with her, watch her. He

would take her to Billy Crow's, the medicine man down
the holler, if her limbs trembled, if foam came from her
mouth, if her breathing slowed too much. He could get
anything for her. He was a magician, a peddler who came
from the woods, from the stars. I knew why she loved
him. He brought magic, like scarves from his pockets,
like a coin where there was no coin, like a silk bouquet.
Any number of pills, brightly colored, could appear in his
hands, or powder wrapped in a paper twist. He coaxed
magic from the ground, made the seeds sprout, made the
plants grow money. Conjured fire and warmth and attention. She had been so lonely with me in the duplex. With
Lobo she would never be lonely.

Like any peddler, people loved him: children, the boys
in the banged-up trucks. Someone was always coming
over to buy something; to ask for something; to sit around
the table, with the gun beneath it like a sleeping dog, and
smoke, talk about smoking, talk about the weather. That
grew old.

Mama was a searcher, Lobo said. She was on some kind
of mission, to experience all sensations, all feelings, to
know the world, to *see*. But that didn't make sense to
me, because dope made you see nothing. It slit your eyes,
dulled them like the dead. It made the world a narrow
sliver. Molly made you love everyone. Opioids turned you
into a doll, a doll who didn't care about anything. Weed
made the world bearable.

I would do none of it. When Lobo said Mama had been
asleep before—before when she was married to my daddy,
when she had cried in the duplex, when she had carried

me...that she was just now waking up and experiencing things in full color, seeking here with him—what did that make me? Someone that didn't matter, didn't register. But I had been with her all along. A ghost beside her sleepwalker.

Things would be better in California.

In the morning, the smell of bacon woke me. For a moment, before my eyes had adjusted fully, I thought I was back before the lost spring, before the farm even. I thought I was waking up in the duplex, into childhood: my daddy standing at the stove in the galley kitchen, cooking while my mama slept. Had he actually ever done this? Been there for us like that? I couldn't remember it. Maybe I made it up.

I blinked. I saw the plastic top of the tent, partially covered with snow, and the shadow of a hanging branch. I felt the ache in my body from sleeping on the cold, hard ground. Sleet tapped on the roof. I slid up. Grayson's bedroll was empty. Dance snored on. I crawled out of my sleeping bag.

It was not bacon, of course, I realized when I unzipped the tent and stepped out into the camp. Something soy-based smoked on a grate laid over a fire. I smelled coffee but couldn't find it. In the hazy, white-sky light, I couldn't figure out what time it was. I knew I had slept late, later than I had in a long time, but there was no sun to judge by, no gap in the clouds. It could be any time.

People walked about the camp quietly, focused on work.

Hammering and sawing came from the trees. Someone was chopping wood.

I could see the camp laid out more clearly in the day: the wide circle of tents, a cook station in the middle with a fire, a cooler, and a picnic table. Those hodgepodge, half-built structures, deeper in the woods. A dozen people, mostly in black, milled about the camp. They were young and wearing coats that looked expensive, long and down. Their skin sparkled with facial jewelry. Nobody smiled at me, but a lot of people looked at me.

"Wil, over here." Grayson, down a small hill on the other side of the camp, was waving.

I headed over to him, grateful to get away from the main group. A white man with dreadlocks stopped chopping wood as I passed and regarded me, ax over his shoulder.

Grayson stood on the banks of a stream, his flannel shirt rolled to the elbows. "You can wash up here. It's really cold, though."

"That seems to be the theme of the day."

"Oh, *them*," Grayson said.

"I don't think they like us here."

Grayson didn't seem bothered. He crouched and cupped his hands in the stream, splashing water over his face, then shook it off like a dog. Ice had formed on the top and sides of the stream, a crust thin as sugar. Grayson washed from a double fist-size hole. The dark water lapped at the edges. It was too cold to fish. The fish, if they were still alive, would be sluggish and clustered at the bottom of the stream, where the heat lay.

"Everybody's cautious," Grayson said. "They just don't know you. You know how people are, especially these days. Nobody likes strangers." He wiped his hands on his jeans. "These are a bunch of college kids. I bet if they knew what your family did, they'd warm up to you real quick."

I looked at a rock on the bank, wondered how far I could kick it.

Grayson was quick to notice. "Did I say the wrong thing?"

"It just didn't exactly work out for me that way back in school."

"Well, high school is stupid."

"So is warming up to someone for what they can get you. Which I can't even get anymore."

Grayson fell silent, studying the camp. I waited for him to say: *You could grow it.*

But he didn't.

I shouldn't have been hard on him. I knew he wouldn't strike back, he wouldn't have said something to make me feel bad on purpose—he wasn't like that. I couldn't really say that about many people. I thought of his flowered sheets, crumpled on the couch at his folks' house; his ham radio that we couldn't get to work. He had taken his turn driving, even though it must have hurt him to shove his injured foot into the cramped space between the front seats and drive on his left, but he did it. He did more than his share. He drove slowly and cracked jokes that were so terrible I almost laughed.

I needed coffee. I was about to say that and apologize

to him when he said, "I think the world is just going to be like that from now on. It's going to be about what you can do, how you contribute to the group, or whatever."

I thought of Skate State: men at the windows of my truck, demanding to know what we could offer them in exchange for our lives. I thought of Jake standing outside the shed, snow filling his flip-flops, his skin chapped and flaking, telling me I hadn't done shit for him.

"It's going to be all about the group," Grayson said. "Your group, whatever it is."

"Skate State was freakish," I said. "It was bad even before the weather turned—Jamey told me. That's not how the world's going to go."

"Maybe not. But look at this place. People all have their jobs. Mica and those women guard the fence. Other people repair it. Some people cook. Some people do construction. They're making something here. Something new. Look." He pointed above the bank.

The trees were bare, of course. No leaves had come back. No leaves were coming. But some of the trees had boughs. I looked closer. The boughs were affixed to the trees, lashed with ropes: props, like the cover the women had used to disguise the truck when we had first pulled into the camp. Below the fake boughs were wooden platforms. They were tree stands, the kind hunters would use. Lobo had chopped down stands like these from poachers perched in our woods without permission.

"Mica said some of them want to move up there permanently," Grayson said. "Eventually move into the trees. Make sure those trees never come down."

"When did you talk to Mica?"

"This morning. I couldn't sleep. Dance snores." Grayson dipped his finger in the stream and began to brush his teeth with water. We had left our toothbrushes—along with everything else—in the tiny house. "So do you."

After we had finished washing up, I helped Grayson up the bank. On the climb, his cast snagged on a root. His jaw tightened and he tried not to wince. "It's fine," he said.

"You keep saying that. But it keeps not getting better."

"The doctor said it would take a long time to heal, re-member? We're on the road. These aren't ideal conditions for healing."

Giggling and crackling leaves: Jamey and the women were headed down to the stream. Jamey had her hair dif-ferent, braided in a mermaid tail, away from her face. It made her look even younger. Her eyes glinted with purple liner, extending across her temples, which I noticed for the first time were freckled. She carried a shower caddy, like she was going to wash up in a college dorm, with a loo-fah and shampoo bottles. One of the women held Starla. Someone had painted the baby's face with pink and blue stars.

"Good conditions for her, though," Grayson said.

I thought I was prepared for anything. I had been raised to expect bad men, men sick with drugs, the unpredict-ability of the harvest, the sheriff. But nothing could prepare me for gas stations closing, the pharmacy running out of meds, the cold that kept coming, the snow that would not end. The swiftness of this change. College kids, living in the trees to try to save them.

Grayson found coffee for me in a stoneware mug, and on top of a hill, I found Dance. He was chopping wood, his coat stripped off and tied around his waist.

"Is that for us?" I asked, nodding at the pile of wood he had already split.

"No."

"You defecting?"

"Just trying to say thank-you to these people." He swung the ax down onto a log, which wobbled but held. "For the beds they offered us last night, and food, and safety." He swung again and splintered it. That aching crack as the wood creaked open, revealing an orange heart that was almost red.

"Are we safe?" I asked.

The camp spread out at the foot of the hillside, tents as colorful as flags. There was smoke and work. On the other side was wilderness. The big hill sloped, grassy in warmer days, now patched with snow.

I felt turned around. I no longer remembered which side Skate State was on, which side was California. Other smoke was rising from the trees in the distance. More people, strangers, in camps or families, trying to survive.

"What are their plans for keeping warm here?"

"I don't know," Dance said. He knocked the pieces of the log he had split into the pile. "Building more permanent structures, insulated ones."

"They're not going home?"

"They say this is their home now. Their ancestors lived like this, built cabins by hand, dug coal scraps out of the ground to keep warm. They made it. They got by on a lot less. Mica says they can do it again."

These hills could hold anyone, I knew that. Cabins and farms I couldn't see, even compounds: trailers and sheds spotting the woods under its woven canopy. The most broken, abandoned-looking shack, leaking and thin-walled, could shelter someone temporarily.

Temporarily could last a long time.

The trees were bare, but clustered together they still gave cover. Rocks could hide. Cliffs could hide. There were caves in the rocks, mines in the ground. Only smoke betrayed the people who might be surviving there.

"What was Ladd Ridge like?" I asked Dance.

"The tree-sit with Mica? That was a long time ago. Spring into summer." He took a break, resting his ax against the stump. "A real summer," he said. "I sat up on a monopod in this tree in the middle of the road they wanted to bulldoze for their fucking pipeline. I guess they did it, after all. I was the tree-sitter. I was the healthiest then, so I was up there, strung up by wires. I had to tie everything down—my phone, my pillow. Mica was part of the support team. She brought me food, took away my buckets. It was pretty lonely up there. I knew I had support, though, down below. I had food, water, people yelling positive things to me from the trees. It helped me keep going."

"Was it like this?"

Dance scanned the hillside, the hiding trees, the smoke from the fires. "No," he said. "This is something else."

I had finished my coffee. Fog might have burned off the mountains by now, but there was no sun, nothing to sear the white mist that seemed to spring from the ground. There was a mine fire near home that had been burning underground for a hundred years, sparked by a coal seam. It might never go out. I wondered if folks had found a way to harness that fire for warmth. I wondered if breathing in the hot, toxic haze of a coal seam fire was worth it to stay warm, if we were killing ourselves to survive.

I hiked down the hill to the main camp. We needed to get back to the truck, back on the road. I needed to rally the others.

Behind me, Dance picked up his ax. I heard the ringing song of the wood being split, the kick and tumble of the logs. This time of year—fall—there still should have been insects, the drowsy riot of hornets, the bees doing their last and best. Mama and I used to joke that the seasons in southeastern Ohio were Winter, Mud, Summer, and Hornet. They were each troublesome, something to dread and deal with on the farm. Now they seemed like children I had named but would never know. Something Lisbeth would have done.

I heard a whistle, high and piercing. Three short blasts.

I looked back at Dance and he shook his head, but he set the ax down, listening. The whistle did not come again. But below in the camp, people began to run.

Someone dumped a bucket of sand on the cook fire. Others pulled boughs and branches over the structures being built. The cooler and food supplies disappeared into a hole in the ground. The whistle was a sign. I started to break into a run down the hill.

The women from Skate State were scrambling up the bank from the stream, Jamey being led by a hand. Grayson stood frozen and I ran over to him. The women with Jamey knew the whistle was an alert, but then they must not have known what to do. No one at the camp had told them more—and no one had told us anything. We stayed by the stream together, looking around.

The man who had been splitting wood in the camp, the one who had stared at me, covered the whole chopping block with boughs. The camp started emptying. People were climbing into the trees, up onto the deer stands. They hauled up backpacks and baskets by ropes.

Mica strode through the camp, calm as it all collapsed around her. She blew more short blasts from the whistle around her neck. She saw us and spat the whistle out. "Get the kid in the trees," she said.

Dance was at my elbow. He lifted Starla out of the women's arms, and reached for my hand. I reached for Grayson. We ran together, slowed by the baby and Grayson's cast. I saw hands appear from trees, ropes fall down like snakes. Someone lowered a big bucket and we loaded Starla inside. She clung to the handle and rose. Jamey clambered up the tree alongside her, helped by the handholds nailed to the trunk. I climbed after her, pulling myself to the platform at the top. I reached back for Grayson, and hauled him up, his boot clunking onto the tree stand. Dance was just behind him.

But then there was no more room. Where were the women, Jamey's friends? I had thought they were right behind us. But they didn't come up the tree. I waited, watching.

We were already crowded, all of us plus a stranger: the one who had lowered the bucket, a boy with a bright blue mohawk. Then Mica rolled onto the platform, smooth and effortless, like she was getting into bed. She lay on her shoulder on the edge of the deer stand, keeping us back from the ledge.

The women didn't come up behind her. Maybe they had run to another tree.

"Don't say a word," Mica said.

The wind rattled through the treetops. It was strange not to hear even the pop of a fire. Something, a sheet of metal from one of the half-built houses or a loose plank of wood, beat against a trunk. It reminded me of a school flagpole, clanging in the breeze.

Voices came from below. Shouting, a whistle through fingers. Over Mica's shoulder, I could see only a small square of the camp. But I could see when the men walked into the clearing.

Two men. I didn't recognize them, but Jamey did. She sucked in her breath.

Mica said, "Shh."

Jamey looked away from the edge. She had lifted Starla from the bucket and was holding her tightly, hiding her face. If she couldn't see the men, maybe they couldn't see her.

I knew that trick. I had done it so many times when

Lobo came home. Hiding from him in the woods. In my own house, hiding from men—not even wanting to glimpse them at the door, believing, though I knew this not to be true, if I couldn't see them, they couldn't find me.

These were Jake's men, then.

"Hellooooo?" one of the men called from below.

"Swear to Jesus, I smell a fire."

"That tree fence sure didn't make itself, whatever the fuck that was."

I heard boots kicking rocks, scattering leaves. One of the men threw something and it bounced off a tree. Then I heard a shriek. Female.

Dance jerked like he was going to do something, but the boy with the blue mohawk stilled him, touching his arm and shaking his head. Blue Mohawk's hand moved to his side. Starla was silent as a doll.

The women from Skate State, Jamey's friends, had not made it into a tree.

I saw them stumble into the clearing below us, pushed forward by the men. One of the women wore a night-gown, so thin I swore I could see her heart beat. The other woman was barefoot.

They had braided Jamey's hair. They had painted the face of her daughter. Now they were kneeling before the men in boots.

"Where are the others?" a man said.

"There ain't any others," one of the women said.

We heard but did not see the slap. On the platform, Starla whimpered. I saw Jamey squeeze her tighter, slip her hand over the baby's mouth.

"There's a fire. We know there's a camp here," the man said. "We know you've got people."

Another woman's voice. "It was our fire."

"You're stupid, then."

"Let's just go," the second man said.

"We didn't get what we came for."

"They're not here."

"You believe these cunts?"

"Look, man," the second man said. "Nobody would stick around here. It's a bad spot. Spooky. I don't like it."

"Scared of the woods?" the first man said.

But he must have pushed or yanked the women forward, pulled them to their feet. The three of them began to move. A scuffling of boots and leaves. The second man came into view. He glanced around for a moment. I saw him pause, peer up at the trees.

I turned my face from the edge. I lowered my head and squeezed my eyes like Jamey. A trick to make ourselves a small stone. Make our bodies inoffensive, forgettable, of too little consequence even to kick.

"It's too quiet. Like the trees are watching me," the man in the clearing said.

But he moved away, following the others.

"We *are* watching you. Freak," Blue Mohawk said after a moment.

Mica shot him a look. She leaned off the edge of the deer stand to see that the men had gone for certain, then she turned back. "Emergency meeting," she said.

No one was running. No one was clambering down

the trees to follow the women, to confront the men, to ask them what the hell they were doing.

"Aren't you going to go after them?" I asked.

"We're going to have a meeting."

"By the time you do that, they'll be long gone."

"We all know where they're going," Mica said.

That was it. No one on the platform raised their head to meet my eyes. No one spoke up for the women, not even Jamey.

"You can't just let them kidnap those women," I said.

"We don't have guns," Mica said. "Those men do. A lot of guns. Just spread the word about the meeting," she said to Blue Mohawk.

He nodded. It was only when he rose off his knees that I saw what was at his side, what he had reached for when the men came into the clearing: it was a knife, half as long as Starla.

11

The meeting was for everyone in the camp but us. We were banished to the truck to wait, led back to the spot by the man with the blue hair.

I should have felt relieved to be returning to my house and my things, but I didn't. The men were out there. The women were missing. We had seemed far away from the main road, from other houses or camps—but the men from Skate State had found us. I could see smoke through the trees. Was it theirs?

Just before the fence, Blue Mohawk tapped the hood of the truck, sweeping off a pile of leaves. He said, "I have to get to the meeting. Can I trust you to wait here?"

"Of course," Dance said.

"Someone will come for you afterward."

He turned back. For a time, his blue fin stuck out, vibrant in the brown and white hills, then it, too, dipped from view. I thought of blue jays. What I wouldn't give to see one now.

"Why don't we just go," Jamey said.

"They still have our keys," I said.

Jamey looked flat and pale. Her eyeliner had smeared. There was a fresh scratch on her face, and her hair was straggling out of its mermaid tail. She had lost her friends. The men had come for her and taken away her friends instead, her sisters: the ones who had waited with her in the meat house. The ones who had braided her hair.

At least the tiny house was unlocked. I held open the door for Jamey, and she slumped inside onto the couch with Starla, and immediately opened up her shirt. The sudden vulnerability: her skin appearing. Starla ducked her little head to nurse. I closed the door.

Grayson sat on the truck hood, his hurt leg dangling like an anchor. "What do you think this meeting is about?"

"Us," Dance said. "Whether we can stay."

"Not going after the women?" I asked.

"The women are gone."

"We don't want to stay," Grayson said.

"They're not gonna let us, anyway," Dance said. "We're strangers. We brought strangers in."

The world had changed so swiftly into something from Lobo's worst paranoias: everyone suspicious, fearful and armed, and out for themselves. It was no wonder the Pumpkin King had been killed. And for what? For nothing.

I felt for the pouch of seeds around my neck. I remembered the gas station where Dance had said the cashier in a bulletproof vest, shotgun propped behind him, had locked the door as soon as the power went off. The world was colder, in all ways.

"Why do you talk like that?" I asked Dance. "Strangers? We brought strangers in?"

"I'm just telling you what they're going to say."

"But they talk like that, the kids in the camp. Self-important. Playing at being a little army in the woods. It's not a game. Jake has guns."

I felt the heaviness in my pocket.

We had a gun.

Jamey appeared around the side of the house, buttoning up her coat. "Starla's asleep," she said. "I put her down on your couch, okay?" She leaned against the truck hood next to Grayson.

The past day had aged her—or maybe it was the woods that made the shadows stretch beneath her eyes, creased with little Xs. Her skin was so dry it looked like paper. Grayson was thinner than I remembered, his coat bunching up at the shoulders. Did I look like that? All of us were covered in a thin brown scrim: dust from the road, from sleeping on the ground, and from the deer stands, dust the color of a dirty river. Snow clouds swarmed the branches of the trees, as if the woods were filling up with smoke.

"Jake's gonna come back," Jamey said—and I couldn't tell if it was resignation or stubborn respect in her voice, the admiration you'd have for a rodent stealing your tomatoes, a stray dog that wouldn't leave your porch. "He won't give up. He's bad like that. Once he gets an idea—"

"What is his idea? What's his deal?" Grayson said. "Why is he so possessive?"

"But Jake wasn't here," I said. Two different men had come into the clearing. "Maybe you hurt him, Jamey. Maybe you took him out."

Jamey didn't seem concerned—or optimistic. Her face turned into that blank slate it got, as expressionless as I remembered first seeing her, outside the shed when we pulled into Skate State. She shut down, wiped the feeling from her face, a window slamming closed. She looked toward the direction Blue Mohawk had disappeared, down a path so slight it was like the trees had closed up after him. "Does anyone have a cigarette?"

No one did.

Mica was the one who came back, not Blue Mohawk. She walked briskly with her head down, trying to book it back to camp as soon as possible, I thought; she didn't want to waste too much time with us. I thought again of how the woods were like a trap, a closing hand. The trees knitted themselves into shadows all around her. She was carrying a loaf of bread.

"It's a *no*, right?" Dance said.

"I'm sorry. We had an open discussion. I spoke up in favor of all of you. But we put it to a vote. And consensus rules."

No one else said anything.

"Can I ask a question?" I said. "Why are you camped here? Why here? You're so close to Skate State, they're always going to find you and hassle you. Why not 'defend' somewhere else?"

"This is our home," Mica said. "Most of us grew up around here before…" She didn't need to say more.

But I couldn't let go of it. "Don't you people have jobs? How do you get your money?"

"Wil," Dance said.

Mica said, "I kinda think this is our job now. Don't you?"

"What's with the bread?" Grayson asked.

She held it out. It looked healthy and hard, probably some whole grain, birdseed thing. It might be useful as a weapon if someone came swinging at us in the night.

But Mica walked past Grayson and held it out to Jamey. "For you," she said. "For you and your daughter. For your journey."

Jamey stared at the bread as though it was a snake.

"Don't we get bread?" Grayson joked. "What about our journey?"

Mica turned. "Oh, you can stay. You and Dance and Wil? You're welcome to camp here as long as you like. You're useful. You have things to contribute. Only the Skate State people have to go. I thought I made that clear?"

"What?" Grayson said.

"We're not Skate State people," Jamey said. "We came from there, but we're not like Jake. That's not our fault. That's not my baby's fault."

"Hold on," Dance said.

"You can't live next to Skate State and just close your eyes to what happens there. What happens to women."

I took Mica's bread. "We're not going anywhere without Jamey and Starla," I said. "That's it."

Mica stared at me. How long had she been in the woods, really? How long had she slept on the ground—or on one of the deer stands, wrapped in waterproof down? How cold would it get before she left? Maybe I was all wrong. Maybe Mica and Blue Mohawk and the others were here for keeps. Maybe they were protecting something I didn't even know needed to be protected, for all of us: the pines, the scarred birches. I had assumed they would always be here, some part of them somewhere, living on. But I had assumed that about a lot of things.

Given the choice, I almost expected Dance to stay. I thought he belonged someplace like this camp, where he could make a difference. Mica turned to him, maybe thinking the same thing. But Dance didn't move.

I slapped the hard loaf of bread in my hands like a baseball bat. "This looks really good, Mica. Healthy. Thank you. Can we have the keys to my truck back, please?"

Her eyes snapped away from Dance, shrinking like crow's eyes. She was not going to act like she wanted anything from us, even her old companion. She passed over the keys and I took them in my free hand. "It was for safekeeping," she said. "You know the way to the road?"

"We can find it."

Dance spoke up. "Good luck with your action."

"It's not really an action anymore, is it? This is just our life now. It's just became our life." Mica turned and went back through the trees. A few steps away from us, she snapped up the hood of her coat. A few paces more and she was gone.

I wondered how long they could make their stand.

When the invaders came, would they look like men with shotguns? Or would they drive bulldozers and limousines?

"Thanks for sticking up for us. You didn't have to do that," Jamey said. We all looked at her and she looked away. I saw her face switch off again, into nothingness, not being hurt, not feeling. She had sparkly makeup and a dirty face. I remembered thinking the camp would be a good place for her and Starla.

"Are you sure you don't want to stay here?" I asked Dance.

He reached for the truck keys. "I'm sure. This place is doomed."

We cleared the brush off the truck, stashing some of the camouflage in case we needed it later. We drove back across the fields slowly.

Nothing was chasing us now.

It was getting dark; it was always getting dark. Or maybe it was just going to storm hard. Dance drove. Starla slept in the back over Jamey's lap. We were quiet and tired. The truck lights swept over the fields, barren and white. Then the lights hit something larger.

"Slow down," I said. And when he didn't: "Dance. Stop."

He hit the brakes hard enough for Starla to wake. In the middle of the field, we halted. Frozen mud and the corn stubble from two years ago made a mush of the ground. There was something moving amid the waste.

Dance turned on the high beams. A figure hurried past the truck. It brushed the side of the hood—so bulky the whole vehicle shuddered.

Grayson leaned over the front seat. "What the—?"

"Cows," I said.

It was a herd. Large and red and white, with tagged ears and faces like masks. They looked big, but thin. I saw the ribs on one, like a corset spreading wide and sharp under its hide. The cows trudged past us. They were headed, determinedly, elsewhere. I counted a dozen, mostly full grown, a few stunted calves galloping along to keep up.

Then Dance said, "Beef cattle."

"We could take one," Grayson said. "Slaughter it. Use the meat."

"Don't hurt the cows," Jamey shrieked from the back seat.

"Just let them go," I said. "They're starving."

We watched the animals in the fading light. What compelled them, what announced to them that it was time to go, other than their own desperation? Where were they going *to*? Except onward. On through the freezing night. Their breath made clouds around them, white scrim the stragglers walked through.

"Do you think they escaped from a farm?" Grayson said.

"Maybe someone just released them," I said. "Couldn't feed them. Couldn't bear to watch them starve."

"Horses!" Starla said, clapping her hand against the window.

"Close," Jamey said.

I made Dance switch places with me and I drove. After the cows had disappeared, I followed the footfalls they had left, and eased the truck back onto the road. I felt relief to drive on the road again, the certainty of pavement. Paved roads meant a town ahead, somewhere. Paved roads meant people, maybe gas or food, though this pavement was holey and slick, black with ice. We moved as swiftly as we could. The house bumped along behind.

We passed a car crashed into a ditch. The car had been there awhile, long enough to get covered in snow. I felt the emptiness of it. Only blackness beneath the snowy windows: everyone had gone. Later, out of the corner of my eye, I saw a church van, abandoned off to the side of the road. I felt like I could drive for a long time, and I did. The others slept, even Dance, his chin jerking back, mouth open. Grayson was right: he did snore.

What did I know about Dance? What did I know about any of them? We were all orphans, in a way. Adult orphans. Dance's daddy was drunk, and his mama: gone. Grayson's folks were off with The Church. Jamey's family...where was her family?

Where was mine?

We had had a lonely, ordinary life in town. My mama had made money—not enough—cleaning offices. There was a bus stop where I waited for a big yellow bus. I cried myself to sleep most nights in a bedroom with thin walls, a roof, a white bed. Glow in the dark stars my daddy had stuck on the ceiling stared down at me. I didn't remember him doing that, caring about me like that, or being in my room. The stars' glow didn't last. Through the walls, I heard my mama weep.

Our life in the country, our life with Lobo, had been different: wild and difficult and gritty and magic. I had seen a comet. I heard coyotes every night. It was also a lonely life, and an uncertain one. I don't think I ever slept soundly, even as a child, especially when the weed was drying in the house: our secret exposed like an exoskeleton. Every crunch of gravel in the driveway woke me, every tread of a raccoon or deer; every rattle of the door meant danger.

The tiny house had been parked well before the big one, in the lower field. If the sheriff—or robbers or men— came up the drive, they would come to me first. Me, who had no dead bolt on the door. Me, who barely had a door. They would see my light burning all night.

I looked at the back seat and realized Jamey was awake.

She met my eyes in the rearview mirror. "I'm sorry," she mouthed over Starla's head.

"Not your fault," I said. "Besides, I was getting sick of all the dudes around here."

Jamey smiled, leaned her forehead against the window, and closed her eyes. Soon, Grayson woke and took over driving for me, stretching his injured leg with the boot out into the passenger side, near Dance, who didn't move. Grayson drove even slower than the rest of us, partially because of his cast and partially because he was just Grayson: cautious, tapping the brakes every few minutes, checking his mirrors, not speaking except to crack unfunny jokes about carpool lanes and commuting. I scrunched into the back seat with Jamey and Starla.

I woke up when the truck rolled to a slow stop. I stirred, sat up. "What now?" I asked.

Grayson's eyes flickered to the dashboard. The gas gauge.

I pulled myself close to his seat. "How much do we have?"

"I don't know. Your truck eats fuel like a monster."

"Did we pass a gas station? We could go back."

"Yeah, but nothing was open. I don't know whether they're running short, or running away, or what."

Grayson had pulled off to the gravel on the side of the road, though I saw no other traffic. More and more of the cars we had started passing were abandoned, dead. They had run out of gas or run into snowbanks, stuck in the drifts like burrowing bugs.

Our way had grown curvier, the turns sharper as we had driven deeper into West Virginia. The roads were jagged parts in the mountains, thin and filling with white. Ice beards dribbled off the cliffs. Grayson said Interstate 77 had been closed; we had passed it while I slept. There were chained gates down across the on-ramp, so even my truck couldn't barrel through. No salt was left to treat the roads, or no trucks were driving around to spread it. No deputies were working to control the skidding, spinning traffic.

I thought we would see more law enforcement, not less, as people panicked and fled. But the law had left us, too. I hadn't seen a sheriff or police car since the West Virginia border, maybe longer. Maybe they knew something we didn't.

With the interstate lost to us, we had the back roads, streaked with snow: the mountain roads where the next rise might plummet us to anything—an unguarded ridge, a face full of poplars, pirates.

Jamey woke up. "Where are we?"

"Almost out of gas," Grayson said.

We went back. The gas station Grayson had passed was closed, of course. Even before we pulled into the lot, I could tell from the dark windows of the little store. Stillness had settled around it, a visible mist. Grayson drove in, anyway, the signal hose setting off a bell. We parked. Nobody answered the bell.

"Let's get out," Grayson said. "I need to stretch my legs."

"Leg," Jamey said.

The gas station and convenience store sat at the bottom of a small rise. Go-carts were lined up at the top, parked and forgotten. A faded, snow-cuffed sign read Boat Trips, Zip Lines, and something else I couldn't read under the snow. Near the back of the parking lot sat a van with a canoe or kayak carrier hooked to the trailer hitch. The van looked dusty and the boats were all gone. Had they been stolen or moved to storage? Had people floated away before the rivers turned to ice?

"I'm going to look around, see if we can find anybody alive to sell us fuel," Dance said.

He disappeared around the back of the station. The rest of us got out of the truck. My foot was asleep. Starla fussed, flinging pebbles against the truck tires. The air was so crisp and cold it felt like it might break, like we were cracking through the atmosphere just to walk around.

"Can I take Starla on a zip line?" Grayson asked Jamey.

"Absolutely not."

"What about if I just put her in a go-cart and push her?"

Jamey looked up at the go-carts. "All right. Wear a helmet, if you can find one."

Grayson raced Starla up the hill, the baby wobbling on her new legs, Grayson lopsided with his boot.

Jamey turned toward the gas station. "I'm gonna try something," she said, more to herself than to me. She walked to the door of the store, pulled something from her pocket—her knife, that she had taken back from me—and knelt in front of the lock. In less than a minute, the time it took me to walk over there, she had sprung it open. She pushed through the door to the sound of jingling bells.

"Jamey." I caught the door, stopping the bells. I glanced up reflexively, looking for cameras.

"Relax. The power's off. Nobody's here. I'm just gonna see if I can get the pumps going again."

I followed her in. A blast of cold air hit me, as cold as the air outside, but stale, like an old freezer. "Jamey, that's stealing."

"You have cash, right?"

I didn't answer. What had she noticed?

"Just leave a wad on the counter for when somebody comes back. *If* anybody ever comes back. I sure wouldn't come back here." She swung her legs over the counter and started fiddling with something behind the register.

"The power's off," I said. "The pumps won't work."

"Hang on." Her hands worked at something hidden from view. She gave a tug. I heard a whir, like an engine cranking, then she stood. "Transfer switch. Should be a generator. The pumps should work now." When I looked at her in surprise, she said, "I used to work at a gas station. Before Skate State."

I glanced outside through the grimy door. Dance had

returned to the truck. He looked at the pump, looked back at me. I nodded, and he lifted the pump handle. It must have worked; he turned to the truck with the nozzle.

I tried to picture Jamey before Skate State. I doubted it was legal for her to work much, but *legal* was a flexible term in the foothills. Jamey in a cashier vest, snapping gum. Reading magazines from the rack, bored on her break. It was both easy and impossible to imagine.

She was scanning the wall of cigarettes behind the counter. "How much cash do you have?" she asked.

"You can't smoke in the truck."

She pulled a carton from the wall. "I'll smoke it here, then."

We sat out on the curb in front of the store. Jamey smoked and I watched Dance pump gas. After the truck was all fueled, he filled our collection of gas cans. On the ridge above us, we could hear whoops and laughter, a go-cart teetering back and forth, as Grayson pushed Starla around.

"That foot ain't never gonna heal," Jamey said. She blew out a line of smoke.

"How did you end up at Skate State?" I asked her.

I didn't know if she would answer, but she spoke right away. It was a simple answer, the simplest answer in the world: "I got pregnant and my folks kicked me out. I didn't know where to go. They were nice to me at Skate State. I didn't have to work, be on my feet all day. Jake gave us a roof and fed us."

I thought of the shack where Kaylee lay on a dirty mattress on the floor. "That wasn't much of a roof."

Jamey took another drag on her cigarette. "Things got worse when it got cold."

I watched her smoke blend with the air and our breath, becoming just another cloud in a low white sky.

"What's your story?" Jamey asked. "You've got a ton of cash, a house, and a gun in your pocket." She sucked on the cigarette. "Yeah, I know."

I could feel the heaviness, without even feeling for it, weighing down my coat. Dance and Grayson knew about the gun. Now Jamey knew.

"It was my mama's boyfriend's."

"The gun?"

"The gun, the money. They left it for me. He and my mama."

"He do something bad?"

"He grew weed."

Jamey took a drag. "That's not too bad."

Dance waved to us. He had replaced the pump, screwed on the cap of the last gas can.

"He's done," I said. I stood up from the curb and dusted snow off my coveralls. "We better get Starla and Grayson and get back on the road."

"Do you really think you'll make it?" Jamey asked. "All the way to California?"

"Sure. Why not." I noticed she had said *you*, not *we*. I held out my hand to her, to help her off the ground. "Do you want to drive for a while?"

Jamey ground out her cigarette and stood. "I don't know how. I'm only fifteen."

12

When the afternoon shadows grew long across the road, and the clouds laced the sky, low, like a storm, we started looking for a place to spend the night.

We passed a chemical plant. The towers and ladders, low buildings and chutes, usually glittered like a city. But this plant was quiet, as still as the snowbanks. I realized why the plant looked strange. The gas flare, which always burned, a tear of orange fire in the darkness, had been extinguished. The stacks of the factory looked as dark and bare as trees, only taller.

We approached a state park, and I made a decision and turned the truck in. Dusk was falling. I expected a gate, a fence we might have to park behind, a lock Jamey could apparently pick. But the tiny gatehouse sat empty, the window shade rolled down. The road into the park was open and clear. It was as though the rangers had left the park for anyone, thrown wide the gate, and ran.

"Where is everybody?" Grayson asked.

"California," Jamey said.

We were off course, I knew. We were taking too long. Skate State had thrown us off, and now we were twisting down hilly country roads, white and slick, afraid to take too many highways, turned away from some of them by blockades and chains. We had to move slowly, but even then the house couldn't take the turns. We'd had to back up more than once and turn around, find another way. The truck was burning through fuel, like Grayson had said. We had filled canisters with gas. Taken—and paid for—every bit of fuel we could find, but even that would only last us so long. We would have to find a better road, paved and straight. We would have to find fuel and water.

I drove through the park until we reached a spot near a cinder-block shower house. A campsite, close to the cover of woods. I pulled the truck in, stopping a few feet before the trees. I turned off the engine and sat for a moment, looking through the windshield.

Silver topped the trees and capped the grass. It was more like the memory of grass these days, more white than brown, knitted to the roots in a frost that just didn't—couldn't—burn away. The campsite had a fire ring and an old grill. The ring was dented and ashy, the grill cast in frozen grease. Nobody had been here for a long time.

"Do you think we should use the camo?" I asked. "Hide the house?"

"Looks safe to me," Grayson said. "This place is deserted."

I looked at Dance but he just shrugged. Jamey was already getting Starla out. "Let's see if there's water," she said cheerfully.

"We could grill tonight," Grayson said.

"Real meat," Dance said.

They slammed the doors and busied themselves setting up camp. I stayed in the front seat, listening to the engine tick and the boys take supplies out of the back. More and more, I felt the roads were *too* empty, the trees too silent. I had the feeling they were waiting—the whole wild world was just waiting—for us to die.

Jamey and Starla ran back from the cinder-block shower house, hand in hand. "Water!" Starla was saying. As excited as a child should have been about candy. "Water!"

"There's running water in the shower house," Jamey said. "It's freezing but on."

"Beats the river," Dance said.

As darkness fell in the early afternoon, we ate deer steaks Grayson cooked on the camp grill, easier than my tiny propane stove. We made a fire in the ring and huddled around it, wrapped in blankets. Our hair, wet from showers in the cinder-block house, dried in the smoke. It was so cold my hair almost froze before it dried, crisping around my ears. Starla fell asleep in front of the fire and Jamey carried her into the house.

She returned with something in each hand, shaking the objects in the firelight before us. Whiskey or wine bottles, it might have been, from somebody else. But that wasn't Jamey.

She held tins of powdered milk and cocoa. "Hot chocolate! Girl," she said to me, "you've been holding out on us."

Jake had called me *girl*. The men who came to the farmhouse did, too.

I watched Jamey try to open the tins with her teeth.

"Now wait a minute," Grayson said, "what if that is the last hot chocolate in the whole world?"

"Then we better enjoy it," Jamey said.

I would bury my money in the ground, hide it in my shoes or a Pepsi can, carry a heaviness in my pocket even if I never could fire it, just to have the weight there. That was my way, that was what my family had taught me. Jamey would pick locks and scavenge and steal. That was what she had been taught by whatever passed for kin and home for her, that was how she had survived.

Dance found mugs and a saucepan, and the three of them bent over the fire, setting the grate from the grill over the flames and mixing the powered milk with water. I sat back and watched.

When Grayson placed a mug in my hands, the steam enveloped my face and chest like a hood. "You okay, Wil?" he said.

I wrapped my hands around the mug. "Sure."

He plopped down beside me on a log we had pulled next to the fire, his leg still heavy at his side. Dance began to tell a story, and Jamey scooted up next to the fire ring, wrapped in a plaid blanket, her eyes as big as headlamps. I looked at the three of them: Jamey; Dance, talking with his hands; Grayson, his hand on his boot like an old man. We might have been friends from high school or college, if any of us had gotten to go to college. We might have been on a weekend trip, a reunion, a vacation.

Except Grayson's boot was starting to smell from rot or infection. He needed someone to look at his foot again; he needed a doctor. Jamey had a scar on her neck. The skin there looked pebbled. I thought it was a burn. A pot handle or a poker or a firecracker had seared her, not long ago. It had not healed right.

We might have been friends, on an escape from our lives, the four of us plus the baby, just camping, except for the stories we told.

"I think it's Earth," Dance said. "Rising up."

"But if spring never comes back, if it just gets colder and colder, won't Earth die, too?" Grayson said.

Dance shrugged the way he did. I had never known someone to make more noncommittal movements. The firelight made his shadow long and spiderlike. "Maybe it's time."

"For everything to die?"

"Maybe. I know we're being punished."

"Maybe you are," Jamey said. "I didn't do anything."

"You drive a car."

I spoke up from my mug. "She can't drive, Dance."

No one else was in the park. No other fires lit up the darkness. Shadows settled in around us like they were there to stay.

I couldn't hear dripping from the shower house anymore. Maybe the pipes had finally frozen after giving us one last fill-up of our bottles and jugs, one last good clean. No rushing sound from the creek that surely cut through the woods somewhere. Maybe its bends were clotted and stilled, fish frozen like shirts on a line. I wondered if the rabbits and groundhogs were alive in their burrows. If the black bears, which had been seen crossing the river in seasons past, had made it, noses white from the icy Ohio, holding their faces above the waterline like a bundle of everything they owned.

I had seen barges on the Ohio: coal topped with snow, little mountains returning to mountains. Were they stuck there, wedged in bergs and flows? Would that coal ever heat anything? Was it all for nothing?

"I fucking recycled," Jamey said. "I collected all the empties in that damn place. We only ate meat we killed or raised. I wasn't old enough to vote before. How is any of this my fault?"

The men were silent for a moment. The fire popped, sending a flare into the sky.

"Well," Grayson said. "You have a kid."

"That," Jamey said, "ain't my fault, either." She stood up, the blanket crumpling to the ground.

"Overpopulation," Dance said.

"Leave it, guys," I said.

Jamey dumped the rest of her mug into the fire. It was careless. We needed the heat. But the blaze only sizzled and kept on burning, and she walked away, mumbling something about checking on Starla.

"What's the matter with her?" Grayson asked when she had gone.

"She's fucking fifteen," I said.

"Jesus."

Silence again, heavier this time. Nobody wanted to break it. We watched the fire fizzle and snap.

I used to love a campfire. It used to be a treat, hot dogs roasting in the lower field. Or a bonfire: an excuse to burn the autumn cuttings and cast-offs—the telltale evidence, branches and leaves that had to be disposed of somehow. I thought of camping trips with Lisbeth's youth group, the boys fighting over who would strike the flint, all of them getting the kindling wrong, freezing, waiting for s'mores, finally eating the chocolate bars raw. The boys teased Lisbeth when the fumes drifted over to her lawn chair: *Smoke follows beauty…* They never teased me. And never, ever let me strike the flint.

I wondered if Lisbeth was allowed to build the fires where she was now, if the cold had gotten dire enough yet that women could do work that mattered, work that men valued. When would that be?

"She's coming with us," I said. "All the way. Jamey and Starla. To California, if they want to."

"Of course," Grayson said.

"You're the boss," Dance said. "Boss lady."

The fire spit and swore at us. I looked up at the sky. Some of the stars were coming down. No, it was snowing again. "We should go to bed," I said. "Who wants first watch?"

Dance put another branch on the fire. "I'll do it."

"I'll take second," Grayson said.

"I'm on third watch, then."

We didn't trust Jamey to stand watch alone. I dumped the dregs of my cup to the side of the log and stood. We gathered our blankets, Grayson and I, and crept inside the house. Jamey and Starla slept on the pullout, the baby's arms thrown over her mama as though she was protecting her.

The stove in the tiny house crackled. I thought the smell of wood smoke was comforting, rich and dark, familiar—but it wasn't good for a child to breathe in. What choice did we have?

I gave Grayson the blankets and found a cushion for him to sleep on the floor. Then I crawled up the ladder to the loft, my loft. Grayson couldn't make it up there with his foot, and it wasn't safe for the baby. But I felt guilty being alone in the loft. A bed to myself. A real bed, quilts smelling of home. I was guilty—and safe. If the cold deepened, soon we were all going to have to squeeze in the house together somehow, all night, and keep watch at the door.

Grayson fell asleep right away, as he usually did. Through the triangle-shaped window at the end of the loft, the night sky looked lighter than it should have, tinged with gray. I could barely see the glow of our little fire, the ring where Dance sat awake, stretched out on the log. His back was to the trees. He watched the road we had come in on, the only road into or out of the park. If a stranger came in, they would come that way. Smoke drifted across my window.

When I woke up the world seemed wrong. Too light and quiet. And cold.

The fire in the house had gone out.

I sat up. Through the window, I could see only white, no sign of the campfire, or grill, or log. I crawled over the quilt to look closer. Cold drafts pulsed from the glass. White coated the camp, a deep layer of new snow. Everything looked clean or gone.

The white of the new snow hurt my eyes, so blinding it almost zigzagged. Was this the way the world ended? I would wake up to everything just *over*. Was this the event The Church had prayed for, the reset that would send them straight into heaven?

How long had I slept?

Too long. The white sun was high. I swung my legs over the loft ladder. Grayson, Jamey, and Starla slept on below me.

No one had woken me for watch.

I climbed down to the woodstove and shoved a ball of newspaper in. The crinkling sound stirred Grayson. He rose from the floor and looked at me, his hair sticking straight up like a bird.

"Put kindling in this," I told him.

He nodded.

"Did we sleep all night?"

"No," he whispered, his voice gummy from sleep. "I took second shift, but Dance didn't want to wake you up. He took another shift after me. He thought you needed the rest."

"Well, I don't."

"He must have fallen asleep."

"Wait. Dance is outside?"

This was a dangerous, potentially deadly mistake. I saw in his eyes that he knew it, too.

Starla mumbled and rolled over, flinging out her arms like a starfish. Her mama didn't move. I pointed to the open mouth of the stove—*feed it*—and Grayson nodded again. I had slept in my clothes. We all did these nights. I had my coat on already, the heaviness in my pocket. I just pulled on my boots at the door, my fingers stiff and clumsy with cold. I stumbled out into the white.

Cuffing, numbing white. The stubborn, useless sun that would do nothing except blind me. It wasn't melting or warming anything. What was the point of it?

Off the little back porch of my house, my leg disappeared to the calf. This was the heaviest snowfall in months, then. I trudged to where the campfire had been last night and saw a white mound, streaked with plaid.

It was Dance. Snow gathered in the crevices of his blankets like the white-capped coal on a barge. He was also wrapped in a sleeping bag. His eyes were shut. I was afraid to touch him. But I had to. I reached out my hand and shook him. Snow rolled off his shoulder, powdered and gritty. He blinked.

I breathed deeply in relief. "You fell asleep in the cold. Are you okay?"

Snow spackled his beard. I repeated myself. Dance's voice, when he finally spoke, sounded like a gravel road. "It's not that cold."

"You could have frozen to death. Damn it."

Then he saw all the snow and slid up. "It wasn't sticking like that this morning."

"Grayson's getting the woodstove going. Go warm up in the house. You should rub your hands and feet. You don't want to get frostbite."

"It's not that bad," he insisted.

He stood with a groan. I tried to assist him, but he waved away my hands. He was standing at least. Tears leaked from his eyes and he shook the snow from his beard. I looked toward the woods to see how wet everything was, if we could find any dry kindling for the fire, and I saw them. Footprints led from our campsite into the trees. Deep and black, like bullet holes in the snow.

"Did you go into the woods?" I asked Dance.

He was beating snow from his blankets. "No."

"Maybe you heard something, you went to check on something?"

"No, I didn't. It was quiet the whole time."

He saw where I was looking. The footprints were heavy. They were human.

The person or people had trudged through a lot of snow, maybe all of it, after it had stopped falling. No new snow filled the prints. They led from the woods to the edge of the campfire, right behind the log where Dance had fallen asleep, then they circled back to the tiny house.

I looked at Dance. He dropped the blankets and we ran as fast as we could through the heavy, dragging snow, following the tracks. The footprints ran alongside the house, close to the walls. They had lingered there, the stranger, outside the kitchen window where we washed dishes, where we had scanned the road and had not seen anyone. We had not been looking the right way; we had not known they would come from the woods.

There was a stamping pattern on the ground, the prints smudged from standing around, shifting, and waiting.

"They watched us while we slept," I said.

The footprints continued to where the trailer hitched up to the truck—no lingering there, just a line, straight to the truck's gate. In the bed of the truck, our tarps had been disturbed, the bungee cords holding down our supplies not just unclipped, but cut with a knife. The stranger had been in a hurry. Our stuff was gone.

"Jake?" Jamey stood on the porch of the house in the furry, impractical boots she had taken from a truck stop a few miles back, no coat. Her face was creased from sleeping, her nose runny and pink. "Was it Jake?" She folded her arms, stamped to keep warm on the narrow step.

"You should go inside," I said. "It's freezing out here."

"Was it him?"

"No," Dance said, without even consulting me. "We don't think so. Just some rando."

I gave him a look, but then I, too, found myself turning to Jamey and saying things I didn't know I believed. "He wouldn't follow us just to steal from us. He couldn't come this far. He wouldn't find us."

"Yes," Jamey said. She hugged her arms closer to her chest. "He would."

Lisbeth would come as far as Crossroads.

But one day—the last day—she came farther, up to the mailbox at the end of our driveway near the road. I heard the crunch of tires over the gravel, then an engine shutting off. In my tiny house, I pulled on boots and another sweater. I don't know who I thought I'd face in the driveway, but not her. Not that day. Then I saw the grille of her truck parked on the other side of the gate, like a horse looking over a fence.

I couldn't keep the smile off my face. "You're here. You came out here. Finally! I have so much to show you." I bent to unlock the gate.

"I can't stay," she said. "Don't bother. It's tomorrow."

"What is?"

"We're leaving. Tomorrow's the day."

I let the chain with the padlock fall. I put my boot on the gate and looked at her over it. "Don't go."

"Come with me."

"I can't just leave. Where are you even going?"

She didn't know. No one knew. Away. Something better was away. A place with safer roads, schools that were open. Jobs and heat. How would we get there? How would they have room for us?

"I'm not sure you can outrun this thing," I said.

"But we can't just stay here, Wil. I'm sick of staying here. Doing nothing. There's no work. I don't even have my own money."

"That's not going to change as long as you're with your folks."

Or The Church. They would always take those things from her. They would always make up her mind for her, what to wear, how long to grow and tie back her hair, what she could watch and listen to, who she would marry—

which would have to be a man, there was no question. A
man from The Church. He loomed over us, a shadow, in-
evitable as a ghost. He was tall. He was silent. He would
want her to be a good kisser, to know how to do the things
we had tried. So she could be pure but also good. Worldly,
but inexperienced in how it counted.

It would never count, any way I might have tried to get
her to stay. Reaching through the gate to pull her close.
Pulling the key out of the ignition. In the crackling trees,
a bird called, the bubbling song of a winter wren.

Lisbeth didn't even turn toward its music. She had a
scarf wound high around her neck like a bandage, hiding
her hair. She didn't take her mittens off. Her truck door
hung agape, letting in the cold air, and letting me know
she was leaving soon. This was a short stop, a last stop.
Nothing I could say would change her mind.

I still tried. "Whatever happens, maybe we should make
a go of it here," I said.

Lisbeth wrinkled her face. "Out here?"

"There's land, a water supply. I can get solar hooked up
like Mama always talked about. We can grow vegetables
in the basement under the grow lights. It doesn't have to
be weed. It won't be anymore. It won't be," I repeated.

"You want the world to end for you here? In Ohio?"

Lisbeth had only lived in Ohio, like I had, like we all
had. It had always been fine for her before, enough to
tide her over.

I realized—it came to me like the cruelest breeze—
the cold was an excuse to get away. Her tunnel, dug with
spoons; her ladder, knotted after many nights, so many

nights of planning and waiting and hoping, never daring to think she would really get out. Why did she want to leave so bad? To leave without really leaving the stranglehold of how she had been raised? There would still be a dress code wherever she went, expectations, dinners to cook, a curfew.

But there might be other people in a new place. She might meet someone.

It was him I felt, standing in the driveway with her, the gate between us. Everyone in the holler she already knew, tired as a bedsheet. But the presence of a stranger, his potential, fell over us as suddenly as the sun, if there had been sun, would disappear behind a cloud. In another place there would be other people.

It wasn't going to happen between us, I saw, a last kiss through the fence, a last chance. Nothing was ever going to happen.

Lisbeth said, "What's here, anyway? What's so special about this town? There's nothing here."

"I'm here. I'm still here."

"Why is that?" she said.

They had taken food. They had taken canned goods. They had taken hand warmers and socks and blankets. And we might have been okay. We might have let it go. We had knives, deer meat, and potatoes stored in the tiny house kitchen. We had the heaviness in my pocket. Dance had a bow and arrows. I had cash. We had a way to hunt and keep warm with the woodstove and the house. We were fine, we were safe, we were warm, as long as we still had the house.

But they had taken the grow lights, too.

I felt for the seeds in their pouch around my neck. I had been meaning to start something. To get seedlings going in the little kitchen. Who knew how long we would be on the road, maybe long enough for something to sprout. But now we were down lights, plastic sheeting, fertilizer. We couldn't afford to lose even these basic items. How would we replace them?

"They must have made multiple trips," Grayson said. "To carry that much."

"Or there was more than one of them," Dance said.

We studied the tracks. A clear line in and a clear line out. The tracks returned the way they had come, from the woods.

I looked up at the sky. Our phones didn't work. None of us had watches. The dashboard clock in the truck had been broken for years, since Lobo had punched it in a fit of rage. Early on, Grayson had switched on the truck radio, trying to find news, weather, anything—but we heard only static. Station after station, the same dull buzz.

I wanted the radio silence to be because Lobo had broken the radio, too, and not because no one was broadcasting, no one was out there, the towers had frozen. We had no idea what time it was anymore. But the sun wasn't too high. It was still only morning, I thought.

"Are you going to include me in this?" Jamey called from the house. She had put on her coat at least, and held Starla, wrapped fat as a snowman.

"No," we all said.

"This involves me."

"No, it doesn't," I said.

"If he did this, then it does."

"Okay. Here's what's going to happen," I said. "Dance and I are going to get our stuff back. You and Grayson, be ready to go. Pack up the camp. When we come out of the woods, you've got to be ready to get us out of here as fast as you can."

Jamey blinked in the sun and hefted Starla.

Grayson couldn't come with us because of his boot, and Jamey because of the baby, but I saw them both cast looks at me as Dance and I wrapped up in warm clothes. It was not a look of anger or of longing to go, but a long glance with dark, furrowed brows. I saw the questions in their eyes. Would we come back to them? How long should they wait? Would this be when they lost us?

Into the woods I went with Dance, the one who had fallen asleep on watch, the one who had not noticed as thieves or Jake made off with half our stuff, stepping purposefully and silently over the ground. If Dance had been a woman he wouldn't have been allowed to just sleep; the thieves might have robbed him of his body, too.

I knew this, but said nothing about it to him. There was no point. I couldn't make him understand the fear that ran through me and Jamey and Lisbeth. It would run through Starla, too, soon enough: a low hum, like a power line always above her. The world didn't want us to just walk through it.

Dance and I stepped alongside the footprints. The snow made a map for us, a dotted line that led, almost certainly, to danger. "If we find these guys," Dance said, "what are we going to say?"

"Why do we have to say anything?"

"I know you have the gun."

I stopped walking.

"It's obvious. You're always touching it."

"I don't have any ammo for it. And the gun—" I paused "—it's been buried. It was in the ground. I don't even know if it works."

"Then why did you bring it?"

I looked at the tracks. They led up a hill. My breath jogged out before me like a wedding veil. "To scare men," I said.

I started walking again.

I remembered when Lobo had bought his new gun, the one to replace the old, battered handgun I carried in my pocket, which apparently I was always touching: it was back when Mama was sick. One of those nights when the light in the farmhouse bedroom stayed on all night, curtains fluttering and ragged as her breath, or maybe on one of those days that she didn't know were days, he went to the gun show. He came back with a black plastic case. I watched him take it from the truck, carry it into the house.

There would be no burying it this time.

She was trying to quit, I remembered that much: the vomiting, shaking, the smell. Stains on the floor. She couldn't quit. Lobo carried more than a gun into the house. He had bought drugs for her. What kind, I didn't even know.

Something crouched in front of me on the hill. A creature, white and furred. It almost blended with the snow, except the white of the thing was dirtier than the snow.

My impulse was to run, not to reach in my pocket for the gun, but to take flight. Selfishly, weakly. My heart knocked in my chest. Dance put his arm in front of me.

Then the white thing lifted its head. I saw that it had been bent down. It was a person. Misshapen by layers— just a person, trying to stay warm. He wore a white coat with a hood he had zipped all the way up, like a ski mask over his face. Bunches of newspaper, balled into fists, insulated the coat and made him appear lumpy and swollen. Cut into the hood, on either side of the zipper, were white mesh screens. Eyeholes. It looked like a monster but it was only a young man.

There was a moment where we saw him, and he saw us. Then he turned and fled.

"Wait," I said.

"Who the fuck was that?" Dance said.

We abandoned the tracks, running up the hill instead after the hooded person. The snow and our boots weighed us down. The person in the hood moved lighter, quicker. Except for his coat, he was not dressed warmly enough. Snow caked his pant legs. He wore ordinary tennis shoes, which must have been wet, but allowed him to run.

He reached the top of the hill and paused for a moment to look down at us. That uncanny hood, eyeholes like a moth, or giant white fly...then he was gone.

I reached the crest before Dance, and looked down. "Oh, no."

A valley stretched before us, broken by a stream. More

white swarmed the valley: people wearing white coats and
furs. Another camp. Another group. In the center of the
valley near the stream was a picnic shelter, and in front
of it: a pile of junk, stacked together like a funeral pyre. I
recognized something in the jumble.

My duffel bags.

"Wait, Wil. What's the plan?" Dance tried to hold me
back, but I shrugged him off.

"We get our stuff. That's the plan."

I was out of breath from running up the hill after the
boy, but I launched myself down the other side of it, kicking up a spray of snow. At the bottom of the hill, people
looked up at the sound. There was no way we were going
to surprise them now. I stumbled down into the valley,
and right into a blanket being held out for me.

I was wrapped in the blanket before I realized what was
happening, like a runner finishing a race.

Two women held the blanket. One tucked the end
around my neck. It was soft and worn, white fleece. But
it smelled of mold. The woman looked willowy and faded,
ethereal but beaten down. She had long, greasy hair beneath the hood of her white coat. She moved with hazy,
dreamlike motions, not looking me in the eye.

"We wear white here," she said, as if it was the most
natural thing in the world.

Dance made it down the hill behind me. The women
were ready for him, too. They threw an old, white sleeping
bag around him. He looked at me, too surprised to resist.

This could have been a kind gesture, strangers helping

us out in the cold, keeping us warm. But I didn't think so. A man was coming toward us through the snow.

Wrapped tightly in the blanket, I couldn't get to my pocket.

The man wore a sheepskin draped across his shoulders. His chest was bare to the waist, pocked with cold, a red rash slashed across it like poison ivy. I thought again of the gun. I did not try to touch it, to draw attention to it, to struggle too much in the blanket. I thought of Jake's flip-flops: of men who were too arrogant to cover up, to dress sensibly, who thought they were beyond the reach of weather. I looked at the man's pink skin.

"Hello, friends," the man said. "You're just in time."

"I think you have our things." I shrugged off a side of the blanket to try to point at the pile, and both the women rushed forward to tuck the blanket back in.

"We wear white," the man said. "It's kind of a rule we made."

The coats and blankets the women wore around their shoulders, the people milling about the campsite by the stream—everyone was in white. They blended with the landscape, though their whites were dirtier than the snow. Maybe it was camouflage. Maybe they wore white to sneak up on people, to steal from them without being seen.

I had been to Skate State. I had seen the Occupied Forest. I had grown up with The Church—and with growers and sellers, who were their own kind of community, a den of watchfulness, resourcefulness, and trickery: a den of thieves. I had even assembled my own group of sorts on the road: the waiter, the scavenger, the grower, the mama and child. Maybe this was how we made it, sticking together in the families we made.

But something was off about this group in the valley. There was none of the busyness of camp. Nobody was cracking ice in the stream or melting buckets of snow for water. I didn't smell wood smoke or food. I didn't see tents. Nobody was even rummaging through the pile of our stolen things, looking for salvage they could use, their favorite canned foods, coats that fit.

"You have our stuff," I said to the man in the sheepskin. He seemed dismissive. "We picked up some junk."

"It's not junk. We're using it. We need it, and it's ours."

The man cocked his head. He had a red beard and a tattoo on his neck, small and black, right on his artery. It jumped when he spoke. It made me feel squeamish. "Really? You weren't there."

"We were sleeping," Dance said. I could hear the exasperation in his voice. "You came into our camp and took our things."

"I didn't see any names on anything. Did you, ladies?"

The women shook their heads. Were they high? They giggled; they had blank and bright faces.

"It was all tied down in her truck," Dance said.

"We're ridding ourselves of our material things."

"Well, we're not," Dance said. "It obviously belonged to someone."

"Do you own this park? Did you pay to camp here?"

"No. Look, man. We're just trying to survive this, same as you."

The man laughed, a little rough sound. I watched his

breath disturb the air. "That, friend, is where you're wrong. We're not trying to survive it."

They had no food. They had no fire. Bones had been tied to the support beams of the shelter house, what looked like a groundhog skull. And I smelled something.

Gas.

"They took the fuel cans, Dance."

The man was staring at us, standing too close.

"What do you want us to do?" I asked him.

"Nothing."

"You have our food, our fuel. You can keep that," I told the man.

I felt Dance jerk beside me, hearing me give it all away. But we needed to get out of this.

"Company. We'd like your company," the man said. "That would be nice."

"We can't do that," I said. "We have somewhere to be."

"Well, we all do, don't we? Have somewhere to be? Heaven. We have an appointment in heaven."

"Okay," Dance said. "Keep the stuff, like she said."

"We need the duffel bags, though." I was sure the man would ask me why, what was in the bags. I felt certain he would check, and take the contents. But he didn't look away from my face. He paced before me, coming near enough for me to see clearly that it was a skeleton tattoo on his neck. Shaky lines, homemade. "All right," the man said. He was so close I could smell his sheepskin. Wet and rotten. "But you have to get it."

He stepped aside so we could see. A woman in a white raincoat knelt by the pile while a second person, the one in the hooded jacket, the boy we had followed into the valley, danced around it, flinging something from a can. It looked like he was throwing flowers at a wedding. But it was gas from our fuel can, splashing over the pile of our supplies. The woman in the raincoat struck a match.

I shrugged off the blanket and ran for the pile. Dance was shouting my name. My vision narrowed until all I could see was the handle on a duffel bag, sticking out of the pile.

A chance to grow again. To make plants live, plants we could eat. A way to live again.

I yanked the bag free, feeling Dance's arm snake around my waist and pull me. We fell back onto the snowy ground. Before us, the gas-soaked pile went up. I felt heat on my face, felt the orange glow light my skin. The duffel bag had punched me in the chest when we fell. I pushed up, scrambling off Dance and clutching the bag. Smoke roared into the trees, as thick and full as I remembered leaves had once been.

Nobody in the camp seemed upset by the fire. Nobody seemed surprised. But it drew them. I was aware of more people trekking through the snow around the picnic shelter to get closer to the flames. People behind us, in the trees all around us.

"We were waiting for enough fuel," the man in the sheepskin said. "We got it now, thanks to you. We're ready."

"Ready for what?" Dance said.

"To be delivered." The man gestured to the valley. Ten, a dozen people in white came close to the bonfire.

Dance grabbed one side of the duffel bag, and I took the other. We turned our backs to the fire, to the man and the others. The bag was awkward between us, but it was not the first time I had run with it. We carried the bag up the hill without looking back at the scene in the valley.

There was no thought of going back for anything else, no discussion. Everything else was gone. I concentrated on climbing, on not breaking the light in the bag. It might be our last one. All the others were in the fire.

I waited for the icy hand of the man on my shoulder, or for a claw in my hair: his women hauling me back, forcing me down onto my knees like the women in the forest, Jamey's friends we had not saved. Halfway up the hill I realized I didn't hear footsteps crashing through the snow behind us, I didn't feel anyone following. They were not coming.

"Wait," I said. I spun around and looked back.

Everyone was right where we had left them in the valley by the stream. The man with the skeleton tattoo, the others in white. They had not even attempted to follow us; they had not cared. Together, they knelt in a line by the bonfire. Orange flames flickered against the white banks. The fire looked dark and greasy. Smoke billowed into the sky. The man and the others had taken off their tops, their coats and blankets, the sheepskin, all their white things. They were bare-chested, even the women. Their skin looked raw against the snow.

I saw the women who had greeted us, the ones who had wrapped us in blankets. They had closed their eyes, put their hands on their knees. They looked like they were mediating.

Except they were going to freeze.

"What the fuck are they doing?" Dance said.

"We gotta go now." I picked up the duffel bag again and Dance followed.

The fire roared on behind us, and we did not speak. It seemed like years before we reached the campsite.

Grayson was gathering kindling by the tree line. He dropped the load in his arms when he saw us. "You got it! You got it back!" He looked behind us and saw there was nothing else. We were lugging only the single bag. "Just one light? Where's everything else?"

"Gone," Dance said.

"Get in the truck," I said.

We shoved the bag in. There was plenty of room in the bed now. The engine was already running, tailpipe streaming exhaust. I thought of the fire; I tried not to think of the fire and the smoke and the people stripped bare. Burning their things. Their appointment in heaven. Dance got in the passenger side, and Grayson and I took the back, beside Starla.

Starla was by herself.

Jamey turned around from the front seat. "Seat belts on, everybody?"

"I thought you said she couldn't drive?" Dance said.

"She can't," Jamey said. She stamped on the gas and the truck lurched toward the woods, turning sharply as she yanked the wheel hard. The house wobbled.

I steadied myself, bracing my arm against the door. "Just

get us to the park gate. Get us out of here. Then I'll take over. I can't drive right now."

"What happened back there?" Grayson asked. "Who took our stuff? Why can't we get it back?"

Out the window, there was nothing to look at, nothing to see. Just white. There was no hint of the people in the valley by the stream. Smoke from their fire hadn't yet reached the treetops. I couldn't tell if anyone was changing their mind, running away, couldn't hear screams.

"It was a group," Dance said.

"I think they were on something," I said.

"Wil, those people were just waiting to die."

I looked away from the window. "We can't save everyone."

13

We avoided the cities and towns. We stuck to the winding country roads, the house looping behind us like a girl's long braid. Sometimes the driver—especially Jamey, when we let her drive—took a turn too fast, and I imagined I heard a crashing behind us, as something fell and hit something else inside the house. Another object was broken from my old life, another supply ruined or wasted; we had so few now.

In the kitchen of the tiny house I had started seeds, tamping paper towels into a glass jar with bean seeds. I had duct-taped the jars under the window, so that they would receive full sun, what was left of it, and wouldn't sail to the floor and smash on one of Jamey's daredevil turns.

I used precious water on the seeds, and the last of our paper towels. I was sure the seeds would sprout, even without grow lights. It was the simplest of setups, and we could

start other seeds this way, too: carrots, radishes, an avo-
cado if I could find a pit. But so far, the brown seeds had
stayed dormant, curled in their secret shells.

I had an aloe plant, useful for snipping off bits and rubbing the ooze on burns, should they come. I felt all kinds
of pain would come eventually, and we would be alone
with it. I had some kitchen herbs, sage and basil, still alive.
I asked everyone to help me look for supplies at the places
we stopped for food and fuel: cups, plastic wrap, potting
soil. Jamey would break in. We would leave cash folded
on the counter, money for dust, for ghosts.

But of course, mostly we stopped at gas stations and
roadside stores that didn't stock gardening supplies. Everything had been emptied by now, anyway, abandoned.
Still, we could usually get the pumps working again.

And then we stopped at the first gas station where we
could not.

We had learned the stations visible from the road would
be trashed, but soon, so too were the places a couple of
miles off our route—and we didn't dare venture much farther than that. What if we got stuck? There was no one
to pull us out of a snowbank or up from a ditch. What if
the truck broke down? Dance could repair trucks, but we
didn't have spare parts; we hadn't thought of that.

I hadn't thought of it.

The first gas station where the pumps had been drained
had a Taco Bell attached to the side. This excited Jamey
and Grayson. I tried to warn them we would probably not
find usable food.

What we found was an open door. It had been barricaded, and the barricade had been broken through. Most of the boards on the windows had been pried off. I entered first through the smashed door, my boots crunching on a floor sprinkled with glass.

"Pick up Starla," I said behind me to Jamey. "Don't let her walk on this. Or maybe just take her back to the truck."

"No way," Jamey said. "I'm not missing out on tacos." Holding Starla, she fanned out behind me. Grayson and Dance took the other aisles.

The metal shelves had been stripped almost bare. The air still smelled of rot, which meant some of the food spoil was newer. Most places just smelled of cold.

I stepped over a smashed jar of pickles. Someone had spilled a bottle of motor oil, and the black slick looked like a dead snack, frozen in a coil.

"Mice have definitely been here," Grayson said from his aisle.

"Mice are still alive, huh?" Dance said.

"Roaches are going to outlive us all," Jamey said. "Those fuckers."

We should have been quiet. I should have warned the others. We should have known better. But I called across the aisle to Jamey: "Any tacos?"

"Everything's gone," she said.

"What about gardening stuff?"

"I think this place is pretty wasted," Grayson said.

We were meeting up at the end of our aisles. In front of us was the Taco Bell portion of the store, its dark and silent counter, familiar shapes looking menacing with the lights off.

"Everything's gone except…this!" Jamey hopped out from her aisle. She wore a rubber Halloween mask: a werewolf. Her blue eyes swam through the eyeholes; her curls overflowed beneath the floppy neck of the mask. Starla clung to her hip, looking calmly at the monster her mama had become. "Happy Halloween!" Jamey said. "It's almost Halloween, right?"

"Is it?" Grayson said. "I don't think so."

I had no idea. It was September, the last time I remembered, the last time we had had our phones. The thought that it might be October sent panic through my veins. We needed more food and fuel. We needed to find and start more seeds. We needed to move faster.

"This mask smells," Jamey said.

There was a boom as a door was kicked open.

It was the door to the drive-through. An old man stood there. He wore heavy black boots, a coat yellowed with dribbling tobacco stains. He had a face of rough white stubble. And he had a shotgun.

"Get out," he said.

I raised my hands. "We didn't know anybody was here."

"Get out. This is my place."

I looked behind him. I could see, in the little alcove of the drive-through window, canned goods, boxes of mac and cheese, tins of tuna, and stacks of plastic-wrapped taco shells. He had bricked the room with supplies. He was making his stand there, in the drive-through.

"How long have you been in there?" I asked.

"Wil," Grayson said.

"Get out," the man repeated. "And drop what you took."

"We didn't take anything, sir," Dance said.

The man nodded his head at Jamey. "Drop that."

"The mask? Are you serious?" Jamey tore it off with one hand. Her face underneath looked red and sweaty. Starla was whimpering a little.

"Careful," the man said. "Slow now."

Jamey dropped the mask on the ground and kicked it across the floor to the man. He was behind the counter, but that shotgun—if it was loaded—could blow a hole through anything.

"Take it," Jamey said. "I was gonna pay for it."

What good was the gun in my pocket? What good was I?

"Do you have any fuel?" I asked the man.

Now it was Dance's turn to hiss, "Wil!"

But the man looked at me. His eyes held the wild, swollen redness of exhaustion. They were runny, his face shiny. "No," he said. "They cleaned me out. They robbed me."

"Who did?" I asked.

"A lot of people. Before I wised up. They unlocked the pumps. They brought a tanker."

Dance's eyes widened.

"How are you staying warm?" I said.

"Warm? What the hell is warm? Who knows that anymore? Now get the fuck out."

He was holing himself up in the drive-through alone. He would die in there.

We began to back up. All of us held our hands up, except for Jamey, who held Starla.

"Dog," Starla said. "Doggy. Want doggy." She was looking at the rubber mask, puddled on the floor.

"Wait," the man said. "Wait one fucking minute." He reached one hand back into the drive-through. The other hand held the shotgun steady on us.

What would he pull out, what would he want from us, what would he take?

He pulled out a can of sweetened condensed milk. Still clutching the gun, he stretched over the counter, and rolled it across the floor. "For the baby."

We couldn't drive the speed limit. Asphalt, gravel—it made no difference. The roads could not be saved. They had turned white, a crumbling, chemical white, as if they had had a shock. The last stab at ice control, at melting the winter that would not be melted, had stained them.

It got over everything, salt and whatever it was: the brine on the roads. I had streaks of it on my coveralls. It sharpened the ends of my hair. When I touched my face I tasted it. The truck was encased like a salt-bake. Starla looked like a beach baby, her hair knotted, her clothes hemmed with grit, as if she had rolled in it. Salt got into all our food, bitter on our tongues.

Where towns had stopped plowing, other trucks and cars would stamp down the snow, making a wild trail, dangerous as glass. And some of the rural roads had seen no travelers for days. We crept through them, an ice-breaker making our way. When we stopped, we had to knock the snow in chunks from the undercarriage of the truck and trailer.

Once we saw a stopped station wagon. At the last moment, right before we passed the car, a woman with long brown hair stepped out from behind the front bumper, her arms raised and open as if expecting a package.

Dance swerved to avoid hitting her. We didn't slow. We didn't go back to see what she wanted. We didn't talk about it, as we didn't talk about the man in the Taco Bell.

I thought the woman may have wanted what the man with the sheepskin and skeleton tattoo had wanted: to die, to take us along. To not be alone in death. I remembered hearing that freezing to death was like burning. You felt warm; you wanted to throw off your clothes. You wanted to bury yourself in the snow. You suddenly felt good in the cold—and that was a very bad sign.

We saw hitchhikers, mostly men with the beards and tattered clothes that showed they had been on the road for some time, packs bulging from their shoulders. They leaned against guardrails. The duct tape patching their coats shone. Their boots were split. Their faces began to blur, and I stopped even noticing whether or not they held out a thumb.

"We ain't stopping for no man," Jamey said.

Nobody argued with her.

The first time we saw a town on fire, it was around sunset. The horizon was a smeared pink line, and above the pink rested darkness. A gray cloud, which just sat there like a front, widening as we came closer. I waited for the scattershot of snow or sleet as we drove on through.

But it wasn't snow that waited in that sky. It was a great cloud of smoke, as wide as a storm. The town ahead was burning.

I could see smoke poured from the highest windows: a church. Flames bloomed below a steeple, which would surely fall. The smoke traveled diagonally up from the fires—five, seven, maybe more structures burning in the town: gray above and red below. Why were such terrible things so beautiful? The fires made color in our winter world.

Dance hit the recirculate button on the dashboard, which didn't even work, and Grayson, who was driving, made a turn off the road, avoiding the town. The others pressed their faces against the windows and craned their necks to see the fires, but I didn't.

After the first fire, we began noticing the aftermath of others. Houses crisped to the ground. Trailer bones still smoking. The abandoned cars piled up, another church van. Once the wrecks were snow-covered, they seemed like they could be anything: a burial mound, the entrance to an ice cave. We passed deserted semis tilting in ditches, their trailers torn open, loads long gone. Already the trucks looked strange to me: too big, part of an ancient, earlier world, a world we no longer knew. There was never anything on the radio.

We passed houses that were little more than foundations, a twisted arm of metal or a stovepipe sticking out of the rubble like a surrender flag.

Up ahead was a charred farmhouse where only the chimney remained, a column of bricks blotched with black: a monument to the struggle of the people who had lived there, maybe died there. Maybe they had just moved on. Jamey said, "Every winter somebody goes and blows their house up trying to get a propane heater or a kerosene lamp to work."

But this wasn't every winter.

"I don't know why we went back for that fucking grow light," Dance said. "There's no power anymore. There's no way to plug it in."

We had not been speaking much, Dance and I, since we ran away from the man with the sheepskin, since we had left those people there. His anger hung over me. I could sometimes sense it, sometimes not—but I knew it was there. Smoke from a distant fire.

I knew, from living with Lobo, not to meet Dance's eyes, not to draw the burning arrow of his anger. I looked out the window when I said: "There *will* be power somewhere. We'll use the light there."

"Sure. In that magical place."

He blamed me, but for what exactly? For leaving those people to die, though they wanted to. For the lost food and supplies—though he was the one who had fallen asleep; he was the one who had not wanted to wake me for watch. Was his anger really blaming himself? Or was he mad at me for bringing Jamey and Starla, but no others. For abandoning Ohio.

"California will have power," I said.

"The coldest night of winter," Jamey said. "That's when it happens." She, too, had lived with an angry man. She knew to soothe him, distract. "That's when the house burns down, every time."

Grayson was driving by the burned farm. Some of the trees around the house had survived, older trees with wide trunks and sheltering branches. I saw an old brick barn and a chicken coop. It was a quiet place, protected by the trees.

"Let stop here for the night," I said. "There's nobody around. We can rest. Scope out what's left of the farm, see if there's anything we can use."

"So we steal now?" Dance said.

"I guess we do," I said to the window.

But the barn was empty, even of hay. The people who had lived on the farm must have burned the hay to try to stay warm; maybe that had caused the fire. What they had left behind was junk, broken tools. Everything smelled of mice and pigeons, and that which was not iced over was coated in a thick layer of gray. Dust and ash. I could taste it on the back of my throat.

I worked in the barn alone, examining the metal parts and trying to think how they might be useful. The others set up camp and started dinner. Soon a shadow fell over me from the open door. Dance stood in the wide barn doorway, switching a flashlight on and off to get my attention. He held the flashlight high like the sheriff. Then he handed it to me.

"Thanks." I turned away from him, but he didn't move. "Are you staying?"

"No. I mean, I'll stay to help you clean out the barn if you want. I'll stay tonight."

I turned back, throwing the flashlight into his eyes. "Sorry." I lowered it. Dance came into focus, thin and purple. "You'll stay tonight?" I said. "What does that mean?"

"I'm not moving on with the group, I decided. I think I should go."

I thought of our long silences, our run up the hill with the duffel bag. Why had I saved a grow light, risked our lives for it? Risked his life?

"When did you decide that?" I asked.

"I don't know," he said. "I just don't I think belong here right now."

"Is this about those people in white?"

"No, it's not about…Snowflake Charles Manson."

"You think we should have tried to save them?"

"No. I think some people are beyond saving." The words sounded so final and true they surprised us both, as hard as the metal parts in my hands. Dance said, "I think we have to try to save ourselves. I want to go out on my own. If the world's different, I want to do something different. I don't think I want to go to California."

"Where do you want to go?"

"I don't know. Maybe look for my mama? My daddy has other kin. Maybe go look for them. It doesn't seem like we're going to get back to Ohio."

"No," I said. "It doesn't."

"Not unless the snow melts."

The roads going down the mountains were treacherous now. What would they be like in a few more snowy months, going up?

I thought of the locked gate that led to the farm. I

thought of the lower field, the poverty grass waving in the wind, in the kind of warm breeze I was starting to forget, heat so heavy it was almost visible, pressing down on my shoulders, waving up from the road, a greasy ghost.

I remembered the thaw, when the creeks would rise. I remembered mud season. I remembered a moment from years ago: spring drips racing off the farmhouse roof. I sat in the kitchen, my phone on the table beside me, and I saw on my phone screen the reflection of the sky from the window, the sun blazing, and the drips, the ice drips, as bright and fast as gold. I couldn't stop watching them. I remember a plane zipped across the sky. I saw its contrail through the window, but I couldn't see that on the phone screen. It was too faint— just the liquid gold pouring as the icicles on the roof dissolved.

I had been waiting for Lisbeth to call. Lobo had come in and yelled at me for wasting work time, zoning out.

It was when I had first got my phone, when we would fall asleep talking, the speaker at my ear. In the loft, there was enough reception; a phone would work. It made me not afraid to be out there, alone, listening until she was only breath. It made me wonder what it might be like to have that in real life, a presence there, breathing beside me, a hard shoulder, warm skin, the beating heart next to me of someone who loved me.

I didn't even know for sure where my phone was now. This thing once so important, so essential, a part of my hand—it had run out of charge. It had picked up nothing for a long time, no service, no signals, and drained itself dead trying.

In the barn, there was an old jelly jar on a musty shelf. I picked up the jar and rattled it, unscrewed the top, and peered in. Corn. A few knocking, dry kernels. I put the corn in my seed pouch.

Dance kicked his boot in the dirt. "You don't need me, Wil," he said. "You've got Grayson."

"Grayson is injured."

"And Jamey."

"Jamey is literally a teenage girl."

"You don't need anyone. You really don't."

He was right. I knew it. But a few feet away from us, Grayson and Jamey were working at keeping everything lit and warm in the tiny house. They were playing at being parents, and had no idea one of us was leaving. The group was breaking up. All groups did, I thought. No family lasted.

"Are you really going out there alone?" I asked. It didn't seem right, to let him just go off.

But then he got excited. "Check this out. Look what I found." He reached for something against the outside wall of the barn, rolling it into the light. A bicycle: ancient, strung with dust and cobwebs. "It was in the chicken coop."

"Sure. That's where I'd keep my bike."

"I bet we can get this rolling again."

"But in the cold, Dance? Are you going to ride up those roads in the snow?"

He looked at the bike, not at me. "I guess I'm going to have to figure it out."

We spent the night at the burned farm. We would have slept well, protected by the chimney and the broken-down barn. They, along with the chicken coop and trees, formed turret walls around us in the tiny house. It did not feel dangerous. It felt sad. In a different time, this might have been a good place to settle. As Jamey said, the bad thing—the fire—had already happened here.

But Dance's looming departure kept me awake. It felt like we were doing something wrong, to lose someone willingly. Grayson and Jamey had taken it well, barely arguing or attempting to persuade him to stay. Were we that broken down that a person's absence didn't faze us? Were we that used to losing things?

In the morning, Jamey made a breakfast of oatmeal and dried fruit, while Grayson watched Starla, showing her the bike. Dance and I stood alone by the truck. He checked and rechecked the straps on his pack. We'd given him what food we could spare—we had lost much of it when we had been robbed—and Dance could only pack what he could carry on his back. No heavy canned goods. Some of the deer meat and powdered milk.

I pulled the gun out. I extended it to Dance, handle first.

Lobo's anger radiated from the gun. It smelled like a grave. I wondered if the gun would always hold the memory of how long it had been buried and why. Maybe that was why I thought I could get rid of it.

"No way," Dance said.

"You're on a bike. You need protection."

"I have a knife."

"We all have knives."

"You should keep the gun. It's all about appearances, right? Hopefully you won't ever have to use it. But a gun's not like a knife. Just the sight of a gun might scare some-body off. A knife, when you use it, you have to get close."

"I know that," I said.

But he kept on talking. "If you pull out a knife in a fight, everybody gets cut, including you. You're going to get hurt, too."

We watched him go. We let him get a start on us. Then we packed up and drove. Too soon we passed him on the snow-freckled road, waving to him out of the open win-dows. Wind rushed into the cab, and we hurried to roll the windows back up, shivering in relief.

I watched through the rearview as long as I could for Dance: a slender figure, a tear in the gray air. A scavenger, gone off to find something to use, something to unearth again.

We were never going to get out of Appalachia.

I felt it in my bones as we slogged over the hills. Roads that should have taken minutes took hours. Starla fussed. We had to stop, then stop again. It seemed like there was always going to be, just around the next hill or the next, a gas station that was open, neon lights shining over the parking lot. A super-market selling fuel, selling *anything*—chips stale in their bright bags, crumbled old chocolate. Even an enterprising stranger by the side of the road, sitting in a lawn chair, wrapped in fur, with gas cans and a cardboard sign: *$100 bucks a gallon*.

We could pay it. We still had cash. What use was cash? There was nothing to buy.

I missed strangers. Just the ordinariness of seeing a face I didn't know. All the faces I saw now were familiar, dirty, and becoming harder. Jamey's cheeks had lost their baby fat. I know I was imagining things but I felt Starla's had, as well, that she was shedding some of the glow she had, her hair dulling to a color like dust. I had never seen a child so quiet, so compliant.

Maybe, even worse than always being on guard like me, like Jamey, Starla *never* would be. She had not learned to flinch and to listen, to trust her gut, to be alert, to brace a door. She went with Jake. She went with Mica, with Grayson, or with me. Grateful for any arms, even a stranger's, able to sleep in any of them. I worried about what that meant.

The light dipped behind a brown mountain and Grayson rolled the truck to a stop. "Any farther and we're out of gas," he said.

There was no other car on the road. There had not been one for miles. Woods alongside of us, woods behind. Mountains before us, craggy and spiked with more trees.

"How far are we to the Tennessee border?" I said.

"I don't know anymore. We've taken so many detours. Maybe we're close."

"We've been driving forever," Jamey said.

"What—" I tapped my finger on the windshield "—is that?"

Orange flared in the trees along the left side of the road, a wink in the drab landscape. It flickered, bright, then dim, then bright again. A lantern? A chemical plant?

"Some other idiot got his house blowed up," she said.

"No, it's too small." I was already pulling on my gloves. "Stay here. I'll check it out."

"Wil?" Grayson said.

"Maybe they have fuel. I have the gun," I said.

I had my knife, too. I tucked the ends of my hair into my scarf and went out, sucking in the shock of air. Cold settled into the folds of my arms and legs.

It felt like it was getting worse. The snowfall the night we had been robbed hadn't ever melted. Nothing had melted, and more snow was coming all the time.

Grayson, Jamey, and Starla all crowded into the front seat of the truck and watched me, their breath steaming the glass. Grayson had left the headlights on to light my way down the road, but the orange light came to me.

Out of the trees, it came, growing and bobbing over the gravel and salt on the side of the road, to where I stood. Grayson flashed the lights. I turned and he blinded me, flicking on and off the brights, some signal I wasn't getting. I turned back around.

A boy stood in front of me.

Eight or nine? I was no good at children's ages. He carried something, and I took a step back, feeling for my pocket.

A gun. I thought he carried a gun. Like me.

But it was a toy. Oversized, with buttons and fluorescent levers that did not belong on a real gun, details that might have been meant to protect him in the world before the lost spring, but maybe would not have. It was plastic. The barrel held a burning wad of cloth. He was using the toy gun as a torch.

"It's this way," he said behind his scarf.

I looked back at the truck. Grayson had dimmed the

brights and was mouthing something to me. Jamey was shaking her head.

"Lock the doors," I said, as if they could hear me. "Be back soon."

I followed the boy.

This was my job. I thought it had always been mine, but I had only just grown into it: to follow with hands in my pockets—knife in one, gun in the other.

The boy blended into the undergrowth off the side of the road. The only hint of him was the torch, which flickered in and out. Saplings gave way to thicker trees as we veered farther away. I turned back to look at the truck, and the boy reassured me, "It's right this way."

What was? Was I wrong to trust a child?

"We need fuel," I said. "We can trade or pay for it."

"Come on, then."

Where were we going? I glanced back one time more to see the lights of the truck still blazing. They were going to run down the battery—but they needed that heat. The boy ducked under a branch, and I followed. He held brambles back for me. Walking along a dirt track, we passed a tangle of metal and rebar. An old road sign. It had been used for target practice, the letters mangled with buckshot. I tried not to feel afraid at this. It didn't mean bad men, it didn't mean Skate State.

TOWN, I read. Nothing more.

Beyond the sign, small white houses lay out in a double row, facing each other across the dirt track. They seemed like blow-up dollhouses, barely bigger than my own tiny house, each with a tin roof, small windows, and a porch.

They were occupied, each window lit by a candle or lamp. At the end of the row—I could barely make it out in the darkness—was a building much larger than the others.

I had seen this before. A coal company town. A company store. And all the little houses, planted down almost on top of each other, were homes for the coal miners' families.

I couldn't believe this company town was still standing. But of course it had been taken over. Shelters like this, with walls and roofs, wouldn't stay empty for long.

The boy with the torch, who had been so solemn in his mission to lead me here, raced off, confident he had done his job, whatever that was. He joined a group of other children playing. Then he became a kid again, in a blur of bright coats and plastic things.

The kids were tumbling in and out of a parked van. It had ice molded to the sides of it, flat tires, and a blue glow that was familiar, and also strange to see again: a TV, hooked up to a generator. It blared cartoons. Whatever they were watching, it had to be a DVD. I was pretty sure TV stations weren't on the air anymore. I saw something written on the side of the van…

Then I was surrounded by women.

"Do you need food? Do you need shelter?"

"Gas," I said. "We need gas. We can pay."

"Are you hungry? Are you in any danger?"

"Are you running from anyone?"

The women had lanterns and flashlights. It felt like being swarmed by fireflies. But one of the women spoke with a musical voice, high and light. I recognized that voice. It both blended and rose above the ones. I parted the women, trying to get a glimpse of the face in the light.

It was her. It was her. It had to be.

Why was she here? How had the boy led me to her? It felt like a year had passed, maybe longer—but it had not been even a season; there were no seasons. I thought of us lying side by side in our sleeping bags, when camping was fun, not survival, just something we did in her room or the backyard. I thought of us running deep into the woods behind her house, branches slapping us, my face stung with tears, when I told her about Lobo: losing my mama to him, his anger, the basement room. There was nothing to do after that but go home. I thought of boys vying for her attention, pulling her hair, flicking notes at her on the youth group trips while I looked down at my hands, rough from work, scratched from stems and the trimming shears. There was nothing to do.

It was her. Lisbeth.

Her face looked both older and younger at the same time. Lines marked her face, fine as telephone wire. She had dark circles; we all did. Hair straggled out of a braid under her hat. When I hugged her, I felt the sharpness of her bones.

"What are you doing here?" Lisbeth said.

"We're on the way to California. Following my mama."

"Your mama? Who's *we*?"

"What are *you* doing here?"

There were so many questions, only questions.

Lisbeth stepped back, and I saw the town clearer. Fires burned in barrels along the path, their sides corroded like lace. People had been told there was a visitor, a stranger to the camp, and they were coming out of the little houses. Many of the windows were broken, I noticed, patched with cardboard and plywood. Rags were stuffed in the holes in the house siding. Gutters had fallen down, packed with frozen moss. A few houses had trees growing through the rotten shingles. The saplings' growth was stunted now.

I saw white shapes in the shadows that might have been the other church vans. The van where the children played had not been moved in a long time.

"This is as far as we made it," Lisbeth said. "The vans started to break down. All of them. One after the other. It seemed like a sign."

"You don't believe in signs."

"Then we found this place. We're fixing it up, making it a real town again. My parents are happy." She was doing that thing when she chattered on, filling the space, when what I wanted, all I really wanted, was for her to stand there. Just to be. "A few other people have joined us. Like you."

I couldn't think of what to say. I couldn't make my mouth say it. She looked wind-burned, raw, and underfed.

"My parents!" She grabbed my arm. "You have to see my folks! They'll be so happy you made it." She wasn't looking me in the eye.

I squeezed Lisbeth's hand and dropped it. "I have to go back to the truck and get the others."

14

I don't know what I expected. That we would drive across the country together, ride through the cold dark, and arrive side by side, alive and safe, in sunny California. Grayson, healed. Starla, healthy. Jamey, happy. And me. Maybe Lisbeth.

But then came the news that The Church hadn't made it anywhere warm, hadn't made it out of Appalachia even, had just given up where they'd broken down.

Dance had said, long before he left, that one thing collapsing meant everything would. Ice froze power cables, crashed tree limbs into lines. Ice stalled water in the pipes, brought trains on the rails and trucks on the highways to a halt. Fuel couldn't get to the gas stations, food to the stores. People stopped showing up for work. I imagined paychecks stopped arriving. Banks were drained. No farmers could grow more food, except for those with greenhouses and grow lights. Generators for the power. Diesel, solar, wind.

And seeds.

I didn't show Lisbeth the pouch of seeds around my neck, or the heaviness in my pocket. I didn't tell her about the Pumpkin King. Or Dance, who was gone. She might have asked me if I had liked him, if he was handsome, what he had meant to me, which were the wrong questions.

Lisbeth and I sat out on the hood of one of the church vans. This one had been repurposed as a laundry room, and the hood thrummed with the machines inside. Who knows where The Church had found them. The coin slots had been jammed with rags, and the machines were plugged into a generator. Long extension cords snaked across the frozen paths through town. At least this meant women didn't have to wash clothes by hand here. I hoped. A pipe expelled the dirty water from the washing machine, repurposing it for something else. Everything had to be recycled, every broken thing remade. Another van had been turned into a chapel, the front seats removed for a mini pulpit. A cross hung from the rearview mirror. There wasn't enough room for the whole of The Church in there, of course, but the preacher spoke with the van door open, congregants stamping out in the cold as they stood and listened, and there was talk of maybe soldering a few of the vans together to make a larger space.

The company store was in ruins, Lisbeth said. The ceiling had fallen down, sodden with rot. Rats and other animals had made a home in there, but then they had died. The Church was fixing it up, but that would take a long time.

"I guess you're here for a long time," I said. The laundry van, the chapel van—those things weren't going to be on the road again anytime soon.

Lisbeth looked in the distance, across the old railroad tracks that bordered the town. Once coal had shuttled through here. Now the tracks were bones under the snow. I wouldn't have known they were even there if she hadn't told me; others from The Church had found them when they had first explored.

"How is this better than home?" I asked.

"It isn't. But it's where we ended up. It's what happened. We didn't know things would get so bad on the road so quickly."

"Yeah, we didn't, either."

"I like it here. I like that we're picking up where someone else left off. We're making it work. I guess we'll stay here as long as it works."

"Is it working, though?"

I thought of the railroad tracks, rusting. What else might be buried under the snow? I tried to remember the last time I had seen a train. Were there train cars stalled, abandoned down the line? Had sleet melded the wheels to the track? Was it all just waiting there, stocked with food or supplies?

I remembered what my mama had said about the year she was born, a blizzard year when schools had closed for weeks. A woman disappeared walking from her house to her barn. A semi had been buried in drifts, found days later, the driver still alive. To get me to fall asleep at night, sometimes she would retell the story: how the roads were indistinguishable from fields—all were snowfields. How her own mama's eyelashes froze. The animals began to starve. That was why the woman had disappeared, trying to get to the barn to take care of her animals. It wasn't a story for children, but I had asked for it again and again.

"I wish that you were singing," I said to Lisbeth.

She turned back to me. "I am singing. Every Sunday and Wednesday night."

"I mean, for a larger audience. For people to really hear you. I wish you had gone to a city like you said."

All that we had said, lying side by side in sleeping bags on the floor. It would be easier when we were older, we had decided. I could leave the farm, leave Lobo far behind. Grow what I chose. Lisbeth could sing on a stage wearing anything she wanted—eyeliner, a skirt that showed her knees.

"Oh, that was just talk," Lisbeth said. She waved away the memories, her breath slowing beside me in the dark. She pointed to a van beside the company store. The tires had been stripped off this one, and the interior of the van fizzed yellow and red with sparks. I heard the drone of a machine. Someone was welding, I realized. "We're working on that one. Trying to turn it into a radio station, to broadcast out. Your friend Grayson's gonna help with that."

"Grayson?" He never did get the ham radio to work.

Lisbeth seemed not to know that. "If we can get the radio station running, maybe we can reach other people. We can find out what they're doing in other parts of the country. What we should do next."

"You're really good, Lisbeth," I said. "I miss hearing you sing. I miss you."

She took my hand. She wore fingerless gloves, hand-knitted. Did she spend her time doing that? Knitting? What a waste, if she did. Her fingers felt cold as roots in the ground. "You're welcome to stay here, Wil," she said.

"Have things changed around here?"

Her hand slackened around mine. "What do you mean?"

"I mean, can you wear pants now? Can you read whatever you want?"

"That doesn't matter. In the long run, that's not important to me. It's just important that we stick together, help each other."

I didn't know which *we* she meant. "I have Jamey and Starla to look after now."

"We can make a place for everyone."

"Have you met Jamey?"

"Wil." She tilted her head and looked at me straight-on.

I was afraid to meet her eyes, afraid that they might convince me—and they couldn't convince me. I had to make sure Mama was all right. Had to find a place for Jamey and Starla. I imagined Mama welcoming them like her own grandkids.

"Wil," Lisbeth repeated. "What if this is all there is?"

The washer grunted and finished its cycle. The sun had all but disappeared, pale pink rust in a sky streaked white. It would snow tonight. It would snow every night.

The Church patrolled the railroad tracks, and the road beyond the trees: that was how they had found us. They had watch duty, food, a school in the little town. They had a Laundromat. I tried to think of what it might be like to stay here: to sleep in a house without wheels, to wake without fear, to live in a place with guards.

But possibilities were like stars. I could go anywhere. I could have a little farm of my own. I could grow things again, everything we needed. "I have to know what's out there," I said.

"What if it's nothing?"

Lisbeth left me to do her evening chores. All these new little worlds had structure, patterns. Otherwise, they would fall into chaos, like Skate State—and even Skate State had a hierarchy: Jake in charge, the men beneath him fixing the cars and guarding the property, scaring up food and supplies. The women, cooking and cleaning, taking care of the children. Doing everything else, everything he made them do. All the work women were going to have to do again.

Lisbeth said she had to feed the dogs, pets that came along and strays that had wandered into the town, drawn by the smell of food. The Church was living off the emergency supplies they had brought with them, stockpiles that would last for months, though maybe not that long if they kept taking in strangers.

Dogs had been allowed to come along with the caravan—but not my mama. I remembered the offer Lisbeth had made before The Church left was just for me. I was still young enough to be saved, she had told me once, because I was a child when I first started breaking the law. When was I going to be too old, beyond the reach of her saving book? Was I already? I wondered if she still slept with her shoes on.

Someone was coming up the path toward me in the darkness. I heard the crunch of ice and a rhythmic thud. It was Grayson, dragging his leg. He hauled himself onto the van hood beside me.

I wished we had whiskey, something to warm us, sitting outside in the cold like stupid kids. We didn't even have a fire. But as soon as we went inside, they would separate us, I knew. Boys in one house, girls in another. The thought made me nervous.

"What did the doctor say?" I asked Grayson.

"I've got to stay off it."

"Why are you walking on it, then?"

"Because you're all the way out here."

Strings of bulb lights lit the company town behind us. Barrel fires bobbed in the darkness, and extension cords wove back and forth across the ground. Somebody was singing as they did their chores. Not Lisbeth.

"I'm not much on groups," I said. "The Church still creeps me out a little."

"Well, some things never change."

"Anyway, I thought you would want to spend some time alone with your folks."

When I had arrived back at the company town with the others, his parents had come out from one of the little houses, two people who looked like Grayson, but smaller, faded. We were the ones who had been on the road, but they were the ones who looked weary. His mama had worry lines cut deep into her face. His daddy sniffed back tears when he saw Grayson, saw it was really him—and that he was limping.

His daddy said nothing more than, *Sorry, son.* But his mama couldn't stop apologizing, couldn't stop asking him what had happened, how could this have happened? I didn't know, after a while, if she meant his cast, the accident—

or something more. How could we have left our homes?
How could we have thought we could do better?

How could it still be cold?

This was what we told ourselves: nobody could have
known. Nobody could have predicted. What an unusual
time. What a ridiculous time. This was one for the record
books. When we wrote new books, we would say: summer was hot sand and burning pavement, growing food
outside in the air, warm earth breaking in our hands like
bread. We got sunburns that flushed and freckled us; we
built machines to cool us. They sent chemicals into the air.

How could we write that, explain that, to a baby like
Starla? What would she remember? Jamey had said she
was a summer birth.

Jamey and Starla had disappeared into the crowd of
women as soon as they had arrived at the town, fussed
and fawned over. I expected to find Starla, the next time
I saw her, in new clothes, her hair washed and festooned
with ribbons, her belly full of cookies. If they had cookies
here. I expected Jamey would be more crabby than usual;
the women would have pestered her about being saved,
about bringing up her baby the right way.

"You should be with your folks," I said to Grayson.
"Spend some time with them. Why did you come looking for me?"

"Well, I have to say goodbye to you."

There was a medical doctor with The Church. Grayson had friends at The Church. His folks were here. Of
course he would stay.

He should stay. I told myself the reasons. I told myself

not to be surprised, not to show outwardly the cold river of sorrow spreading through me.

"Are you sure you want to stay?" I said. "It's just…"

The men patrolled the perimeter, only the men. The women had served dinner that night: canned green beans and rolls and hamburger casserole, and the women had cleaned up after alone. They had refused Grayson's offer of help.

"They left you," I said.

"Your family left *you*."

"I didn't want to go with them then."

"Well, I didn't want to go with my family, either, at the time. But times have changed. It seems like we should be with family now. Doesn't it? Whatever that means."

I felt an ache. It wasn't like the awful thought of leaving Jamey and Starla behind in the compound; it wasn't even like watching Dance disappear off on his own. Grayson wouldn't be alone here. But I still didn't want to let him go. It didn't seem right. It seemed like, once we had found each other, we should stick together.

"Are you going to be safe?" I asked him.

"Of course."

"It seems a little cult-ish."

"It is. But you can't blame people for wanting to believe in something, especially now. And the assistant pastor's a woman," he offered hopefully.

And the pastor was a man.

Power was power, I thought.

"Do you believe this stuff?" I asked.

"Not really. So what? So I have to go to church sometimes."

"A lot. Sunday and Wednesday night. Probably more. A lot."

"I'll do it. It's temporary. Nothing is forever now. It's not a big deal. I want to get this thing off me as soon as I can." He kicked his leg and we both looked at the boot. If he did get it off, it would feel light for him. It would feel like flying. "I want to survive," he said.

I hugged Grayson. Above the layers of flannel and thermal and fleece, his coat was stuffed with balls of newspaper. We had learned to do this miles ago, insulating ourselves like old house walls. When I hugged him, it crunched.

Beneath all of this was a person I had grown to trust, to even love a little. I tried to imagine the road without his dumb jokes and hesitant driving. I didn't want to think yet if Starla would miss him. If she would ask where he was, the limping, bearded man who would sometimes carry her around on his shoulders, though it must have hurt his foot. He saved the softest lumps of meat for her. What could her life be like if she got to grow up with someone like him? I had stopped trying, years ago, to imagine a life where my daddy hadn't left when I was little, or Mama hadn't met Lobo—or Lobo was different. Just different. That was all I had dreamed.

There had been other men before him but I didn't remember much. They were flannel and beards and beer, indistinguishable from each other. I was still not sure, after all these years, why Lobo had stuck. He yelled at the sky, at the eggs burning in the skillet, at a series of dogs who ran away. He didn't plan on being a daddy, but he loved my mama and part of the way he showed that love was by putting up with me—Mama had told me that once. We always had food, though it was often deer meat, and potatoes and tomatoes he grew. We had warmth, though it was woodstove heat. There was money for school supplies and clothes and gas. Lobo provided. Was that why she had gotten stuck? Because he kept us from dying? I wanted something more.

We didn't talk about keeping in touch, Grayson and I, because how could we possibly do that? How could we manage that now? Our phones were rocks. The internet was dead. The Church might not stay in this company town if invaders came, or tragedy came, or something better came along.

"Get that radio station working," was all I could say.

He held my shoulder. "Get to California."

Before turning in for the night, I double-checked everything in the tiny house: that the windows were locked, the stove off, that no one from The Church had stolen anything. I looked in the cupboards, counted our dwindling packages of deer meat. I should have felt grateful that I still had the keys to my house and truck, that I had been allowed to park close to where we were staying. I was telling myself that when I noticed them.

The beans by the windowsill. The seeds in the jars I had watered faithfully, for a long time, for nothing.

They were sprouting.

I ran to tell Lisbeth, the first one I thought to tell. She was tucking extra blankets on the bed in the house where we were both staying. Extra blankets for me. And her smile, when she heard my news, when she turned to me, was bright with the kind of open-faced joy I hadn't seen on her—on anyone—in forever. She looked like spring.

"That's great!" she said. "God provides."

"But it was me," I said. "It was me. I grew them."

I don't know what I expected. That news of the seeds sprouting would make her change her mind, would make her want to come with me. That it was a sign—and she had started to believe in signs.

But not this sign, not the seeds bursting from their brown casings like butterflies, spreading green wings.

She turned back to the blankets.

I didn't tell Grayson about the seeds.

It was supposed to be nice to sleep in a real bed in the company town, under a real roof—Lisbeth and I had a nonleaky one. To sleep on a bunk, the mattress stuffed with hay and leaves. Guards patrolled the wild outside. The ceiling in the house stretched high enough I wouldn't hit my head if I stood, unlike in my loft. And Lisbeth lay on the mattress beside me, her back pressed against my side, like we were on one of our old sleepovers.

But when she woke in the middle of the night to find me still awake, staring at the moon through the cracked window, she didn't ask me if I had had a nightmare, what my dreams were, if I liked Grayson or not, if we had kissed. She only said, her breath sparking in the moonlight, "I'll pray for you."

I turned to see her hair fanning over her shoulder, pale as a mermaid's. Her hand reached back to hold mine. Cold hands, warm hearts.

Her hand was bonier than I remembered, sliding into my palm. She fell asleep again instantly, shivering in her nightgown under the quilts and extra blankets, her tennis shoes that wouldn't protect her. How fast, how far, could we run?

I had lost my friend a long time ago. Frost fractured the moon through the window into a million more shards.

We left after breakfast, Jamey, Starla, and I. It felt good to hear the truck start again. The sound meant freedom, survival. The truck heat, stale and sharp, had a dry smell like hay. How long would trucks have heat? I wondered. How could we slap this together with duct tape and wire?

We fueled up at the company town. They were sending us off with food we hadn't asked for and extra canisters of gas. I wanted to refuse it, but we hadn't found any place to buy or borrow since we had been robbed by the people in white, and the faces of the women pressing canned goods into my hands were so hopeful, so sure of what they were doing: giving survival away. I had never felt that sure about anything.

Some of the women cried when they said goodbye to Starla, passing her into the arms of Jamey, who rolled her eyes. That made me feel a little better.

"Let's just get this over with," Jamey said.

She buckled Starla into the back. She tucked heavy blankets around her, which Starla immediately kicked off. Jamey got into the front seat, pulled the visor down and put sunglasses on, even though there was no sun. The sunglasses were heart-shaped, cracked on one lens. Everything that wasn't already broken was starting to break.

I hoped that Grayson and Lisbeth would protect each other from whatever The Church would demand of them. I hoped that I would see Grayson again; maybe he would be walking. Maybe Lisbeth would think of my hand in the dark.

They both had come out with the rest of The Church to say goodbye, lined up outside the miners' little houses as if for inspection. It might have been easy to lose Lisbeth among the other women. They all wore long denim skirts, thick woolen leggings or slouchy sweatpants tucked into boots underneath. They all kept their hair in braids down their backs. But Lisbeth was different. There was a spark in her. It radiated off her, a kind of humming light. When she was onstage, singing, I knew that everyone saw it: a golden glow, buzzing around her. But now—waiting to get into the truck, Jamey checking her hair in the passenger mirror—I felt I was the only one who could see it still.

Grayson stood with his folks. People like us left home both earlier and later than people in cities, I knew that. The pull of the holler was real, a kind of invisible mist or vine swirling around our ankles, tying them fiercely to the red ground.

But it was also practicable to stay. Where would we go? How would we live? What jobs were there? How could we afford to get them and start over in a town with no kin to float us gas money or food, or offer us a couch for sleeping, even reluctantly?

"I don't feel useful," Grayson had said to me last night. "You grow things. I'm a waiter."

"You're great with kids," I said.

"I'm just a waiter." Grayson looked around the company town. The lights in the houses were all going out. I didn't know if there was a curfew, and someone would come around and yell at us, the generators wheezing off, or if people just wanted to save their candles and kerosene. Grayson's boot thudded on the van hood. "If I stay here, I can at least help my folks."

"Don't sacrifice your life to help your family."

I was aware, as I said it, of the postcard from California in my truck. Of the reason we had left the farm. Of the farm itself. Not my idea, not my dream, just a dream I had inherited.

"What life?" Grayson said. "Back home, maybe I could've worked my way up to manager eventually, if the restaurant had stayed open. I could've squatted in a trailer on somebody's land, or in a house with a bunch of other folks until we got kicked out for being late on the rent or noise or some other crap. It's not like I could ever own my own house. It's not like I could have a great job."

With the lights off, the town was turning silver, crested over with snow. It was too cold to sit outside, but still we sat, watching the shadows around the houses. There was a sliver of moon, as thin as a razor. It slid in and out of the clouds.

"Maybe this weather is a great big equalizer," Grayson said. "Everybody has to start fresh."

I thought of Mica in the forest. "Some people are starting out with more."

Grayson slid off the hood. The newspaper in his coat made his arms rustle. "Damn, Wil. If anyone knows how to do more with less, it's us."

As we readied to leave, I knew Grayson was there, but if I didn't look closely, he blended into the congregation, bundled in his warm things. It was like when The Church had left, when I couldn't find Lisbeth in the vans. I was losing her again. I was losing two people.

I got into the truck.

Was this what a wedding was like—everybody standing there, watching, waiting for you to do the thing you already knew in your heart was wrong? When my mama married my daddy, leaving was already in him, like searching was in her. There was something in the blood, some kind of pull. I couldn't change my mind now and stay, or insist Grayson and Lisbeth come with us. It was too late. People were lined up on either side of the truck, getting impatient and cold. Jamey was making faces in the mirror. Starla needed to nap.

I made my body move, close the door. I had done this before, willed my body into action: in the truck with the boys from the bar, in my loft. Mindlessly, rotely, I belted myself in. I put the truck into gear. I drove. Just drove.

Straight ahead, slowly. I didn't look back.

"Let's get out of town," Jamey said. "Get on a highway already."

The engine was comforting, its rattling purr. I heard the

rustle of Jamey settling into her seat, a sigh from Starla in the back. Then we were out of sight of the little houses. The trees were a tangle that hid the access road to the town. The Church didn't need camouflage to hide their camp. Maybe it would all be fine. I tried not to imagine everything burning.

I saw a blur in the rearview and felt my heart jag. Grayson or Lisbeth, come to call us back?

No.

It was a little girl. She was dressed as a rabbit in a fuzzy, full-body suit. A Halloween costume. Either The Church had run out of warm winter things, or she had persuaded her minders to let her wear it. It had long ears that wouldn't stay up, a hole for her face.

I kept driving, but slowly, in case she darted forward. She followed behind us until our tires hit the main road, then she stopped. Some invisible line halted her, some mental fence. Someone had yelled at her or hurt her for going farther. She believed them; she was afraid of them. She looked like a magical creature, guarding the town.

I didn't want to speed up until I saw her turn around, until I saw her at least start for home. The truck idled.

"What?" Jamey said. "Did you forget something? Why aren't we going?"

The little girl just stood there. She didn't turn around. She just watched us. I looked back at Starla, but she was asleep.

We got used to things. After our first night alone as a trio, the days developed a rhythm, as they had back on the farm. We drove, stopping often because Starla needed to run around and stretch her legs, and because the sight of too many cars now made me nervous. A few cars were okay, but a caravan with tires roped to bike racks, gas cans strapped to roofs, scorch marks or spray paint—meant people organizing, traveling together: groups with an agenda. And a leader. Groups meant trouble. A leader meant power. People together could not be trusted. Our house would draw attention, attract too many questions.

Parts of the roads we traveled had crumbled. Some were closed, gated or chained. Sometimes people had driven around or through, anyway, splintering the gates onto the ground. At nearly every gas station, we stopped. Most of them had closed signs, but we tried, anyway. We filled the fuel cans when we could. We collected kindling. We collected tins of little sausages and noodles in red sauce and we ate them cold as we drove, passing the cans back and forth across the front seat, like other girls might pass a joint, and I dissuaded Jamey from giving too many packages of candy or cakes to Starla.

Everything was stale.

In the afternoons, we found a place to stop for the night, somewhere sheltered, capable of hiding the house. We used the painted boughs from the Occupied Forest. We had our jobs that we had decided on. Jamey fed Starla and started the fire. I cooked, aware that I was not as good as Grayson, and was painfully reminded of him every time I stabbed at a hunk of frozen deer meat with a spoon, or tried to do something with a potato.

"This is some of the last meat," I said to Jamey as I

handed her a plate of it, warmed with nubby brown potatoes, which we were also running low on.

"Good," Jamey said. "I'm sick of deer meat."

"You and Starla need protein."

She looked up from her plate. "Don't do that."

"Do what?"

"That mama thing. Saving the meat for us? Giving us the biggest piece?"

"You're younger than me."

"So? That doesn't mean you have to die for us. I didn't ask you to." She fed Starla a potato off her fork.

The trees shone silver with frost, like they had been shellacked, like the snow globes Mama and I made one winter for presents: saving food jars, gluing trees from model train sets onto the lids, and screwing them on upside down. Glitter snowed on the miniature world, and it was pretty, safe, to look at the fake cold, contained behind glass. I had given one to Lisbeth, and she had saved it on her windowsill for years. She was thoughtful like that, careful. I wondered if she had packed it. I hadn't seen it in her room in the company town.

Jamey and I had parked for the night at a county fairgrounds, up on a hill by the horse barn. The barn was large enough to hide us, even the house, but we could see anyone approaching from below. The animals were long gone, of course, and the buildings probably cleared of anything useful. Snow layered the roof of the barn like old paint. The gutters held sprays of ice and frozen spouts.

I took the first watch; I took most of the watches.

When Jamey came to relieve me a little after midnight, I

had found the demolition derby track and was sitting in the stands overlooking the snowy dirt circle. A car rusted in the center of the circle—what was left of a car: a banged-up shell that reminded me of Skate State. I tried to imagine the stands around me filled with a cheering crowd, drinking beer and eating popcorn and flushed with the warmth of summer. Where had all those people gone? How many had made it?

Jamey plopped down onto the bench beside me. "This place is huge. I looked fucking everywhere for you." She scanned the bleachers. A banner, half-ripped or rotting off the grandstand, read: PEP... "Anything useful here?"

"Nothing works," I said.

She pulled something from her pocket. It was a small pepper, a jalapeño, dried to a husk. "I found it in the barn," she said. "It's still got seeds." She shook the tiny pepper, and it rattled like a baby's toy. "Thought you could use them, for your collection."

"Thanks," I said.

Her breath puffed out. "Thinking about that boy?"

"What boy?"

"Exactly!" Jamey laughed, stretching her legs across the bleachers and crossing her feet at the ankles. The metal stands groaned and shifted, reminding me of high school for a minute, enduring pep rallies and assemblies with Lisbeth. Kids smoked under the stands. I could tell from the scent whether it was Lobo's weed or not.

"What's the thing you miss most about spring?" Jamey asked.

It was such a short season. It always had been: a blip that meant more work.

"I don't know," I said.

"I miss mud." She laughed again, uncrossing and kicking her heels. The bleachers gave little answering thwacks. "In the thaw, it got everywhere. It was kinda funny, you know, how everybody just gave in to it. Kinda like now, just giving in to the cold. We're all just dealing. Of course, I liked mud *before* I moved out to State. Out there, mud just meant more laundry, more shit I had to do."

I didn't ask where Jamey's home was before Skate State. There were only so many places it could be. I knew her parents had kicked her out. She had probably come from one of the villages by the river. Tar paper houses, toys on porches. More stuff in the yard than in the home. Wood smoke and weed smoke, the occasional bitter wind from one of the chemical plants or coal refineries.

She had probably been born there. Jake had probably dealt drugs to the kids at her middle school. I bet that was how she had met him, on the blacktop after school. I could picture him, leaning on a chain-link fence, blowing smoke rings to get her attention.

"What's the first thing you want to do when we get to California?" Jamey asked. She had shoved her fists in the pockets of her coat and was propped on her elbows, leaning back to look at the stars. When I didn't answer, she said, "I want to swim in the ocean."

I pushed my hands deep into my own pockets. I felt the heaviness there. "It might be too cold to swim, Jamey."

"Well, I want to see the ocean. I want Starla to see it.

She's already seen more than I ever thought I would." *Violence, hunger, depravity*, I thought, but Jamey said, "West Virginia, Virginia, Tennessee," ticking off the state names like we were on vacation.

"I want to find my mama. I want to get her free from her boyfriend."

"You and everybody else." She didn't look at me. "What do you think is gonna happen when we get out there?"

"I think I'm gonna find her and that we should strike out on our own. We can make it work—the four of us women. We have shelter, wheels, a way to keep warm. We just need to hunt and chop wood. We can do that anywhere."

"Well, not anywhere. The beach don't have trees. Well, palm trees."

"We can grow them ourselves. Mama is the fastest trimmer. We can grow vegetables for food. Sell or trade the extra. I can grow anything. Lobo taught me. And—" I paused "—I'm better at it than him."

"I know you are," she said. "Why do you think Jake kept you around? Tried to keep you all there? He didn't want your damn house. He didn't want you to dance. No offense, but there are plenty of girls to dance, better dancers than you, I bet. Jake wanted a grower."

Jake knew my secret.

At any other time, I might have been upset: my family's identity spilled open on the floor. But secrets seemed not to matter anymore. A lot seemed not to matter.

Of course he knew. How would he *not* know. We had grow lights in the back, weed ground into the seams of the truck, crushed into powder on the floor mats. I was sure I smelled of it still. I would smell of weed forever: my winter gear, my boots, my skin. It didn't matter that I hadn't smoked, that none of us had on the trip. It was *in* me.

Jake could have found out a million different ways. Our farm was so close to West Virginia, just across the river. The boy with the station wagon could have sold to Jake. A kid, a girl, could have smoked something good at Skate State, brought something to a party, something that attracted attention, something strong and sweet. Maybe she was asked where it came from. Maybe she was still there and recognized me when I pulled into the compound with a truck, two boys, and a tiny house.

Maybe Jake himself had bought from Lobo. Maybe he had been one of the men at the farmhouse who smoked at the table, who laughed at my mama. Had he seen me there?

"How did Skate State make its money?" I asked Jamey. "How did you eat?"

"Stealing, shows, and drugs. Same as everybody else," she said. "I guess that's not gonna work now."

"I guess not." I had been sitting in the cold stands for too long. I stood and my knees and back felt stiff, the bleachers groaning. The sky was too white for stars.

Jamey was still looking down at the track. "Do you know I saw a girl win once?"

"Derby night?"

"Yeah. Only we didn't know it was a girl at first. She had a helmet on. Black car, some shit sponsor like the pet store. She got pushed into a corner at the beginning, but then she reared out of it. Came out swinging, striking everybody. She got hers, pinning them into the corners, every car that ganged up on her in the beginning. By the end we were all rooting for her. And she won. They called it for her. Jake was on his feet, fists pumping like crazy. Then she crawled out of the window and threw her helmet down. She had pigtails, little purple bows. She was a *girl*. Jake was so mad." She shook her head. "Her name was Starla. I just thought that was a real pretty name."

"I should go back to the house. You okay to keep watch for an hour or two? I should get some sleep, check on Starla."

Jamey didn't look at me. "Starla's fine."

15

It always felt right to leave in the morning, like we were headed off to something good. There was always the chance that we'd find an open gas station. Maybe they'd have a carton of ice cream, frosted over and forgotten in the back of the freezer. Maybe we'd run across a flock of fat turkeys. Maybe we'd hit a stretch of clean, straight road.

In the morning, nothing had turned desperate yet. The frost sparkled, looking like a bright pretty thing, not like a killer. Maybe today the sun would break through. You never knew. Maybe this day would finally be warmer than the last.

We brushed the snow off the truck with our gloves and a straw broom, and we put away the boughs we had used for hiding, kicked snow into our cooking fire. Jamey took the first turn at the wheel. I was grateful that we had been teaching her to drive before Dance and Grayson left; I wouldn't have had the patience to do it myself. She bumped down the fairground path and lurched onto the main road without looking. I glanced in the back seat, but Starla, full of milk, slept on.

"I did some looking but I didn't find any food at the fairgrounds," Jamey said. "Other than that old pepper."

"I wouldn't think that you would."

"But I did find…" She turned from the wheel to look at me, her eyes flashing like a gremlin, and I had to restrain myself from redirecting her attention to the road. "A bag of powdered sugar! I broke into the funnel cake shack, and there was a big bag of powdered sugar just sitting there."

"You broke into the—"

"Unopened. Nobody had touched it. No bugs or anything."

"The bugs are all dead, Jamey. And that's all Starla needs, a big bag of sugar."

"You say that now. But one of these cold nights, you gonna be glad I took it."

"Did you at least pay for it?"

"Money doesn't matter anymore."

I wondered if that was true.

"French fries," Jamey said, thinking aloud. She slapped the wheel. "I wish I had found some of those. I loved funnel cake, but I really loved French fries, didn't you? The best part of the fair. Second best, after derby night. A big cup of thin, greasy fair fries. Eat 'em as you walked around."

I remembered. It seemed like a funny thing to have to remember: cheap junk food that you could have found anywhere once. "You had to eat fast because the vinegar made them all soggy."

"Gross. No vinegar. Just salt and ketchup, baby."

Jamey talked about cotton candy and caramel corn and cigarettes. More and more of the gas stations we stopped at had been ransacked. Not just abandoned, but trashed: windows broken, locks jimmied long before us. We stepped around glass shards to enter, empty chip bags scattered about the floor. We dealt with smashed bottles and sour smells, the smell of unplugged coolers, of things left to rot. Sometimes the gas pumps would be destroyed, consoles shattered or hoses ripped off, not that that did any good, not that it would bring fuel out of the ground. It made me nervous to go inside these places, after the man at the Taco Bell, but we had to try. We had no other choice.

There was never any unspoiled milk, and fewer and fewer cigarettes. Not the brand Jamey wanted. "People steal the good stuff," she said. We would pass the cash register with its drawer hanging open, empty as a mouth, but I still left a little money, folded on the counter, to pay for the things we took, though Jamey said I was being dumb.

We saw our first dead body at a rest stop.

We had parked the truck and gotten out while Starla napped in the back, just leaving the baby for a moment in order to see if the vending machines right by the parking lot were full.

But they had been looted, of course, smashed and emptied. Jamey was picking up a few snack bags dumped on the ground and shaking them when I saw the shoe sticking out of the snowbank.

I left the little vending machine alcove to look closer. The shoe was attached to a foot, a leg, unmoving as something unnatural—or the most natural thing of all. The dead body looked like a branch, a rock, part of the wild like it had always been there. A bone going home, back to ground.

"Don't look," I said to Jamey.

But she was already at my elbow. "Is he—?"

"Yes. There's no point even in checking."

We thought the semi truck parked to the side of the rest stop, the only other vehicle we could see, must have been the man's. The dead man's. We couldn't get into the back, the lock was jammed—probably it was trashed back there, anyway, Jamey said—but she managed to break into the cab. She scavenged a thick pair of mittens, some instant coffee. A crate of oranges sat on the front passenger seat. The oranges were all greenish-white and solid, but we took them into the tiny house kitchen, anyway, in case they were only frozen and not rotten. I was thinking of what the man at the flea market had said about scurvy.

Then Jamey took the empty, wooden orange crate and shoved a blanket down inside it. "For Starla. She's supposed to have a car seat," she explained to me, as if I wouldn't have known.

We looked down at the little seat she had made. It was a good idea. There was a faded illustration on the side of the crate: leafy trees, plump glistening oranges.

"If we don't get to California, that would be okay,"

Jamey said. "I mean, if something happens, it would be okay to stop somewhere for the rest of the winter. Try again for California in the spring, maybe."

I think we both knew there wasn't going to be a spring. I think we both knew that if we stopped, we were going to stay.

"The first good place?" I asked.

"The first good place," Jamey said.

We fought after I took over driving.

We had gone through a train tunnel. The tracks had rusted and been torn up years ago, long before the first lost spring. But the old brick tunnel remained. It might be here forever, I thought, through a hundred winters, bearing the snow on its humped back. At the top of the entrance was a little keystone, with a date I drove under too fast to read. There were things in the tunnel, junk in the shadows lining both sides, between the walls and the road. I saw an old van parked along my side. Other objects flashed out of the dimness: what looked like chicken wire, trash.

Jamey said she saw a big cord of firewood. She thought we should go back for it.

"It's somebody's wood, Jamey," I said.

"I didn't see anybody in that tunnel. Did you?"

"Well, they're obviously storing it there."

"What if they don't need the wood?"

"How could they not need it?" I said. "It's freezing."

"Maybe they died."

I ignored her.

"What if we take it and leave money for it?"

"I thought you said money didn't have value?" I didn't want to start taking if we didn't have to. She had stolen the sugar. We had stolen—though paid for—gas and snacks. We were going to have to start taking a lot more. We were out of deer and potatoes. "We're completely capable of chopping our own wood," I said. "What if somebody's sick and they can't?"

We were through the tunnel. Wooded hills rose up on either side of the road, and through the branches I thought I glimpsed something winking in the dull sun. A sparkle, like light on glass. I thought I could see a little house.

"Jamey," I said. "Can you see what's on that hill?"

"You're changing the subject."

"I can't look because I'm driving. Is there a greenhouse up there?"

"Looks like it," she said.

Was it possible all its windows weren't broken?

"Looks like a camp on the hill. Another group." She fell silent for a moment, then she said: "It looks nice, Wil. Real nice."

I didn't say anything.

"Like a good place."

I shot a look at her. Her head was firmly turned away from me, staring through the glass.

"You can't tell that from here," I said.

"Well, I don't hear screaming. Or gunshots. That's a good sign."

"Jamey, it's too soon to stop." I wasn't ready to give up, not yet.

"But what if this is the *last* good place?"

"The truck is driving fine," I said. "We have those oranges now. And we still have food from The Church. Canned spaghetti, meat. I saw some peaches in there. In syrup."

I realized Jamey had stopped arguing. I glanced in the rearview, but Starla slept on. "What's wrong?" I looked at the side mirror.

"Po po," Jamey said.

And when I still didn't get it.

"It's the sheriff, Wil."

I snapped my attention back to the road. We had returned to the highway well before the tunnel. The back roads were too bad, and hardly anybody was driving even on the main routes anymore.

But here were flashing lights. So strange in the white air, in the drab loneliness of the landscape. Here was the law, waiting in a dip of the road, in the middle of the path before us, blocking our way.

It was a sedan—older, dented, but what car wasn't dented anymore—startling in its gray paint, its red sheriff star. The lights on top still worked. They swept bright across the colorless road, blue and red over the snow.

The law. What were they doing, why had they stopped us? And where had they been all this time, through all these broken windows and burned houses and looted gas stations? And a dead man? I slowed down.

I felt ordinary fear, fear from before the lost spring. It took me a moment to recognize what it was, to remember it. Such a jolt. It took me back. Flashing lights meant trouble. Meant stop. Meant don't get caught, don't give anything away, don't say your real name.

Sarah. You're Sarah.

Maybe they'll take your stepdaddy.

A man stood outside the sheriff's car. He held a rifle behind his head like a lamb. That didn't seem right. Then he set the rifle to the side, leaning it against the car, to throw something onto the road. It unrolled before us—a magician's trick—becoming a carpet, silver and barbed.

A spike strip, glinting in the snow.

I slid the truck into Park. We weren't going anywhere. At least not forward. One move and I would shred the tires. The man picked up the gun again.

"What the hell?" I asked.

"That ain't no cop," Jamey said.

The man with the rifle began to walk toward us. I kept my hands clearly visible on the wheel. I had the heaviness in my pocket.

Jamey was staring through the windshield. "That's Jake's man. He's got somebody in the car with him." Her voice had turned to ice water. I felt it flood through my own body. "It's him. I can see him. It's Jake in the car."

"What is his obsession with you?" I said. "To track us this far?"

"It ain't me," Jamey said. She turned to look at me. Her eyes held a familiar panic. I had seen it before, in my mama's eyes. My mama telling me to hide, he's coming. Telling me to be quiet, be still, be good. He's coming.

"It's Starla," Jamey said. "She's Jake's daughter."

I didn't have time to be surprised, to ask any questions,

to ask anything of Jamey at all. "Jamey, there's a knife in the glove box," I said. "Another under Starla's seat."

"I got my knife," Jamey said quietly.

The man knocked on the driver's side window. I looked at Jamey, at Starla sleeping, then rolled it down.

"I'm gonna need you to step out of the truck, miss," the man said.

I decided to pretend a little longer. "I'm gonna need to see your badge."

"Out of the truck. Now!"

The man wrenched the door open. I grabbed for the handle, trying to close it, but he yanked hard, like he was tearing off a chicken leg. He forced me out of the truck and onto the ground. I hit pavement, but snow cushioned me, clung to me. I pulled myself up by the door and closed it, prayed that Jamey would lock it. My heart was hammering too loudly to hear.

The man leaned close to me and spat on the ground. "We want the girl."

"She doesn't belong to you."

"Like hell she doesn't."

"She's fifteen!"

The door of the sheriff's car popped open.

It was him. I knew it would be him, but he was different. Jamey had done something to him. She had hurt him.

He moved strangely, with a slow drag that reminded me of Grayson, though it made me sick to think it. But like Grayson, Jake had a hurt leg. He had to slide his body forward and lean on a cane to walk. Something was wrong with Jake's eye. He wore an eye patch. There was red behind it, over his forehead. Old, dried blood, or a bruise or burn stretching into his hair.

But the hurt, the injuries, didn't make him seem weaker, or slower. They made him seem scarier. Less to lose. Less alive.

"Not that girl," Jake said. His voice had changed, too. It was thicker, deep with clots. It had lost its joking, maniacal joy.

He didn't move like Grayson, I decided. He moved like a snake.

"You can keep Jamey. That bitch. I want my baby."

"You stay away from them," I said.

"And I want the grower."

Me.

He wanted me.

The man with the rifle, the man pretending to be a deputy, had not told me to put my hands up—he was not pretending very well. I stood with them at my side. The heaviness in my pocket dragged against me like a stone.

"We can't live on deer meat forever. Apparently!" Jake spat the word. "If this weather don't get fixed, we're gonna need somebody who can grow things. That's you, girl. I remember you from your daddy's. I know what you can do. *Did you know that weed was grown by a girl?* they told me. *A little bitty thing? Like magic*, they said. *Like a witch.* Well, we're gonna need a witch now. We're gonna need to grow things to eat."

I could barely believe what I was hearing. "You want me to grow...vegetables?"

"Yes. And we're gonna need weed."

"I don't have any weed."

"You can grow more."

"I don't have any clones."

"I do!" He slunk closer to me, his body wobbling with the effort. "But those idiots I got for help can't make them grow. They got rot, they got bugs, I don't know. I got idiots, that's the problem. What I need..." He tilted his head. The eye patch was like a well, a bottomless empty well—there was nothing in there, but I couldn't look away from it. "Is *you*. I need a grower, and I need my baby girl. And then everything—" he wobbled on the cane "—will be right as rain back at Skate State. Don't you want that? Order returned to the universe?"

I had left the key in the ignition. I prayed that Jamey saw it. I prayed that she started the truck, reversed it, left me, and got her and Starla the hell out of here. I wished she could read my mind. I thought of Lisbeth, holding my hand in the dark: all the things I tried to transmit to her, the love I tried to make her understand.

"Look at you!" Jake said. "You're a grower. You're more talented than any girl I ever had! You have the ability to bring happiness to this hellhole of a world we apparently got stuck with."

"How did you find us?" I asked.

"Bitch, you're dragging a house. You don't exactly blend."

"Let Jamey and Starla go," I said, "and I'll go with you. I'll grow for you. Whatever you want."

Jake shook his head. "I need my baby with me."

"That's never gonna happen. You raped her mother."

Jamey turned the key. The truck engine started with a roar behind me, and we all turned. The man with the rifle yanked on the handle of the door, but she had locked it.

I shouted at her, "Go! Get out of here!"

Her face through the dashboard looked small and bleached, too little. How could she go, how could she get away, how could she do this? We had just taught her to drive. She didn't even know how to turn around. She put the truck into Reverse and I heard a high squeal.

She was going to burn rubber all the way back to West Virginia.

Jake started forward, but I stopped him. I felt very slow and calm. I felt it was not me who removed her hand from her pocket, who showed him the gun, who pointed it straight at his head, at his missing eye. It was a perfect black bull's-eye, meant for a bullet, though I didn't have a bullet. I had the gun: heavy, so heavy. It seemed to pulse with energy, potential, and heat. And death.

I willed my hand to be straight. "I have a gun," I said.

"Cute," he said. "So do I."

It was already in his hand. How had it gotten there, a dark extension, fitting better in his palm than mine ever could. And then it was popping. I heard firecrackers, popcorn. I heard the sound of breaking glass, then a splintering. I turned to see the truck keep going, backing up. The house started to tilt. Then it hit a tree.

Crashing as the windows of the house broke. The back porch shattered against the trunk. The truck engine was still on, tires spinning. I didn't see Jamey behind the wheel anymore. There was a spiderweb of broken glass on the windshield, a bullet hole as its eye.

I ran to the truck. I forgot that Jake had a gun, forgot the man with the rifle. I forgot everything except the back door. I had to reach the back door of the truck.

I yanked it open. Starla was screaming. I tried to get her out, then realized my hand wasn't working; it was too heavy. I had a gun in it.

I shoved the gun back in my pocket. I unclicked the seat belt from around the orange crate, smashed now, grabbed the whole bundle of blankets and baby, and pushed them to my chest. There was a backpack on the floor. I couldn't remember what was in it. I pushed the straps over my shoulder with the hand that wasn't holding Starla. I couldn't reach anything else. There was no time to think, to look for what we might need, no way to carry everything. The money, the food, the grow light.

"Jamey?" I said.

She was slumped over in the front seat, hair hiding her face. There was blood on the hole in the windshield. Blood in Jamey's hair.

"Jamey?" I shook her. Blood came away in my hand. Jamey didn't budge, didn't respond. Her body moved only because I moved it. "Jamey!"

The man with the rifle had reached the truck. He clawed through the door, coming for me. His hand clamped onto my ankle and I let Jamey go, kicking at the man. My boot sent him sprawling against the open door, but he lunged with his other hand. He was stronger than me. I would have to run.

Lobo had taught me: if they were bigger than me I could not be stronger, I could only be faster. I scrambled across the back seat, over the splintered orange crate. Starla's hands gripped my neck as hard as iron. I didn't need to hold her; she wasn't letting go. I pushed open the other door and shot out of the truck.

Then I was running across the road and into the trees. I leaped over a ditch, running up a hill. The baby and the backpack weighed nothing. I felt nothing. I tore up the hill, then crawled, yanking on saplings, pushing off of leafless trees. I ran and ran. Up the hill, down another one. Branches lashed past me. The forest floor, leaden with snow, weighed me down. I nearly tripped over a hulk of rust.

It was an old washing machine, thrown out in the woods years ago, grown over with vines, rattling now and dead. I got my balance, hauled us around it. Starla pushed her face so hard into my neck it hurt. I don't know how long we ran through the forest, long past when I realized no one was following us.

Jake and the man weren't coming.

Only then did I feel the pain: pain from falling, pain from being pulled out of the truck and onto the ground, pain from carrying Starla. Pain in my legs, pain in my back. Shadows were doing things to me, skittering like lizards over the leaves.

I saw a shape perched on the next hill and thought it was another piece of junk abandoned in the woods. But when I came closer, moving numbly, on automatic now, my body slowed by pain and the baby, I saw it was much larger than a washing machine. It was a tarp, half-covering a frame.

A house-shaped frame.

The greenhouse we had seen from the road.

It was real. It was solid. None of the panes of glass that I could see looked broken. Snow had been cleared around the greenhouse, making a path to its little door.

I looked around but didn't see anyone. No footprints marred the snow except my own—but new snow had recently fallen. New snow was always falling; it could have covered up any tracks. Starla whimpered in my arms.

I whispered, "Starla, somebody's growing something."

She lifted her head a tiny bit. Legs trembling with fatigue, I approached the greenhouse and pushed at the tarp. I fell at the little door and it sighed open. The heavy, wet air that greeted us seemed like an embrace.

Home. I had almost forgotten what it was like.

I stepped into the greenhouse, Starla clutching my neck. Inside the glass walls, it felt like another season, one I thought I might never see again, never smell the air like this: earthy, mineral. I was too hot in my coveralls and hat. It felt like spring, like summer. I remembered. I remembered everything.

I saw tables lined with soil-packed flats, little green dots that were seedlings. Maybe carrots? Green shoots packed closer together might be radishes. I saw clay pots, trowels, a coiled hose, a bag of fertilizer. There was a worn, striped recliner in the corner of the greenhouse, a crank radio tied to a beam with twine. A kerosene heater blasted, casting out waves of heat. Its coils glowed red.

Above the rich, peaty scent of the greenhouse, I thought
I smelled wood smoke. I peeked my head back out of the
door—against my neck, Starla whimpered, to be thrust
into the cold, into the world again—parted the tarp, and
glanced up beyond the greenhouse.

Smoke from cooking fires drifted down the hill. The
wind carried the scent along with the murmur of speech.
Lower, deeper voices. There were men on the top of the
next rise. Another camp.

This must have been the camp Jamey had spotted from
the truck. This must have been their greenhouse, their
seeds. At least they knew to start vegetables. I listened, but
did not hear shouting. No guns. No crying.

I listened for a long time.

Finally, convinced they were not Jake's men, they were
not coming for us, I ducked back into the greenhouse,
closing the door. The tarp settled down around the house.
The warm air enveloped us.

All at once, I felt sleepy. We could bed down for the
night in the greenhouse, move on very early in the morning. The camp on the top of the hill, whoever they were,
would never even have to know we had been here. It was
nearly dusk, and I doubted anyone from the group would
check on their plants in the dark. We could leave at dawn.
I didn't have to sleep.

I doubted I would be able to for a long time.

I put Starla in the striped recliner, tucking her blankets
in around her. The blankets had been in the car seat with
her. One corner was sopped in red. Blood.

There was more blood flecked across the blankets—

how had I not seen it before? Frantically, I searched Starla, lifting up her hair, pushing up her sweater to stare at her skin, searching for the source. She had fallen asleep in my arms, the stress trying to protect her, shutting her body down, but I jostled her, pitched her nearly out of the chair, looking for her wound.

I couldn't find a mark on her.

Her cheeks were flushed and streaked with dried, slimy tears. She stayed asleep, despite my rustling. She looked so much like Jamey. It wasn't the baby's blood on the blankets, I realized. It was her mama's.

What would I tell Starla when she woke up?

The backpack had slumped on the floor, where it had fallen from my shoulders when we entered the greenhouse. I bent down and unzipped it. I pulled out a makeup case with a star-shaped glittery key chain tied to the zipper, and a paperback novel, yellow and waterlogged; I didn't recognize the title. I flipped to the back of the book. There was an inked library stamp. From a junior high school.

The only other thing in the backpack was a bag of powdered sugar.

I looked around the greenhouse. The seeds were tender, the heater blared. The people in the hilltop camp would come back here to check on their plants first thing in the morning. Starla wouldn't be alone—if it came to that, if I didn't come back—for long.

"I have to go back for your mama," I whispered. "I have to try."

From around my neck, I took the leather pouch of seeds. Seeds from the Pumpkin King, from the flea market, from the burned farm, from Jamey. Pumpkin, millet, corn, apple, pepper. Almost enough for a garden. A new start. The cord was black with dirt, and the pouch reeked of road salt. I laid it at Starla's feet.

The sun hung low, and as I shut the door on the greenhouse, letting the tarp settle back down after me, it started to snow—the kind of snow that didn't announce itself with white light. The air didn't smell sharp; the snow didn't come from clouds that had gathered, lowing like cows, all day. This snow just appeared in the air like it had been conjured, as sudden as buckshot or tears.

I hoped the snow wouldn't cover up my tracks. I had to find my way back to the greenhouse. I remembered my mama's stories of the blizzard, the woman disappearing. I didn't have a rope to lead me. I didn't even have a flashlight anymore.

I cast one more look back, and then I ran. Down the hill. I didn't glance behind me again. I listened but did not hear Starla waking and crying, or anyone coming down from the camp on the hilltop. I passed the washing machine. Another hill. I was close. Snow got into my eyes. My feet felt frozen. There was slush inside my boots.

Then I could hear Jake and his man.

I hadn't even doubted that I would find the truck again, find Jamey—and there the men were. They had not left the scene.

As suddenly as it had started, the new snow had stopped falling, which stopped muting everything. I slowed, conscious of the crunching sound I made, blundering through snow and leaves. At the edge of the tree line, I froze. Before me, the hill sloped down to the ditch, and then to the road.

I saw my truck, my truck that had crashed against the tree. A little smoke rose from it. Otherwise, it seemed frozen in time. Nothing moved, even the snow on the hood. It looked etched there. The glittering and broken glass had been on the ground forever, part of the road. I didn't hear the engine anymore. Had it been turned off? Or died? The truck looked as still as the dead. It waited, a part of the woods now.

Down the road, I heard the men's voices again. They were arguing.

The man with the rifle had put down his gun. He was examining things they had pulled from my truck and laid out on the road. Our stuff. The man and Jake were debating what was useful, who should get what. I felt a hot surge of shame, seeing our belongings splayed out—my long underwear, Jamey's fuzzy boots—and I felt anger. We needed those supplies, the warm clothes, the food. We had paid for them, been gifted them. And we had nothing now.

"I don't see any ammo," the man with the rifle said. "Or weed. And this knife is shit."

"Whatever," Jake said. "It's a blade. The grower is gonna come back for this stuff. She's gonna come back for this *house*. She can't survive out here. We just gotta wait her out." He clapped the man's shoulder. "I gotta piss."

In the trees, I drew the heaviness from my pocket.

My hand trembled, but maybe it was from the weight of the gun. I stilled my hand against my side, keeping the gun pressed close to me. I crept right behind the trees, parallel to Jake's path, his dragging, shuffling walk. Snake walk. He headed alongside the ditch, farther down the road.

I shadowed him. When he stopped, I stopped. I put my head down, my heart knocking in my chest. I hardly dared to breathe in case he heard me, turned his face to see me. And I listened.

The woods were still. No birds sang. Had they fled or had we killed them? No deer pulled the bark off trees. Had the deer escaped or been hunted to death? Or wasted away? No other cars came. I listened.

This was my real secret: control. I controlled what I could, which was not much in this world. I had barely been high, beyond contact buzzes from living at the farm, from having to go up to the big house some nights for a battery or flashlight. I avoided the upstairs where smoke hung around the rooms like an extra person; the crackling laughter of my mama and her lover, who would kick me if I came in at the wrong time, who would accuse me, eyes wide as marbles, with the look of fear that everyone wore around now, of taking money, of counting it wrong, of trimming too much or too little, of snipping some buds for myself. I could still feel the grip of Lobo's hand around me, remember how it burned. I was surprised I had never received a scar like Jamey's.

Or a child.

I had spent my life around shirtless men with skeleton tattoos, men too arrogant to put on shoes in the cold, men who would take it too far, who wouldn't stop at weed, who wouldn't stop, who wouldn't ask how old I was, who didn't care, who rattled the tiny house door, a quick shudder that shook me forever.

I waited for the unzipping. I heard it.

Then I sprang.

I hit Jake before I could see him. I jumped out of the trees, hammered the air, and collided with bone, thwacking, then soft, sick flesh. I gripped the barrel of the gun and beat with its heavy handle. I hit his face, surprising him and knocking him off balance. Beat his groin to bring him down, his throat so he couldn't scream, then knees— one, two—then eyes—one, two. That part was easy; he was half-crouched already in the ditch—his narrow, seeing eye; his dark, bottomless patch. Then his nose: a spray of bright red, which I jumped to avoid, straddling the ditch and him below me. Then I hit his throat again, silencing his voice, which had only grunted.

"You're a predator," I hissed at him, hardly above a whisper. I didn't have breath beyond the work of hitting him, which took everything, all I had. I didn't want the other man to hear, and the words I said, I said for me: "Jamey was a kid. She was just a little girl. You ruined her life. You took her life from her. You decided."

Lobo had decided I would be tough. I would be a grower, a fighter. Any child of his, under his roof, would know these things. I had seen him: how violence needed to be fast, surprising, and followed through. A darted punch, followed by a kick to the stomach, followed by a lot of kicks. Once a man was down, he needed to stay down, Lobo said.

Lobo had taught me, had made me practice, springing

on me when I came home from school, or with my arms full of groceries, grabbing me from behind.

I knew these things. Groin, knees, eyes, throat. Where to hit, how to hit. To hit until I heard the sickening crunch, the wet sounds of blood, the gurgling—and then to keep hitting and kicking. Keep going beyond what I felt was safe. Nothing was safe. Nothing would ever be safe, not for me.

Jake was down in the wet, red snow. I was kicking him after I hit him, my hand burning, striking at the giving surfaces of his body with my boot until he curled into a ball too tight for me to find a space to beat. And then I hit his head again until he uncurled, useless now, relaxed and bloody. He barely cried.

I put the heaviness back in my pocket. A string of blood leaked from it. My gloves felt sticky and the smell was overpowering, salt and mineral mixed with the clean scent of snow. It made me want to vomit.

I didn't look at Jake. I staggered back through the trees.

The man was still standing in the road, looking at our stuff. He was paging through one of our books, shaking the leaves, checking for money. Grayson had forgotten to take the book with him, or maybe he had left it for me. Maybe it was Jamey's, another one she had never returned from the junior high library when she dropped out of school—when would that have been? When the lost spring came, or when her pregnancy started to show? When she was thirteen? What was the title of the book the man held? I would never know it now.

I stepped from the trees and pulled out the gun. "I'm just here for Jamey."

The man turned. He dropped the book and held up his hands. "Shit. Where's Jake?"

"I just want my friend. My family. Then I'll go."

I kept the gun trained on him. The barrel of the gun was red, leaking a stringy line. I sidestepped to the truck without looking at it, staring at the man. The back door of the truck hung open. Still keeping my eyes on the man, I opened the driver's side door.

"Jake's dying. You should fucking see to that," I said. I waved the gun at the man, dismissing him.

"Fuck." He dropped his hands. He ran to the edge of the trees, then ran away.

I climbed into the truck. Jamey lay where I had left her, tipped over awkwardly on her side, across the front seats. There was blood on her shoulders and her neck, blood flecking her hair like bits of red ribbon. I remembered her story about derby night, the girl with the bows who Starla had been named for. I remembered our fight about the firewood. I wished we had stopped and stolen all their wood. I wished we had taken a different way, stayed on the back roads forever.

"Jamey?" I touched her arm. "Jamey?"

The man would be back in a minute. Maybe Jake was alive, or maybe Jake was dead, but the man would be back, angry. I tried to pull Jamey across the seat to me. She left a red streak on the cushions.

I looked for a wound, not exactly sure what I was searching for, and afraid to feel for it. I pushed the hair back from her head. A lump was rising on her forehead; she must have struck it on the steering wheel. I couldn't see any rips in her clothing. My fingers trembled, looking, until...there: the side of her hip had a red gash, torn and raw.

When I found the wound, her body shuddered with a breath that almost made me scream.

She was alive.

It was a small gash. The bullet had just grazed her; she must have been knocked out when she hit her head. I propped her onto my shoulder. She was heavy but not as heavy as I thought.

And she was breathing.

It was too hard. It was too much weight. I couldn't do it. I was trembling. I took her down off my shoulder, resting her on the truck seat again. She made a rattling sound. Her eyes stayed closed, but her chest moved, up and down. I had to do this. I put my hands under her arms, trying to avoid touching her wound, then dragged her.

I pulled Jamey around the front of the truck to the ditch, then balancing her back on my shoulders again, I took a breath, stepped over the ditch, and hauled her up the hill. At the first sapling, I paused to breathe. I set her down, then began to drag her again. I couldn't rest for long.

From the direction of the truck, I heard a cackling, like Lobo coming up the stairs to grab one of us, whoever was closer would do. Things never sounded like what they were: guns, fire. Everything terrible sounded much more innocent.

This wasn't laughter. Not at all.

A fuel line in the truck must have been cut in the accident. The tank had punctured, was dripping gas. It found its spark. It caught.

From the woods, I heard the whoosh of the flame finding fuel, finding the box of matches in the glove box, or the last cans of gas. The truck caught fire, then the house did.

The kerosene lamp would burst. The woodstove would glow for one last time. The little stained-glass window would shatter into a million shards. All the books would burn, all my pictures of Mama and Lisbeth. The loft where I had made love, the window where I had looked out on the woods and wanted more. The maps, the dead phones, the last grow light, the postcard with the address in California.

I turned away from the fire and carried Jamey up the hill. No voices called back to me. No one ran after me.

It was quiet in the grow room, I remembered. And though I preferred working outside, feeling the sunbaked soil in my hands and the light warm on my back, the dirt in the basement room was warm, too, heated by the lights. When I cupped a tiny plant with its root webs and thick, dark globe of dirt, warmth radiated through me. I would hold each plant in my hands longer than necessary, each time I transplanted them to a bigger container. It was like holding a baby chick, something alive and beating with hope and potential. I imagined I could feel them breathe. I imagined that it mattered that I was down there, that *I* mattered. And when I was in there, in the grow room, I couldn't hear the shouting from the farmhouse above. I couldn't hear my mama crying, or smell the vomit or smoke or worse. I was making medicine, I told myself. I was making medicine.

I was a witch, I had told myself when I was even smaller, not too much older than Starla, the first time my mama had taken me out to Lobo's farm, to meet the magic man. I was a witch girl, and only I knew the secrets of the wild plants. They whispered to me, like wind through the long grass. *Slippery elm bark for sore throat, boneknitter for sprains, jewelweed for poison ivy, elderberry for cold.*

I broke a pebbled leaf of spearmint for Lisbeth to chew the first time we met, in the fields behind the elementary school. She trusted me, took the sweet taste from me. The bright surprise of lemon balm, the peppery wild onion. Only I knew where the nettles grew, gathered willow bark by the stream. Only I could heal the maiden's heart, find the warmth in the cold cold room, deep underground.

I carried Jamey.

Over the hills, the greenhouse glowed in the distance like a lighthouse, leading me onward, getting us there where the heater was warm and the seedlings grew, where the radio might work. Tonight I would tend to our wounds. In the morning, I would bury the gun in the snow. The people in the camp on the hill would cook us breakfast, if this was a good place. I would let them help. I was ready. Inside the greenhouse, Starla was stirring. She reached for the seeds at her feet.

★ ★ ★ ★ ★

ACKNOWLEDGMENTS

Thank you to Eric Smith, who is a champion among agents; to Margot Mallinson, my dream editor; and to everyone at MIRA. For their friendship, encouragement, and assistance with this story, thank you to Ellee Achten, David Dodd Lee, Angel Lemke, Geri Lipschultz, Robert N. Solomon, Michael Stearns, Christina Veladota, and Carrie Ann Verge. I am grateful to Alyssa Stegmaier, Erin Perko, Erin Glaser, Katie Miller, Morgan Hyatt, Angie Mazakis, and Sophia Veladota for their time and patience. Thank you most of all to my family, especially Andrew Villegas and Henry. I'll take first watch.